Bullets, Rage and Bourbon:

A Love Story

By

John T. Fisherman

Acknowledgements

To Mike and Jax, my brothers.

To A. for loving me, even when I make that very, *very* difficult.

To H. and L. for being just the coolest.

Table of Contents

"God will not have his work made

manifest by cowards."

- Ralph Waldo Emerson

Chapter 1

The night my daughter died visits like a spurned lover. The panic and grief, the anger, they come back. I remember sitting in a sterile hospital chair in a semi-private waiting room. One of those huge, ancient tube TVs humming in the background. I sipped the kind of coffee that insults your sense of modesty in a way few things short of bodily fluids can. The low, warm lights only adding to the tension coiled in my muscles. Old magazines, undoubtedly soiled with unspeakable disease, littered the end table. Beige paint; that's what I remember most. And a handful of landscapes dotting the walls. A floral wallpaper runner splitting the monotony of color.

The whole room gave the impression that the decorators had tried, but not that hard, to create a mellow feel. As with all hospitals, the stench of death mingled subtly with the cheap air freshener and antiseptic they use to clean. If you are uncertain what death smells like, it's that somewhat warm, acrid feeling you get in the back of your throat. Something like bleach mixed with spoiled fruit. The next time you find yourself in treatment, concentrate a little.

Denial, that was my mindset, as I thumbed through random

pages on my phone. Like being there was somehow off; like a mistake. I occasionally glanced up to watch another family sharing the space as they suffered their own tragedy. Faces weak with exhaustion and dripping with fear. Intellectually, I knew it was likely my daughter would die too, but at that moment, I couldn't help but feel glad not to be them. Their pain was palpable and immediate. I pitied them.

My brother, Virgil, sat next to me. His bandaged head in his hands. The cast for his broken arm making his posture awkward. His wounds were fresh; blood still drying around them. His surgery had been quick; well, relatively quick. Kat had been in surgery for eight hours. The doctors desperately trying to put her back together.

I'd like to just quickly look at the modern American emergency room doctor. They often work twelve hour rotations, three to four days a week on a variable shift. This means on any given day they are either beginning, in the middle of or ending forty-eight hours of people dying. I know we like to imagine our hospitals as gleaming centers of miracle healing with cutting edge technology and compassionate care, but in reality people go to hospitals to die. So, you take this high mortality rate, long hours and crushing debt from medical school. You sprinkle in the patients and their families, our belief in the resiliency of the human body and you get men and women who are passionately trying to fix the unfixable, in the shortest amount of time possible, before moving on to the next billable corpse. Anyway, for my sake, we'll say Kat's doctors were working desperately.

Virgil's face was pale except for the red puffy skin around his eyes. He bled guilt and despair and I hated him. He had been driving her home after a fun day away from mom and dad. The early evening had been wet with rain and mist. He came over a hill on the highway and was not prepared for stopped traffic. He lost control and I lost the love of my life. He had managed to slip back into his soiled clothes after waking from his surgery. I had been sitting in silence, judging the weeping family across from me when he sat down.

My wife was out of town when I called her. I lied about everything. She was weeping on the phone and all I could muster was a meek "everything's going to be OK". I knew she couldn't handle reality. I would have had to deal with her suicide had I told the truth. I was selfish. She promised to be on the next plane home and asked that I tell our daughter "mommy loved her very much" when she woke up. I knew she wouldn't.

It's a funny thing, being told your child is going to die. The calm I felt was unsettling. Like the moments before a tornado destroys your town. I'm not sure how I thought I would react, but this…this was surprising. I said that I hated my brother, but that's only what I thought I should feel. After all, he was driving, he was responsible. I should hate him. I wanted to feel something, anger, rage, pain, anything. Instead, just sterile understanding. My mind had formed a wall between thought and emotion.

Virgil's movements were slow and deliberate. The contorted grimaces and low grunts betraying a tremendous amount of pain. His light blonde hair was matted with sweat and his clothes were filthy; caked with dirt and blood. He was about two years younger than me. Thin and athletic, great career; he lived a happy life. We sat in silence. Both too tired to carry a conversation neither of us wanted. He sobbed slightly. I was annoyed. His tears felt more like manipulation than grief; a lazy way to get my attention. I ignored it. This went on for some time before he finally worked up enough courage to speak.

4

"John...John, I am so sorry," he said.

I thought about the other people he had killed in the accident. I imagined their parents and siblings and children all fostering the same hate I pretended to have. We had spent so much of our childhood together; often with the same group of friends. I remember times when our father was angry with one of us, we would try and take some of the blame for the other. We attended the same college. He was my best man at my wedding. I remember that jittery moment right before the ceremony. I was too excited to even sit. He took me by the shoulders and said "be a man." Great advice. We were close. But seeing him quivering, looking pathetic, it made it easy to invent feelings.

"I...please don't look at me like that," he pleaded; tears running down his cheek.

"Like what?" I asked

"I can't...I can't say how sorry I am," the words sort of spilled out of him, like a confession.

I was silent. I'll admit, I was being an asshole. I knew, I could feel in my very being that he wanted nothing more than to be told I still loved him. That it wasn't his fault. That he could still lead that

5

happy life he had created.

I turned to him, placed my hand on his shoulder. I could feel his muscles relax in my hand. This gesture, more than anything I could say, was relief. He breathed deeply. I contorted a smile and looked him in the eyes.

"I will never forgive you," I said.

Can you blame me? As you can imagine, this had an effect. All the tension and pain and hopelessness that had melted away moments before flooded back into his body. It was physically manifested and I could feel it through my skin. Those feelings whelmed up more than can be expressed in words. I didn't care. It made me feel a little better. He placed his head in his hands again, crying softly, just as our parents walked in.

My father struggled with a cane. I wondered if he hated coming to hospitals. If they reminded him how much closer to death he was than the rest of us. Ironic that we had all gathered for the youngest one in our family. His straight slacks well creased ending in no break, giving them a military precision. He wore a blue suit jacket, which hung open revealing a white button down shirt, but no tie. His hair, still a dark brown in most places, was straight but

6

obviously windblown.

I often consider how I will dress when I am his age. Will blue jeans and a t-shirt still be acceptable? Does everyone, regardless of generation, dress in slacks and oxford shirts when they hit their 70's? The real questions of our age.

My mother, her makeup smeared from crying, ran directly to my brother. She wore a long skirt and blue blouse. Her hair cut long and wiry. She always treated him more tenderly than me. He was the baby and was regarded that way regardless of his age. Together they sobbed in unison. That hardly seemed fair, since I was the one actually grieving. My father placed his hand on my arm, which felt out of place, somehow. I wondered if he, as I had done with the other family in the waiting room, looked at me with pity. He was not me.

"John, we got here as soon as we could," he said.

I nodded my head, acknowledging his prompt arrival. I was tempted to lash out at him as I did Virgil, but my words were lost in the sudden need to welcome my guests. Politeness too ingrained; too automatic to be ignored.

"Please, Dad, take a seat," I said.

7

He welcomed the opportunity and made himself comfortable next to where I had been sitting. This whole ritual made me feel ridiculous at a time when manners would surely not be missed. My mother and brother continued to weep. My father and I ignored them. A product of our self-imposed need to be resilient, even in the midst of losing a child.

"So have they told you...what to expect?" my father asked.

"Yes," I said. "She probably won't make it."

My mother looked at me. Such great pain in her eyes; tears streaming. I knew she was too afraid to ask, to pry into my own emotional state, but her face so clearly conveyed she did not understand me.

"So that's it then?" he asked.

"Yep," I said. A long moment and then, "I don't know what else to say. They said her skull was crushed on impact and the fact that she made it to the hospital is a miracle."

I trembled as I said the words out loud; reality cracking the barrier my psyche had hedged. I felt tears for the first time. "No, don't think like that; don't let that in." I managed to dry that well of thought and we sat in silence for some time. I can't remember

8

exactly how long. The other family received good news at some point. They suddenly began holding each other and crying. I know that doesn't necessarily sound positive, but their cries were cathartic, almost light, like the air that escaped from them held all the weight of their trouble. A father, mother and sister. The doctor hadn't stayed long, another patient to tend, I'm sure. They and my family were now split on either side of the emotional spectrum. My mother and brother tightly wrapped in each other. Dad and I carried on an empty conversation.

"John, how's work going?" my father asked.

"Hmm, what? I don't know," I said. I was distracted, my mind unable to focus on anything concrete.

"Any word on that promotion you were hoping to get?" he asked.

"No," I said.

I stared off into the distance. His tone felt like he was trying hard to connect, but didn't know how. I felt guilty for being so abrupt. I knew this was impossible for him, too. He had always cherished his granddaughter and spoiled her un-apologetically. Now, he would never be able to again. Just like the rest of us, he had lost

9

something precious forever and would never be whole because of it.

"I'm sorry, dad," I said. "I'm just not feeling very talkative right now."

He nodded and kept silent. The guilt gnawed at my gut. I tried to think of something to talk about. He was always eager to discuss some new topic he had found; politics, art, literature, sports. He was the kind of man that was only truly happy when he had a captive audience. I desperately wanted something to say, but there were just no words. None that came to mind, anyway. As I frantically tried to invent an excuse to speak, the silence becoming more and more awkward, a nasty, little thought dug itself into my mind: it was my fucking daughter that was dying and fuck him for making me feel this way. I felt better.

The silence was broken by fresh sobs as my wife's parents arrived. I had called them just after mine. I knew that my wife would have wanted them to be here. Her father was younger than mine, wearing jeans and a sweatshirt. His thinning hair having lost the majority of its color. He walked briskly with his wife's arm around his. She had not accepted growing old with the grace. Perfectly manicured nails, seamless make up and designer clothes. She spent more money on her appearance than anyone I have ever met in my entire life, which frustrated me, especially when her mascara ran. She felt enough pain to cry, but enough embarrassment to paint her face. That's stupid.

Her father, more emotional than mine, joined the women and my brother. They prayed too, I think. I can recall intense fury listening to them begging god to spare my daughter. Truly if the creator of the universe wanted to spare my little one, he could have kept her skull from being crushed. Now that the damage was done, it seemed even crueler to ask for her to live some kind of half-life in paralysis. I played out in my mind the impossible task of ending her life, should she be brain dead. I'd have my father in one ear denouncing me for even considering letting her suffer on; totally righteous and passionate, safe from being the one to actually do it. In total opposition, my tear ridden mother begging me to let a miracle happen; to just believe. Somehow, her broken body would be healed by the power of the almighty. All this while, I assume, my wife, completely emptied by the situation, would barely function and be no help at all.

I imagined the devil masturbating to my torment; truly

enjoying my hopelessness and the blasphemy in my heart. There may or may not be a god, but I absolutely know there is a devil. All of us, manifestations of his debasements. Every lustful thought creating a man; women from jealous flashes as he watches us worship something other than him. Those truly broken, born from the love he has for himself; people like me. We are spawned from moments of drunken self-obsession. We carry with us always that belief, in our heart of hearts, that we are special.

Kat's doctor walked to the middle of the room and stopped. His head swiveled, looking for someone. His green scrubs splashed with my daughter's blood. She had spilled all over him. He carried himself as if my computer had died, and, apologetically, he was unable to retrieve the sex tape I had hinted at repeatedly for him to save.

"Mr. Fisherman?" he asked. His voice horse and tired. I'll give him that.

"Yes?" I answered. My father flashed his eyes briefly, instinctively responding to our name.

"I'm sorry, we did everything…," The words died in the space between us. I remember feeling like my heart stopped; my lungs not willing to breath. It was if time stalled and I was alone with the knowledge Kat was dead. I was later told that I began screaming and had to be restrained from strangling the surgeon. I was not so much aggressive as manic. I was yelling at the doctor over and over to bring her back; the logic part of my brain caught in an endless loop. My brother, of all people, was the one to hold me back. I passed out at some point.

I'm not sure how much later, but when I finally came to, my mother was sitting next to me in a vinyl covered chair. My head was pounding and I was lying in a hospital bed. They had taken me to a private room after blacking out. There was a light murmur from the heater and muffled voices outside the door. It was late; the sky was dark. Yellow luminescent parking lights cut through openings in the blinds.

"How long was I out?" I asked.

"Just a few hours, sweetheart. How are you feeling?" she asked.

"Pretty shitty," I said; wincing as I touched my head. "I feel like I got hit with a bowling ball."

"Security had to restrain you after…after you started

13

punching that doctor in the...in the groin," she said.

"What?" I asked. I sat up, trying to recall the day's events. I realized I was wearing a hospital gown. My clothes folded in a plastic "bio-hazard" marked bag on the ledge. They were stained; apparently I had bled a lot.

"Yes, you had to get a few stitches when you hit your head," she said.

Poor memories, gray and hazy were fighting for consciousness, but I couldn't quite make them clear. Silence fell over us. I waited, thinking she had more to say, but she just sat watching me.

I asked, "Did everyone go home?"

"Your father is asleep downstairs. Everyone else left," she said.

I was relieved. The things I did remember weren't particularly good examples of my character. I laid back on the bed and looked over my mom, her eyes swollen from crying. Her clothes were wrinkled and she sat with her arms draped over the sides of her chair, like she didn't have the energy to lift them onto her lap.

I thought about asking if Virgil had left, too, but couldn't find

14

the strength. I was so tired. Hours of stress and waiting; exhaustion doesn't even begin to describe how my body felt. I was drained, completely, and I knew talking about my brother would only sap what little energy I had.

"Have you had anything to eat, mom?" I asked.

"No, I'm not hungry," she said. "Are you feeling better?"

"I don't know," I said. I searched for my cell phone, curious about the time, eager to have something other than Kat to discuss. "You really should eat something." I found it on a nearby rolling table and tapped the screen to life. "It's, uhh, wow, 10 o'clock. I'm a little hungry. I'm sure we can order something, pizza maybe?"

I was searching for open restaurants, swiping through menus, muttering to myself, when she said, "You are going to have to forgive him, sometime."

I let my hands fall into my lap, the words hanging in the air like fine dust.

"What?" I asked; a spark of anxiety burning in my chest. The glow of my phone casting shadows on my face.

"Your brother; you can't hate him forever," she said. She adjusted the blanket on her knees, folding the edge into a neat crease.

15

"I, uhh," I stuttered through my words, trying to put together something coherent.

"Someday your father and I will be dead too and all you will have left is each other," she said.

"Jesus, Mom. I, don't really want to talk about this, right now," I lifted my phone and resumed swiping through pages. "I don't think you really know what you're saying."

She straightened up, placing her hands on her lap.

"You need to know that. You've already lost so much, don't lose him too, not because of this," she said.

"What did you say?" I asked.

"This can't be the reason you stop loving him. You need each other now…now more than ever and..."

"For fuck's sake mom, he killed my fucking daughter. How the hell am I supposed to forget that?"

"You watch your mouth," she said sharply. "I raised you better than to use that kind of language."

I took a deep breath. "Mom, I feel dead inside, alright; completely empty. Kat is...was the only person in my life that ever truly made me happy."

Tears started to gather in her eyes. I stopped, trying to find words that would, somehow, hurt less, "What I'm trying to say is, I don't know how I'm going to get out of bed tomorrow, let alone, forgive *him*."

I waited a long moment, waited for her to agree, to stop crying, to suggest a pizza place, anything. Instead, she just sat there in silence; dabbing tears with a tissue. This made me angry. It started small, just a twinge in my chest. But it grew, roiling over into rage.

"Fuck him," I said, putting my phone back on the table and rolling over. "I hate him. I want him to die and for her to be alive. Do you think I fucking care about forgiveness?"

My mother tried to keep from crying, but couldn't. She sobbed loudly. I didn't care. I was supposed to be comforted; cared for. I was the one who needed a mother. But no, like everything else in my fucked up life, somehow, my own mother was preoccupied. She only cared about him.

I listened to her for as long as I could and then called a nurse. She seemed annoyed, to have to escort an elderly weeping woman out of the room, but after a brief moment of judgment, they left and the silence was a relief. I spent the rest of the night at the hospital

17

and checked myself out in the morning. I had to wear scrubs home because my own clothes were, um, soiled. I passed the surgeon who had operated on Kat on my way out. He ignored me for the most part, except for a quick glance. It was a solid "fuck you" with his eyes. He walked with a bit of a limp, so we'll call it even.

I spent the rest of the day ignoring calls and texts from everyone. Uncles, aunts, cousins, dear friends, occasional acquaintances, for some reason, they all felt compelled to try and comfort me. It was a steady stream of notifications and I hated it. I just wanted to be alone. The weight of everything being much lighter when there was just a whiskey glass for one.

Every time my phone buzzed, though, it sent a vibration of panic through my stomach. There was really only one person I was truly avoiding - my wife. She had been traveling for work, something pretty common in our lives. She had taken an executive position at a decent sized company and was always flying somewhere to handle something. She was damn good, too, at what she did. Although, I'll admit, I never really understood, specifically, what it was. I'm all about female empowerment, though.

I had always appreciated the time apart. It had given me an

opportunity to build a special bond with Kat. Something I think a lot of fathers miss out on. Although, no matter how awesome a time we had, playing super heroes, running a restaurant or having a tea party, the moment she saw Sephie, I was basically invisible. The mother's bond or whatever.

Anyway, it wasn't until late the next evening that Sephie was able to find a flight home. I had lied to her throughout the day, inventing different excuses why Kat couldn't talk; terrified to tell her over the phone, to tell her the truth. I kept waiting and waiting, hoping for a good segue into Kat's death. I realize, now, how selfish I was, but at the time, it made perfect sense. I still blame the head trauma.

As she got off the plane, she gave me a hug and we kissed and my guilt was unimaginable. She complained about her meeting and how pointless it was and how much she missed us. And I remember the exact moment when she noticed Kat wasn't with me. There was this brief pause where she looked around, a look of expectation, that she should be right here, at my side or in my arms.

I was watching the carousel of suitcases spin, passengers standing in awkward silence, and I couldn't hold it in. What was left

19

of my soul demanded me to tell her, and I wanted to just explode with emotion and grief, but mostly, I didn't want to shoulder the burden of telling her all to myself. I told her right there. I was too weak to bear her pain alone. I couldn't be the only one to absorb it. Watching her heart tear, alone, it would have been too much. I would have blown my brains out right then (might have done a lot of people a favor too). So, I included the strangers at carousel 3 in our intimate family tragedy and somehow felt better.

Pro tip: if you want to cause the most awkward situation imaginable, tell your spouse in a public place that your child died and that you have been lying to them about it. Then ask the person next to you for tissues, because of course you forgot some and this is just so embarrassing. I did this to a random traveler. He was wearing ear phones and his face was so full of confusion that he must have convinced himself that he had misheard me. But the crying woman next to me must have prompted his sense of gentility to comply. He slowly reached in to his carry-on and handed me a sample sized package of Kleenex. I thanked him profusely. He actively avoided eye contact with us after that.

It wasn't long before a police officer tapped me on the

shoulder. I'm sure they see a lot shit, but probably not too many

passengers crying hysterically in the concourse. His thick mustache

covered the upper lip on the greasiest face I have ever had the

displeasure of looking at. His girth, molded by a tight fitting

uniform, brushed against me as his right hand flirted with his

sidearm.

"Sir, what the hell is going on here?" he asked. Sephie had

collapsed to the floor by this point, holding her head and just rocking

on her knees. His eyes darted between my wife, the tissues placed on

her back, the empty package in my hand and other passengers

nearby. I can't say for sure that he looked directly at me because

each time his eyes were about to connect with my mine, they jumped

to something else.

"Our daughter died, my wife just found out," I said.

His head tilted slightly sideways, from my perspective,

unconsciously, as if his bewilderment was literally too heavy for

him.

"What?" he barked, placing more weight on his pistol.

"We just found out, well, my wife just found out our

daughter died," I said. I tried sounding normal. I nodded and said

21

"car crash." Like, you know, kids die all the time. All this while also trying to pull Sephie off the floor, but she was so heavy; completely dead weight. To the cop I'm sure I seemed more bully than supportive husband.

"You told your wife that your child died in the middle of an airport?" his puzzlement was thick. I will admit that I was surprised at his spot on assessment of the situation. He may have been the most physically unfit police officer of all time, but his detective skills were not bad, not bad at all.

"Are, uh, are you OK, ma'am?" he asked.

Sephie continued to sob, but shook her head yes.

"Really, we're fine it's just the shock of it all," I said, pulling harder to get Sephie to her feet.

"You both need to leave," he said, his voice stern and commanding, "now."

"Of course, I just need to get my wife's bags, then we'll be on our way." I let Sephie go and she crumpled back to the floor.

The cop watched as I pawed through several pieces of luggage until finally finding hers.

The airport was sparingly furnished in the baggage area. It

22

gave the impression it wanted you to leave. I found a very uncomfortable bench to leave her while I searched for something to drink. The tears had streaked her makeup and puffed her cheeks, but it was the shrieking that really did her in. Her voice had faded to the point that only gravely, guttural sounds could be produced. It was really difficult to have a conversation. When I left her, she was partly catatonic. She responded to my questions with grunts, but stared off into the distance, avoiding my eyes. Her coat hung loose on her shoulders, her blue blouse showing through. Her hands laid folded on top of each other. Even in her broken state, her face, the lines of her brow and the soft curves of her body, the structure of her being; she was beautiful.

I had to exit the building and re-enter to find a vendor selling something, anything for her to sip. The closet thing I could find to tea was some really shitty coffee and a bottle of water. I wound my way back around to the sitting area I had left Sephie. She was gone. Her coat, bags, purse everything left in a pile on the bench. I set the drinks down and ran from one end of the room to the other, trying to find her. I darted from bathroom to bathroom asking women as they exited if someone was crying uncontrollably inside. I was met with

23

mostly disapproving looks. I think they assumed I was the cause of the issue; they weren't wrong I guess.

The baggage carousels faced large glass windows that opened to a street that cars, buses and other vehicles used to pick up passengers. As I checked every possible location for my wife, I heard the screech of tires outside. I turned to see her narrowly missing traffic. Buses swerved, cars dodged and taxis were pretty much indifferent. I sprinted out and threw my arms around her.

"What the hell are you doing, Sephie?"

She shoved me back.

"No, no, don't touch me, don't you fucking touch me you motherfucker, asshole. You lied to me, you fucking lied to me!"

Sephie slid down to her knees again. The tears pouring from her face, she couldn't find the strength.

"Sephie, I," my daughter, pale and dark. Her body limp and incompletely sown together; the metal operating table caked with what was left of her life. This burned into my consciousness like the shadows of Hiroshima. I joined her in the middle of the street. The blaring horns, angry curses, they crashed over us. I wondered, holding her as she cried roughly on my chest, whether, if they knew

24

our pain, if they would be sympathetic. Those drivers, all frantically trying to get to where ever they thought they needed to be. Would it matter to them at all to know? All of this faded away as I held Sephie close, trying to find words or kisses or anything that would help.

We sat like that for too long probably. We were eventually handcuffed by our chubby detective friend and led to the airport police station. After we had sorted through everything, he was just about to let us go when he got a call from one of the airport employees about a set of abandoned and suspicious looking luggage. We were rearrested and spent another several hours sorting through that mess. Anyway, about half a day after my wife's arrival, we were pulling onto the highway to make the long and very quiet drive home. I don't know what song you should have for that sort of situation, but apparently Blood Hound Gang's "Fire Water Burn" is not it.

The night was cold and a soft snow fell on the road. It had been sufficiently plowed, but there was still need for caution as temperatures dropped; melted snow starting to refreeze. We saw several cars stranded in snow embankments along the highway. I wouldn't normally consider pulling over to help other motorists, too many stories about people getting shot that way, but at that point the empathy part of my brain had completely melted and I felt nothing watching their yellow caution lights blinking in the distance.

The drive took longer than usual because of the weather. It was solidly night by the time we pulled into the drive way. I helped shuttle in my wife's bags.

Walking into the house was difficult. Emotionally that is, although the ice on the sidewalk didn't help anything. The old wooden floors strewn with toys and clothes. Kat had personality. She was also pretty disobedient but in that "too cute to really be angry" kind of way, you know. I stood in the doorway regretting every moment I didn't spend with her and every moment I was angry and every moment. I had five years with her and I didn't spend every single second holding her close. I was a failure. I had chased money and fun and friends and sex and now I had absolutely nothing.

Sephie went straight to Kat's room. I'll admit, I was too scared. Instead, I opened a bottle of very expensive bourbon, a gift from a recent birthday. The liquid vapor stung; the sweet burned sugars covering over the boozy tones of alcohol. My thought was to sip it. I even grabbed a nice glass from our bar. But when confronted with actually drinking it, I just opened my throat and gulped it down straight from the bottle. I choked and spat as my belly ached from the acidity.

Sitting down next to the fireplace, I pulled out my phone. A small light blinked in the corner indicating more notifications. I tossed it into the next room, the glass face shattering on what I assume was the dining room floor. I waited for my whiskey to kick in. At the rate I was drinking, it didn't take long.

I finished the bottle and, now sufficiently drunk and numb, tried to stand. The room swam with the weight of alcohol poisoning my nervous system. My legs and feet tingled and I felt that exhilarating shift in balance in my gut, like crashing down the first drop of a roller coaster. I vomited into a nearby trash can and collapsed back down into my chair. I thought about just letting myself pass out, but being alone was strangely too much. It was all I had wanted for the last 48 hours, but now that I had it, it was terrifying. I steadied myself on a nearby table and then stumbled my way upstairs. I found Sephie curled up in Kat's bed with a few stuffed animals and our dog.

"Why are you in here?" I slurred. It felt wrong, somehow, being in there. Like if she had known, she would have thrown a fit; pissed that mom and dad were violating her space.

Sephie didn't respond. She hadn't spoken a word for hours.

"Damnit, answer me," I demanded. "Why are you fucking in here?"

"Fuck you, John," she said, not bothering to roll over.

"What the fuck did you just say to me?" I asked, leaning against the door frame, trying to choke down another round of vomiting.

"You fucking heard me you lying, fucking asshole. Get the fuck out of her room," she said.

"I'm sorry I was the one to tell you our daughter is dead. You're right, it should have been some asshole doctor. It should have been you, by yourself, having your fucking heart ripped out. It shouldn't have been me having to deal with all this shit by myself."

Sephie shot up from the bed, "Are you fucking kidding me? You told me she was fine. I told my boss, I told my fucking mom she could come see her in the hospital tomorrow. God, she must think I'm a fucking lunatic. You told me, in front of a million

28

fucking strangers that our daughter was dead. She's dead John, she's dead and I was in public."

"What fucking difference does it make? Did you even consider what that was like for me? To have to deliver that kind of news to fucking everybody? I was alone...all alone. If you hadn't taken that stupid fucking job...," I stammered, trying harder and harder to focus past the booze overwhelming my mind.

"God dammnit I don't want to have this argument again. I can't be here to hold your fucking hand every day. We've been through this a million times. If I'm not out there, providing for our family, none of this works. Someone has to pay the bills, put food on the table."

"Is that what you think? You're providing for the family? Well then fuck, help me understand. How is providing never being here? When was the last time you actually spent time with us without your fucking cell phone going off every five minutes? I'm pretty sure Kat wouldn't recognize you if it wasn't in your hand. You're so fucking eager to fly away, to be anywhere other than here with me, with her," I shouted.

"That is not fucking fair. If it wasn't for me and how hard I

29

work, you wouldn't have *any* of the shit you love so much. That fucking truck you wanted so badly? The piano lessons from a private tutor for Kat. The trust fund so that she doesn't have to work during college. You think all of that just happens or on your salary? I work so that we have decent lives. I push myself; give up everything so that you and Kat can be happy. Do you have any idea how hard it is to wish your daughter happy birthday over Skype? Do you think I want it that way? Apparently, though, all this shit is just so you can sit around and drink yourself to death," she said.

"That's right, I am drinking myself to death, so when you are here, I won't have to deal with your bullshit," I said.

Sephie picked up the nearest object and threw it at me. I flinched as Winnie the Pooh bounced harmlessly off of my chest. We continued to scream at each other, often at the same time. It was an incoherent jumble of rage and pain. As bold as we were in our curses, neither of us were quite brave enough to say what we really felt, *I blame you for her death.*

After we were both horse, I went back downstairs, freshly out of imaginative ways to call Sephie a bitch. I sat back down on the couch. Our living room was finished with the fittings of an upper-middle class family. The drapes were a perfect match for the carpet and expensive floor lamps provided ample mood light for the large area. The house had been an older home in an established neighborhood that we had bought relatively inexpensively, when we were young and foolish. We had grand plans to turn it overnight into something showcased on cable television.

Although we had many opportunities to move over the years, every time we considered it, there seemed to be this nagging feeling between the two of us that we were giving up too soon and that we would regret moving the rest of our lives. Instead, we spent a small fortune on updating and renovating. It had started as a labor of love, me proving my manhood by doing most of the repairs, not very well I might add. Sephie was able to make it an artistic outlet, experimenting with different styles and color palettes. Over time though, it became a nightmare of unexpected repairs, disappointing aesthetics and judgmental neighbors.

It was often a source of contention between the two of us as we were continually frustrated by our lack of progress and sense of completion. Although, it might just have been the fact we were drifting apart emotionally.

31

We didn't fight as often now that she was traveling for work, only because we saw each other less. We were a stereotypical marriage for our generation. We were in love, got married, were happy for a while, wanted more out of life, questioned our decision to be together, but not at the point to actually leave. Instead, we would make each other miserable to ensure no one was happy.

Then we had Kat, well Katherine, with a *K*. Sephie insisted since we would call her Kat. She didn't want her to be self-conscious about the nickname, in case she was a dog person, I guess. I tried to explain that using a K wouldn't change the pronunciation and that it really didn't matter, but I lost that battle, obviously.

Life with Kat was good. Even if her mother and I still fought, the time in between our epic bouts were filled with happiness. Kat's personality was such an even mix of us both that it was impossible to criticize the other's parenting without opening yourself up for an equal amount of punishment. Kat had my biting sarcasm and sass, which is very becoming of a toddler, and Sephie's ability to pick out the absolutely most expensive thing anywhere and insist on buying it for no other reason than it was "really nice."

I sat in silence, desperately hoping Sephie would come down

and apologize and just want to be with me. Despite everything we had been through the last couple of years, the last couple of days, the truth was, I still loved her and it was becoming clearer and clearer to me that I needed her. Of course, I wouldn't be the one apologize first, though.

I turned on the TV, hoping to distract myself. It was awful. We are such consumers of absolute shit, it's amazing we haven't all collectively devolved into primordial sludge. Do you know they have TV shows now where they interview serial killers? They give them a microphone and camera and say "go ahead, sir, please tell us your reasons for skinning that mother of three alive." I mean, what the fuck? Whenever there is a mass shooting, we are submerged in photos and commentary on the inner workings of the killer and there is righteous outrage from normal, decent people, demanding these killers do not get an audience. But, give it a few years and appeals, and fuck it, put it on cable television. It's educational now.

We allow greedy, repugnant parents to whore up their small children and parade them like cattle in front of *judges* whose job it is to *judge their physical appearance and provide a numerical rating in which to compare other children...on their physical appearance.*

33

You know who else was really into judging physical appearance and providing rankings? Hitler. You know who else? Doesn't fucking matter because you're in the same category as Hitler. Don't let anyone ever tell you this world isn't fucked, because it is.

As you can imagine, it didn't take long for me to turn it off. I'm not sure what I expected to find in such a stupid thing, but at that point I was pretty hammered. I decided to pass out in my own room, but my feet carried me, without realizing it, to Kat's room again. It was quiet now. The yelling had stopped when I left...like usual. I laid down beside Sephie and finally gave in to the warm embrace of booze driven sleep.

I woke to the sun pouring into the room. It was painfully bright. The flower printed comforter lay crumpled on the floor. There were books everywhere. She loved to read and then make up her own stories, changing costumes five or six times in an afternoon to really sell the characters.

I rolled over and realized Sephie was gone. I sat up, placing my foot in lukewarm puke for my trouble. Apparently I had gotten sick in the middle of the night and threw up on the area rug. Kat would have been pissed. Even for a five year old, she had a temper and was very proud of her room decor. I wiped my foot clean and crept downstairs, the hangover making my insides hurt. My head pounding, I opened the fridge, took a long draw of orange juice straight from the box, puked blood in the toilet and then sat down in the living room with a bottle of aspirin and the largest beer mug I had full of water.

Sephie lay on the couch, her face red still; fixated on the ceiling.

"Did you sleep at all last night?" I asked, flipping the pill bottle into my mouth and swallowing however may fell in.

She rolled over to face the back of the couch. I rubbed my head and felt raw stomach acid boiling in my gut. We sat in silence for a long time, me watching the sun move across the room counting the seconds between rolling waves of nausea. Sephie was motionless, except for the soft breathing of an exhausted cry. We were a pitiful sight for sure. I kept thinking in any moment she would throw herself into my arms and just let me hold her, but for however long we sat, that never happened. It was just a hollow, painful quiet.

I knew how much of bastard I was, but dammit, I was only

human. How do you act like a good person during all of this? I wanted to yell more, but frankly would have been at a disadvantage with how much my head hurt. I needed to say something, though, anything. The lack of sound was suffocating.

"Sephie, please," the words were difficult to form in my mouth, "I...I'm sorry, so, so sorry. I didn't know how to say it over the phone. I just...I just couldn't."

She didn't move. This angered me for some reason and I lashed out, "Goddamnit, she was my daughter too. I'm fucking sorry if I wasn't perfect in telling you she was dead. I mean, how do you even start?" I realized nothing I had done was right and it couldn't have been and now I was just shouting nonsense, rather than address the situation rationally. I broke down in tears.

Sephie rotated her head just enough to take in the sobbing mess that I had become. I held my head in my hand and just cried. To this day, I don't know if she took my apology as sincere or just felt like she had established her moral high ground, but she sat up, walked over to me and sat in my lap. We held each other for some time. I didn't even try to move. My joints and muscles had that tired soreness from sitting in the same position for too long, but I didn't

36

care. This moment was the first since Kat had died that I felt human. It had been days of just total isolation and emptiness, but now that was gone; swept away in a tide of soft skin.

What they don't tell you in parenting class is that when you lose a child you stop being a person. I mean you have a body and need to eat and sleep, but your soul dies. It dies completely and utterly. You lose your conscience and sense of morality. You want the world to burn and not figuratively. The pain you feel is consuming and it wells up inside; it has to escape and violence whispers in your ear. It tugs on your heart. It takes you by the hand and shows you wonderful relief. But when Sephie wrapped her arms and body around me, for a brief, wonderful time, I felt love again. We fucked.

It wasn't the most adventurous lay I've ever had, but it was the most intimate experience in my entire life. When it was over, we were tangled in each other, just breathing. We fell asleep and when we woke, it was like the first time we had ever seen each other in bed next to the other.

The sun was bright, maybe mid-day, when my stomach made this audible rumbling sound. Sephie smiled and asked, "So, are you hungry?"

"Starving," I said.

"I think we have some eggs or something. Do you want toast?" she asked.

"Ugh, I think Kat ate the entire box of English muffins by herself this week," I said with a smile.

That thought hung in the air between us for a long, long moment. I didn't even realize what I had said until tears started to well again in Sephie's eyes. I kind of chuckled at her, like when she would break down over life insurance commercials. But then it hit me, all of sudden, Kat was dead and I understood.

"I know, I know," I said. I held her close again, but that spark of hope was gone. We both knew that no matter what happened, no matter how happy we were, for the rest of our lives, everything would collapse into despair when we remembered that Kat was gone and gone forever and nothing would fix us.

Chapter 2

It was dark. The stars and moon hidden by thick clouds. The kind of night that makes you sprint back to your bedroom and throw the covers over your head after finishing that agonizing midnight piss. A twinge of terror as your reflection flirts in the dimmed mirror of an empty room.

Aleela was shaken awake by her older brother Elim. "Ikaato, little one, wake up! Wake up!" he whispered sharply in her ear. A yellow half-light crept in to the closet she used as a bedroom from a bare bulb down the hall. She was small for her size, but beautiful. The short locks of hair fell in her auburn eyes. She sighed heavily and rolled over sleepily.

"What…what do you want Elim? Go away, I am asleep," she said, laying back on her side, away from her brother.

He roughly rolled her over and brought his hand across her cheek with a sharp smack. Her eyes shot open; her brain switching on so fast that her senses were overwhelmed. Her cheek burned. The light from the hallway hurt and she was suddenly cold in the chill air. The sounds of shouting and laughter floated up from the first floor. After a disorienting moment, she was able to focus. She noticed Elim's sweat stained clothes and tense muscles. His face had never been so stern. Her stomach turned sour.

She rubbed her sore cheek, "Why did you hit me?" she asked.

"Get up, get dressed," he said, looking over his shoulder "You have to go, you have to go now." The house was old. The paint had long since faded from dirt and the wood floors were warped and bent from use. Doors closed in the sense they filled a space between the frames, but some blew open from drafts; others had to be opened with significant force. It had been a farm house long, long ago, but had was bought and sold and abandoned and burned so many times, it was a house only in the loosest sense.

Their uncle had acquired it after retiring from the military and had intended to restore it, but as the work and costs compounded, he increasingly ignored projects until the house resumed a state of perpetual disrepair. They came to live with him after their parents died. Aleela had been very young. Elim was a few years older. They spent most of their days in school and nights working the fields. The few hours for sleep were precious.

"I am not going anywhere with you at this time of night,

brother. You must be mad," she said.

Elim whipped his head around and slapped her again. She cringed in anticipation, softening some of the blow her hands. His shorts and shirt hung off of him. He wore well-worn shoes tied tightly around his ankle. She looked up at him with shock.

"Get your skinny ass up," he said. "You have to go."

She hesitated and he raised his hand again. She threw the covers back and sat up.

"Alright, alright, let me get dressed," she said

"Hurry up, quickly," he said firmly.

He turned his back as she slipped on a shirt and shorts. Elim turned around and grabbed her by the hand; pulling her roughly down the hall.

"Brother, what is your problem?" she asked.

"Shut up," he said.

He stopped at the end of the hall and leaned around the stairwell corner. The voices from the first floor were loud and erratic; a party. Uncle had a habit of drinking every day, often into the long hours of the night, swapping war stories with friends. This sounded different to Aleela, though; maybe there were more people than usual or the atmosphere was different, but that, and her brother's manic mood, coiled anxiety in her stomach.

"Now," he said, almost pushing her down the stairs. They sprinted into the kitchen, which was nearly pitch black. Aleela shook in the cool night air and was still trying to find her night vision with the quick transition from sleep to wake to dark.

"Please, Elim, tell me what is going on," she said, shivering.

Elim peered out into the living room through the adjoining door; raising his hand to silence Aleela. The kitchen was filled with dirty dishes, an old table and an embarrassing number of empty wine bottles.

Aleela followed behind her brother and leaned under his arm to see into the next room. Their uncle sat at a large table. The walls were yellowed by faded paint; illuminated by a single, bright light at the center of the ceiling. He was joined by several men his own age. They played cards while snacking on the remnants of fried fish and potatoes. They laughed, jeering each other with each hand and sipping from sweating whiskey glasses. A few younger men, either attendants or relatives of the guests, sat in the corner, nursing a few beers and watching their elders enjoy the lion's share of fun.

Elim slowly let the door close and pushed Aleela back into the pantry. She starred at him with sleepy eyes and waited for him, expectedly, to send her back to bed; to laugh and say he was joking.

Instead, he said, "You have to leave. These men...they're terrible and Uncle has agreed to something terrible. I packed a bag for you. Run out to the road and follow it into town." He pulled a small backpack from a cupboard and slipped it around her arm. "Here is all the money I have. Now, please, run. Run and don't come back." Elim forced a few crushed bills into her hand.

Aleela, stood awkwardly, the pack hanging loosely off her outstretched arm and her fist hugging a wad of money. She didn't move, but stared at the contents of her hands to her brother and then back to the door leading to the living room. A small smile worked itself across her face.

"Ha ha, Elim, very funny," Aleea said. She let the pack slide to the floor and set the money down on the kitchen island. "I'm going back to bed. You didn't have to slap me so hard, you know." She turned to leave and heard the faint gasp of a man trying to hold back tears. Elim was crying. Not sobbing or convulsing, just tears. Ice water filled her veins.

43

"What, Elim? What is going?" she asked, grabbing his shirt.

"That bastard, Uncle, he…he made a deal with those men out there. They take children, Aleela. They take them. Do you know what that means?" he said.

She tilted her head, studying Elim's face. She had never seen him cry.

What her brother was implying started to congeal in her mind and she said "You mean, they…they force them to..."

Elim shook his head "yes"; she couldn't finish her sentence. She leaned against the island; steadying herself. Her brain trying to process everything, but creaking against fatigue and the weight of it all.

"But Uncle, why would he do that? He loves us, right? He took us in when no one else would," she stammered.

"He doesn't love us," he said sharply, almost spitting the words. "We're his bastard family. Forced on him by his mother. He couldn't say no when she was alive. Now he can do whatever he likes."

When their parents had died, their grandmother took them in; loved them like her own children. Aleela loved living with her and

44

Elim. So many nights under the stars eating cookies. Even with the sting of losing her parents, it was somehow a little better there with her. After about a year, though, she became ill and wasn't strong enough to care for them. Her father's brother had agreed to let Aleela and Elim live with him as he cared for his dying mother. Now she was gone, too.

"What? Why would you say that?" she said.

"Uncle is an evil man," Elim said. "He needs money, I don't know for what. He is selling you as a whore."

Aleela sobbed quietly, "Why are you doing this?"

Elim grabbed her shoulders and started pushing her towards the door that led to the yard.

She let out a loud sigh and shuttered in his arms. "No Elim, no. God, please don't make me go. No, no, no!" she screamed.

He forced his hand over her mouth and all the noise in the adjoining room died.

"What have you done, Ikaato?" Elim whispered harshly.

Their uncle, a large man with Kenyan military tattoos on his arms, pushed through the door and ignited the ceiling light. Elim spun and put himself between his sister and him. Uncle's khaki

45

pants, stained with sweat and dirt, clung tightly to his muscled legs. He wore a loose fitting, short sleeved button down shirt. Greying beard stubble gave him the appearance of a world weary man. Several on-lookers from the kitchen stood and watched over his shoulder as Uncle stood motionless in the door way.

"Children, it is late," Uncle said in a very sympathetic tone, but with enough slur to make it obvious he had been drinking. "Why are you still awake?"

Neither Elim nor Aleela moved, but she kept her eyes on her brother. Hoping he would just go upstairs; act like nothing happened.

"Come on, let's go back to bed," Uncle said reaching out for Elim's hand. Elim pulled it away; causing Uncle to stumble half a step. Those in the living room started to crowd the doorway, eager to see what was happening. Uncle straightened himself and brought his hand down heavily on Elim's face; a sharp *smack* echoing around the room. Elim bent at the waste, covering his jaw, but maintained his position protecting Aleela.

"Now, I am losing my patience," Uncle said. "And you are embarrassing me in front of guests. Get upstairs, immediately," he stabbed the air with his finger, pointing in the direction of the door.

Aleela, bewildered and so very tired, turned to go up, but as she took a step, Elim produced a knife from his pocket and lunged at Uncle. The blade caught him mid-way down his rib cage, slicing a very shallow, but bloody gash across his side.

"Ahh!" Uncle screamed, grabbing his newly minted flesh wound. "You crazy son of a bitch."

Elim moved his head slightly and looked back over his shoulder at Aleela.

"Go, you must go, little one, run!" he said.

Aleela's feet were rooted to the ground. Her wide eyes unable to convey her level of shock. She watched as her brother took a step toward their Uncle, raising the knife.

More of the guests, hearing the commotion, rushed the kitchen. They produced much larger and much more lethal knives; ready to retaliate. At first, their confusion matched Aleela's as they tried to piece together their bleeding comrade, the teenage boy with a bloody Swiss Army knife and a petrified middle school girl. Then they laughed. The site of Uncle cursing and clutching his chest was apparently funny.

This seemed to enrage Uncle as he lunged at Elim, who

countered with a wild thrust of the short blade. Uncle caught his wrist in mid-air and snapped it; the little pocket blade falling to the floor. Elim screamed as the bones in his arm splintered.

"Run Aleela!" Elim shouted.

Uncle reared back and hammered his elbow on Elim's forehead. The boy went limp in Uncle's hands. Aleela, tears pouring down her cheeks, couldn't move. She wanted to say something, crawl, run, do anything but her body wouldn't obey. Uncle turned his attention to her and let Elim fall to the floor.

"Aleela, everything is OK. Just stay there," Uncle said, reaching out to her; one hand on the red stained portion of his shirt.

One of Uncle's companions took a couple of tentative steps towards her, then another stepped forward and another until she was nearly cornered. In that moment, surrounded by all those strange men, her bleeding Uncle and her brother laying on the ground, looking dead, she finally found her feet. She turned and sprinted out the back door. The shouting behind her blended into the pounding of her feet on the wood and then dirt and she ran out into the night.

The house was situated on the edge of old mangroves The jungle had reclaimed much of the plantation and replaced it with the

48

natural order of the area, but the fruit trees to the back of the property were a hybrid of man's will and the sheer force of the surrounding wildlife. Untamed vines grew over decayed utility sheds and out buildings. Civilization stopped very suddenly outside the walls of the house. The town had grown exponentially over the last 100 years, but this house and the surrounding acres had remained a boundary to the growing and emboldened urban area.

Aleela's shoes were drenched in dew as she sprinted through the trees. Her heart was a broken symphony in her head and her chest ached as she sucked in shallow breaths. She could hear her uncle bellowing into the darkness. His rough voice carrying on the wind. She stopped behind a large fruit tree, finally inhaling deeply to stave off the burn in her lungs and legs. She leaned out from behind the massive trunk to look back at the house. Figures passing in front of the glowing windows were the only motion she could make out from her distance.

"What am I doing?" she whispered.

She had sprinted to the end of the yard furthest from the road that led to town. More voices carried on the wind. She peered around the tree again and saw men moving towards her.

"Little One!" Uncle shouted, "Come back! It's very dangerous at night! Please, I have presents for you!" There was pleading in his voice. Aleela almost felt guilt. After all, Uncle had taken her and her brother in. He had fed her and clothed her; helped her with her homework. He was a good man and had always been sweet with her. Elim was the one who started the fight. He had cut Uncle with that knife. Anyone would be angry.

She very slowly stepped out from the tree. There was a clear line of site from her to Uncle. Apparently, it was too dark for him to see her because his head kept moving back and forth.

"Aleela, you get back to this house, right now!" He screamed. "Your brother is going to hurt more if you don't hurry!"

She took a step back.

"Little One! This is the last time I am going to ask!" Uncle walked back into the house and she watched intently, waiting for him to reappear. She had to stay very still as the men walking towards the mangroves were getting closer. Uncle returned, dragging Elim's limp body into view under the only light on the porch. He moaned just enough for it to reach Aleela's ears. Tears trickled down her face. Blood was pounding in her ears, her muscles ached; she was cold and wet and terrified.

"Alright, Little One," Uncle said. "I am disappointed." He took out a large hunting knife from his belt and held up Elim's hand. He stretched out his right thumb and cut the digit of with a wet *thrack!* Elim screamed.

Aleela lost control and knelt on the wet grass, sobbing as her brother writhed in pain.

"See, Aleela, see what your bad behavior is doing? Do you want your brother to hurt more?" Uncle boomed into the night.

Elim, half conscious and with blood pouring down his hand, tried to thrash free of Uncle's grip. Uncle held tight with what seemed like very little effort. He leaned over and whispered something in to Elim's ear. There was silence now, just the slight rustle of leaves in the wind. Something caught Uncle's attention, because he pointed and harshly ordered something she couldn't make out. More men from the house started in her direction. The original pair had stopped about 100 feet away, waiting for their companions.

Uncle leaned over and again whispered angrily into Elim's ear. Uncle waited a moment and then used his knife to slice off another finger, sending new howls and shrieks into the chill air.

Aleela felt warm urine run down her leg as she watched her brother wretch in agony.

Elim, barely able to catch his breath, spoke in a broken and hoarse voice, "Ikaato, please help me, please come back to Uncle. He promises he won't be mean any more."

Aleela, placed her hand over her mouth and sobbed. All of the men in the yard sensed the muffled noise and moved toward her, beating the tall grass with long sugar canes. She desperately wanted to stop her brother's pain, but imagined her own fingers being cut, or worse. Her mind telling her to freeze and her heart begging her to stand. She finally decided she just didn't have the energy stay concealed, listening to Elim's screams. She was completely drained and perhaps going back to the house would calm things down.

As she once again stepped out from behind the tree, Elim mustered what little strength he had and screamed, "Aleela! Run away, he is going to kill you! Run!" As he struggled to finish, Uncle grabbed him with an arm around his neck and another around his forehead. With a quick *pop*, Uncle twisted Elim's head until his spine snapped. His body went limp and Uncle let him fall to the ground.

"Aleela, your brother is dead," Uncle said, "You disobeyed me and he suffered for it. Now, come back and I will forgive you! You don't have to hurt, too."

Aleela's life had been a pocked record, spinning endlessly with tragedy and loss, but she had always held to the melody of good that surfaced through all the pain. There were lots of happy memories and hope for the future. She was in school; wanted to become a politician. She was studying local government with her class and longed for the opportunity to help lead her country into the future. She liked a boy at school. She had many friends.

Losing her parents and grandmother were so hard that she never imagined really ever feeling whole, but Elim had been with her, every step of the away, to shoulder some of the burden. He had shown her how to be happy even when the world fell apart. He had been a rock in stormy and cruel life. Now he was gone. Taken from her by somebody she had loved as a father. She was completely alone.

Her tears stopped. The fear and loneliness of the dark vanished. Everything was replaced in that instant with pure, unadulterated hate. The kind that the devil himself would envy if he could love enough to have someone taken from him. She moved herself back into the bush and began crawling on hands and knees; the dirt and rocks cutting into her skin and untold writhing things crawling over her. She waited for the breeze to blow the tall stalks of grass, biting her lip as she felt many tickling legs crawl over her hands; waiting so that her movement would be concealed. Working in short bursts, she moved around her pursuers. It was probably only a few minutes, but in what felt like a lifetime, she traded places with them, as she worked her way toward one of the empty sheds on the property. The whole time, Uncle screaming her name over and over.

She stood next to the collapsed wall of what use to be a tool shack, and kept her line of sight on the house. Men walked between Uncle and the mangroves. He leaned against the porch column, smoking a cigarette, finally resting his voice. Her brother's body lay sprawled on the ground at the foot of the front steps. The tears came in waves as she watched. Her eyes darting from Uncle, to her brother to the men searching for her. Watching her brother's murderer laugh and drink while ignoring his body was a pain Aleela did not think was possible.

Her concentration was broken, though, as the sound of

54

breaking sticks and cut foliage pierced the relative silence. Several people were making their way with sugar canes and machetes, cutting down low handing branches and tall grass. She moved inside the remnants of the shed. Two walls had collapsed inwards, giving the impression that the building was a deflated balloon. The wood framing having warped perfectly in the constant exposure to give the impression of ripples and waves. She crawled under broken beams and pulled pieces of torn sheathing over her body.

Three men walked up to the shed, talking loudly and laughing.

"That little bitch better be worth all this," a man with a red baseball cap said.

"Josef seems to think so," a man with a machete said. "Can probably fetch a premium price in Malindi."

"Then why the hell doesn't he come out here and beat the bush for her?" the man with the cap asked.

A third man with a sugar cane and flashlight said, "You better watch your goddamn mouth."

"Oh yeah, and what are you going to do about it?" Baseball Cap asked.

Flashlight Guy raised his stalk and wrapped the man on the rib cage.

Baseball Cap cursed and doubled over.

Flashlight Guy whipped him again on the back. This time Baseball Cap shrieked in pain and fell over.

Machete turned and stared off into the trees.

"Now, I know you're new here. I get that," Machete said. "So, I'll be kind and give you this warning: I here you talk like that again and I will beat you to death. Understand?"

Baseball Cap shook his head and slumped over. Flashlight Guy lit a cigarette and took a drag, enjoying the night air. Slowly, Baseball Cap came back up to his feet. Machete lit a cigarette too and had a low conversation with Flashlight Guy; laughing with each other. They peered into the shed as they smoked. Aleela kept herself absolutely rigid and prayed they wouldn't come any further.

"I tell you what, even give you a chance to make up for being so stupid," Flashlight Guy said to Baseball Cap. "You go in there and see if she's hiding."

This was loud enough for her to hear. The fear in her heart was so strong, she could barely control the trembling. She willed herself to remain still, but it took every ounce of strength.

Baseball Cap looked into the dark of the shed, the flashlight only piercing odd shadows as the crooked structure blocked most of the light.

"Look, I…I can't crawl in there. I'm…scared of small spaces," he said.

Machete and Flashlight Guy looked at each other and laughed out loud. Flashlight said, "Get the in there or I'll cane your fucking face."

"What if there are snakes or something in there?" Baseball Cap pleaded.

Flashlight Guy finished his cigarette without taking his eyes off of Baseball Cap and threw it into it into shed.

"Get. The. Fuck. In. There," Flashlight Guy said.

Baseball Cap looked back into the shed and said, "Can I at least take the light?"

Flashlight Guy lit another cigarette and handed him the large spotlight.

Baseball Cap went down to his knees and sort of squatted into the shed; crawling under low hanging beams. The wood was damp and slick from the moist air. He carefully tested each spot before shifting his full weight, in case the rotted floor boards snapped. He made slow progress, getting caught on old rusting nails and broken posts.

Aleela, watched, holding her breath as long as she could between gasps; only letting in the essential amount, when her lungs screamed for air. She felt the tingling, spastic pain of muscles tensed for too long, her legs bent at awkward angles. She tried to fight it, will herself to ignore the growing throbbing in her knees, but couldn't, the sensation taking up her whole world. She slowly adjusted her position, uncoiling her twisted legs so that they could stretch. A piece of wood to creaked with the change. Baseball Cap froze and lifted the flashlight. The broken pieces of walls and the discarded tools casting insane shadows on the far wall of the shed. Aleela compressed her body as much as possible behind the sheathing. Baseball Cap turned his head to see Machete and Flashlight Guy smoking and talking, totally uninterested in him or the shed.

He forced himself under the second wave of debris and squeezed farther into the shed, completely on his stomach now. Her terror grew as every moment passed, and he got closer. She heard him muttering under his breath. His boots made a creaking sound along the broken boards. Her eyes followed the moving light. She felt tingling again, but somehow different. She peered down and stretched her foot and leg into view. The low light scattered by the random debris was enough for her to make out writhing shadows. No, that wasn't right; not just shadows, *driver* ants.

They were known for moving in thick columns along the jungle floor and eating everything that had the unfortunate luck of living in their path. They could even cross bodies of water when needed; millions of ants sacrificing themselves to build a bridge the colony would use to continue their bloody campaign. There were legends of cows caught in their march and being completely picked clean. They were now marching on her and they were swarming. She watched as they moved out of a hollowed out beam her leg had been resting her on. She hadn't been bitten...yet. They more curious than anything; investigating her for hostility or as a suitable meal. Baseball Cap was nearly on top of her now. A few more inches and they would be face to face.

Thump, thump, thump her heart was deafening. She wanted to run; to stop existing, to become an ant and just disappear into their endless walk. Baseball Cap pulled himself within a foot of her now. Aleela could smell him; nowhere else to go. She was trapped; he was going to find her and she was going to die. Why didn't he see her? The anticipation was unbearable. Baseball Cap placed his hand on the beam with the ants. She kicked it. The swarm frenzied. They rushed both her foot and his hand.

Baseball Cap screamed; tiny stinging mandibles tearing into his skin. Thrashing wildly, he broke beams and floor boards. He pushed himself back out of the shed, cutting himself along every inch.

"Fucking ants, Jesus Christ," Baseball Cap bellowed. "It hurts!"

Machete took off his jacket and raked Baseball Cap's arms and legs, whipping it back and forth. Flashlight Guy stood away, teetering on each foot; careful not to get in biting distance. A few others came to check the commotion, shining their lights on the ground and carefully stepping around clumps of ants.

Aleela watched as they retreated back to the house. Once out of ear shot, she crawled out of the shed; crying in agony as hundreds

60

of ants swarmed up and down her legs, ripping bits of flesh. Free of the broken wood, she used clumps of dirt and rocks to rub them off her skin. It took forever. Each time she stopped, pain shot through her nerve endings from fresh bites. Her eyes and face burned from tears and heartache and venom; the night had pushed her body to the absolute limit and now every part of her ached. She limped to the cover of a large thicket not far from the gate; certain to check for ant hills before settling in. She leaned against the base of the plant; too tired and her legs too swollen to keep moving without a rest.

The search continued most of the night but no one came near the shed again. Aleela was left in relative peace, except she couldn't move any closer to the exit. She was an easy catch for anyone with a flashlight and two working legs, had she tried for the main gate of the property. The men seemed settled in for the night, too; smoking cigarettes and sipping beers. As the adrenaline subsided in her system, exhaustion set in. She felt the pull of sleep, the dream of a warm bed, but the pain in her legs, wet clothes and the constant fear of being found kept her eyes open. The night was a fitful, waking nightmare of sound and sensation. Every bent blade of grass, every animal call, sent a new pang of panic through her stomach like blades. She prayed for daylight, but wasn't sure what she would do when it came.

When the first streaks of morning light broke over the horizon, Uncle finally moved inside and slowly, one by one, the others followed; probably giving in to their own fatigue. She waited until just before the sun came above trees and began moving slowly toward the road. She took a few steps and lowered herself to the ground; waiting and listening for movement or talking or any sound at all. She crept this way to edge of the tall grass.

It was about 30 feet from her place in the grass to the long gravel driveway and then 100 yards to the gate and then 8 miles to the police station in town. She took several deep breathes and checked above the grass again. Still alone. The blistering sores from the ant bites seemed to die down as fresh waves of adrenaline provoked her body to flee. New tears rolled down her cheeks. The calm of the morning somehow made her more anxious. She raised herself above the grass, now ready to sprint, ready to escape and came eye to eye with Uncle; stepping onto the porch with a cup of coffee steaming in the early light. It took him a moment to process her figure, but then rage flared in his eyes. She was between him and the open road. She ran. He jumped off the porch; his mug shattering on the ground. He shouted for his comrades as he pursued.

Sleepy and drunk, his men stumbled out of the farm house. At first, they just stood and watched; unsure of what to do next, confused by his sprint down the driveway. After several moments though, one of the less inebriated pointed out that Aleela was also on the road and the group followed.

Aleela could hear Uncle as he followed. Her legs burned, the muscles only half working. Her lungs burned, starved of oxygen. She pushed herself to the point that it felt as if her heart would explode in her chest. She turned to see how close Uncle was.

"No!" she huffed as he gained with every step. The road turned down and then up a hill, then finally following a shallow creek into town. For a brief instant, Uncle lost sight of Aleela as the ground raised up in front of him. As he crested the hill, she had vanished from the road. He stopped, breathing heavily.

"Aleela!" he shouted between his breathes, "You are going to die! Come on out and end this!"

Aleela hid under brush and mud just behind the crest of the creek bed. She tightened her chest with every bit of strength left in

63

her body to force her lungs to relax their desperate grasp for air. They obeyed. She watched Uncle like a deer, totally still and quiet.

"Listen, Aleela. I have an agreement with some of my friends up at the house. If they catch you first, they are going to rape you over and over and then kill you," he said, taking a step toward the creek while scanning the tree line for movement. "If you come out now to me, I will make sure they treat you well. Stop running. Your brother has already died. Don't make this worse. Those men paid good money for you and they *are* going to collect, you understand, me? Aleela?" he asked.

She lowered her head into the mud. She laid still, waiting; the anticipation of being found, that was the worst. Not so much what would happen after, just the vibrating anxiety of waiting for it to happen, knowing it would happen. She heard more voices and raised her head just enough to see. Uncle's men had caught up and he was whispering instructions to them. They split off into the surrounding trees and began beating the bushes with their sugar canes. Uncle remained in the road for a few minutes, then stepping down into the creek a few yards from Aleela. He slipped down the smooth rocks and fell back into mud, cursing loudly for his trouble. A few nearby rushed over to help him; having trouble staying upright themselves. This provided the one opportunity to move while they were distracted. Aleela jumped back up the creek bed back onto the road; picking solid looking stones that would dampen her steps.

She pumped her legs like a wild animal, the thought she might actually escape, pushing herself to cover as much ground as possible in each step. She turned her head and felt a slight twinge of relief as the road was open behind her. She ran for as long as she could, longer than she thought possible with such little sleep and no water and no food. Her body was a bloody mess of cuts and blisters and pulled muscles. Somehow, she kept putting one foot in front of the other; feeling the sun grow hot overhead.

The thing about adrenaline is that for as much as it gives you superpowers, or in Aleela's case, the ability to run 5 miles in her condition, it will totally crush you when your brain stops production. It's a bitch. Her legs went numb and then buckled, almost without warning. She collapsed into the grass near the road. Exhaustion, real exhaustion, the kind that fills your whole world, the kind that can kill you, intercepted every bran signal in her body and her eyes closed.

She woke some time later. There was no way to tell exactly

how long except that the sun was lower in the sky than before. Her throat ached and she longed for a muddy puddle on the side of the road. She looked around, but found only dust and rocks. She listened on the wind for voices, but all that was to be heard were the calls of birds and buzzing of insects. She sat up and cringed with pain. Her muscles, sore and aching, rebelled. She managed to stand, but stumbled and fell. Picking herself up, she dusted the gravel from the road off of her knees and tried walking again. This time, making deliberate movements with her feet.

Her stomach twisted with hunger and her mouth was so dry it hurt. As she walked, her mind now free from immediate danger, she kept picturing Elim, his broken body crumpled on the porch. His screams echoing around her skull. The scene of his death played over and over in her mind; watching his head twist and limbs go limp. It was all she could focus on. As she kept moving, though, her body found a rhythm. The repetitive sound of her feet moving against the road, it became almost trance like; compassionately distracting.

The loud screech of a buzzard in the trees shook Aleela out of her trance. She demanded her muscles move faster, although running was no longer an option. The weakness in her legs was not something she could will to overcome completely, but she was able to increase her pace. She overtook another hill and saw dust trails in front of her…a vehicle. Hope sprung up in her chest. This was a rural area, surely they would have water, a radio maybe to reach the local constable. A place to sit in the shade, maybe even air conditioning, although, she thought, that would be almost too much to ask for.

Her relief quickly dissipated as she considered, just how rural an area this was. Not many people had a use to be out this far from town. She thought about how many friends Uncle had. How many of them were combing the road for her. She ducked behind a tree and watched as the whirls of dirt grew and grew until they were nearly on top of her. The truck, she made out, had something different about it. Its roof was taller somehow. She studied it, perplexed as the odd shape rounded the nearest corner and then all the knots in her stomach released in an instant. The local constable was out on patrol. The police had found her.

She waited for the truck to drive by her hiding spot and stepped out, waiving her arms and shouting. The truck skidded to a stop, nearly striking her. The driver emerged, weapon drawn, looking confused. He looked Aleela over.

"What in god's name are you doing out here?" he asked. His head swiveling back and forth. "Are you alone?"

"Please help me, oh god, he killed my brother, please take me, please take me away!" Aleela pleaded. She collapsed at his feet, half conscious and muttering incoherently.

The constable holstered his pistol, "What?" He slid to his knees and cradled her in her arms.

"Water," she mumbled.

He retrieved a canteen from his belt and poured a few sips into her mouth. "Take it easy."

Aleela tried to tip the canteen into her mouth and suck down all the water at once, but the constable held it firmly in his hand, keeping her from choking. They sat like this for several moments, letting her sip water a few gulps at a time.

The constable asked, "How did this happen to you?"

"My uncle, he killed my brother, oh god. He chased me into the bush. I've been out all night. Please you have to help, please, please!" Fresh tears on her cheeks now. Her body completely limp in his arms.

"Jesus, yes, of course, here let's get you in the truck," he said, opening the door and lifting her into the passenger seat.

He walked around to the driver side while speaking into his shoulder mounted radio. She couldn't make out the exact words from the other end, but she didn't care either. Her fear and pain eased as she sat leaning against the door. Sleep crept into her eyes again and she felt the truck rock gently as the constable closed the door.

She slipped in and out of sleep as the officer tried to talk with her.

"Hey, hey, can you tell me your name?" he asked, gently.

"Aleela," she said.

"How long have you lived in Meru County?" he asked.

"My whole life," she said, "I moved out this way a few years ago when my parents died, but I lived in Meru, in the city, before."

"You said your brother was killed. What can you tell me about that?" he said.

Even with dehydration wreaking havoc on her body, tears still worked their way down her cheeks. She told him the story of how he had tried to rescue her, and how he died. When she had finished, the constable placed his hand on her shoulder and gave it a light squeeze.

"Jesus, girl," he said.

She curled up in her seat and watched as the trees passed. The setting sun created ribbons of light passing through the bush. The truck bounced along the road and she remembered the best moments of her life, those with her brother. The tall grass whipped by and she felt troubled, like there was something she was missing. The deep layers of her mind began itching her conscious thoughts, then began drumming, then screaming. Her sense of security vanished and she desperately felt the need to throw herself out of the moving vehicle. Why? Why? She couldn't place it, a sense of dread consuming her.

"When we will get to the station?" she asked.

"Soon," the constable said.

"Like in a few minutes? I have to go to the bathroom," she said.

"Just soon," he said.

Her stomach turned to ice. Then the truck took a corner and

started up a hill next to a shallow creek. She wasn't moving away from the house; she was on her way back to it.

"What, where are we going?" she stammered. "What are you doing?"

The constable ignored her. She reached for the door handle and it was locked. She reached for the lock mechanism and he threw her head into the dashboard. Lights flashed behind her eyes and she swooned. The pain in her head pulsed and blood trickled down her forehead and nose.

"Why?" she stuttered.

"Does it matter?" he asked. "No hard feelings. It's just business. You aren't the first and won't be the last."

She fought to stay awake, but her concussed brain went haywire. She couldn't control anything, everything was limp and then darkness. The truck sped up the road and the plantation house rose into view.

Chapter 3

I sat on my front porch, sweltering in late summer humidity; sweat clinging to my skin. This time of year in the Midwest is what most people imagine Hell is like. The heat is palpable and thick, like a hot, wet blanket you wear all day.

I had been drinking since dawn, switching to beers by the afternoon to slow the steady march towards blackout. It was Saturday and I had already decided I wasn't going to work on Monday. My boss was a good man who genuinely cared about me and my family. He was about twenty years older than me and I think I reminded him of a son; maybe. I never asked him about his life. He spent time with Sephie and me though, even before Kat died. He came to dinner; gave us presents at Christmas, remembered my wife's birthday. Things no reasonable person would feel obligated to do.

He saw us at our happiest and he hugged me at my worst. He told me to take all the time I needed, no matter how long that meant. He told me to take care of my marriage and focus on healing. I took advantage of that sympathy. I just didn't show up most days - too drunk to drive or too hungover to function.

The thing is though, even if I had known he would fire me for missing another day; even if he had called me and begged me to come in, to save my career, to make even the tiniest effort to get my life back, it wouldn't have mattered. I was so consumed with self-pity and alcohol that losing my job really didn't scare me. Running out of booze - that was terrifying, but being homeless? That didn't really register.

Working sporadically had gone on for months and looking back now, I do feel some regret; treating my boss and the people who worked for me like shit. They had been so patient and understanding, so much more so than could have possibly been expected and I drank in the bathroom stall between meetings.

Sephie opened the front door, walked to her car in the driveway, kicking over empty beer bottles along the way. She rummaged from the front passenger side door, and then returned. She stood in front of me, hands on her hips, blocking my view and trying to get my attention. She had lost weight over the last few months, looking tired and unhappy.

"Have you seen my wallet?" Sephie asked.

"Sorry, I haven't," I said.

She sighed heavily, "Alright, thanks."

We still lived together, although, only technically. She had taken over Kat's room and I slept on the couch. I rarely ate anymore, just throwing down handfuls of chips or pieces of bread when my stomach was capable of not immediately throwing it all back up. This made having meals together difficult. She spent a lot of time at work or with her parents. I drank. We created separate worlds without ever actually deciding to separate. It was nice; took the burden off of having to actually deal with our problems.

"Have you checked the bedroom?" I asked.

Turning her head slightly as she slipped through the door she said, "Yes."

There was silence, the two men on the porch with me sipping beers in the buzzing heat, trying to ignore the awkward tension between me and Sephie.

Mike, wearing moccasins and jeans, even in the heat, because he is an idiot, broke the tension "Damn," he said.

"What?" I asked, throwing my beer back.

"Things that bad, huh?" Mike asked. I shook my head "yes".

74

"Sorry," he said.

"It is what it is," I said.

Mike nodded, sipped his beer, and shifted his hat so that the sun was less intense on his brow. His long beard, matching mine, made him look homeless. He declared upon leaving the armed forces "I had to shave every day for the last six years, I am never touching a fucking razor again." He was passionate about the subject.

Growing up, he was constantly lighting something on fire, stealing his parent's car, or just generally running amuck - you know the type. This behavior translated well when the Army recruited volunteers for stupid, dangerous shit. He had been a pathfinder. These are the soldiers responsible for identifying and eliminating improvised explosives ahead of friendly convoys. This often meant that if there was going to be an ambush, they caught hell first. And sometimes, because they were often ahead of friendly units, they would be called on to assault the enemy so that others could retreat. As you can imagine, if you are asked to cover a withdrawing American military element, something has gone terribly wrong. Mike never seemed to mind, though. He was just that kind of person. He just wanted to be in the middle of whatever was going down.

You might remember a hotel resort that was attacked by insurgents in Iraq a few years after the "end" of the war. Bunch of rich bastards holed up in their rooms while terrorists swarmed the compound. Mike and his team were the first to arrive on scene. It was one helicopter against twenty or thirty hardened mujahedeen armed with heavy machine guns, rocket propelled grenades and bad attitudes. Not to mention potentially high value hostages. Well, Mike got the job done. Just him and a handful of ballsy paratroopers. That was the kind of man he was – equal parts precision and crazy.

Deep down, he was a good guy; thoughtful and reserved. He was the kind of man completely aware of his surroundings and totally in control. When he told you everything was going to be OK, you believed him. I think that is why, when all I wanted to do was drink myself to death alone, I felt so comfortable with him. I just needed someone to tell me I wasn't dead yet, and when he did, I believed him. I'll never understand why he thought hanging out with such a miserable bastard, like myself, was a good idea, though. Maybe I made him laugh, I don't know.

"You think about moving out?" Jax asked.

"Shit, where would I go?" I said, "Just another day in

paradise."

I finished my drink in one long slow gulp and opened a fresh one with my wedding ring. The cap rattled between the empties at my feet. Sephie reemerged from the house and stood with her hands on her hips again, looking pissed. Her wallet clasped around her wrist.

"Did you put my wallet in the freezer?" she asked. Her head cocked to one side; sunglasses hiding most of her face.

"What?" I asked.

"Did you put my fucking wallet in the freezer?" she asked, her voice stern. Mike and Jax chuckled lightly as they checked their phones; politely pretending to ignore us.

"Why would I do that?" I asked.

"Because you're a goddman drunk, that's why," she said; kicking over several bottles with her feet, dregs of beer spilling on my bare feet.

"Jesus, alright, I got it," I said; her head twitching. She didn't respond, but instead got in her car and drove away.

"Did you put her wallet in the freezer?" Jax asked.

"Probably," I said, taking a deep draw off my bottle.

"Sorry things are so shitty," Jax said.

"You know man, two months ago, I might have cared. But now, fuck it, fuck everything. I just don't care anymore. All I want to do is get drunk." I finished my bottle threw it into the yard and opened another.

"Hell yeah, brother," Jax said.

Mike finished his bottle, tossed it into the yard and grabbed another.

"I'll take one," Jax said.

He was tall and muscularly built. His patchy side burns and beard giving him a rough look. He took the beer from my hand and popped the cap off with his lighter. I counted 13 bottles around his chair. It was two in the afternoon. He was mostly sober. That's the thing about alcoholism, its goddman expensive. He sipped his drink and smiled as Mike showed him an internet meme of a man with a fist in his ass.

Jax had been a combat medic in Afghanistan. I don't know how much exposure you have had to the reality of war, so I'll just assume you're like me and have no fucking idea how awful and terrifying it really is. Medics are not the Red Cross volunteers you

78

might imagine in some fairy tale version of conflict. No, they are hardened men. Men who hold their buddies hand while they scream and gargle in their own blood. They sear open wounds from infection with chemical compounds that are as dangerous as the wounds they treat. They decide who lives and dies on a battlefield because there are only so many people you can treat in a firefight. They are the men who shoulder their weapons on patrol to examine a young child with pneumonia, hoping their mother isn't concealing a grenade in her hijab…sometimes they did.

He told me how he and his platoon had once escorted an all women mountain climbing expedition in Afghanistan. The Freedom Climbing Club had been receiving death threats and asked for military protection; one young girl had even been attacked with acid; her face scarred for the rest of her life. Even though the Taliban was mostly shit at that point, a lot of just regular people hated the idea of a woman doing, really, anything. Tough girls, though. They were dead set on climbing. Jax's unit was tasked with protection. His commanders thinking it would do a lot to win "hearts and minds".

Jax saw some of the most violent fighting of his career on that climb. A lot of good people didn't make it; stranded, frozen and starving on that mountain. Jax had seem some shit. I loved him for it. He was broken, like me.

We sat, drinking and throwing empties pretty much where ever all day. Our aim got lazier the drunker we got, bottles eventually breaking on the porch and sidewalk; landing in the rose bushes next door. I know my neighbors hated me, but mostly because I wouldn't stop passing out on their lawn. That and Mike's preference to piss off the front porch, again theirs, not mine. Anyway, I guess they couldn't find the moral high ground to call the cops on a grieving father for his asinine behavior though, because they never said anything. But I could tell, the way the stared at me while driving or walking past, they knew.

It wasn't long, after losing Kat, most of our friends and family stopped trying. They distanced themselves from me and Sephie and I don't really blame them. I sure as hell wouldn't know what to do. Still don't.

At first, everyone was so eager to do something, anything, to comfort or even distract us. One of the directors at work offered us his private yacht for a cruise to the Bahamas. A cousin of mine showed up at our door step with cocaine and just smiled as he dangled the bag in our door way. Sephie's mom and dad offered to buy our house so that we could move. That was the most beautiful thing anyone did. They understood that being in that place, surrounded by Kat's laughter echoing off the walls...it was agony.

When we didn't just carry on, though. As our pain became more of who we were. As I got drunker and Sephie got angrier, people faded away. The calls, the texts, the random visits and offers for prayer and condolences, they became less and less frequent until it was just us.

At the time, when her parent's offered more than what our house was worth, I was so, so angry. How dare they try take us away from us the only pieces of her we had left? Were we going to just throw away her stuff when we moved? Would we leave and act like nothing happened? Start a new life and pretend that she never existed. I told them to "get the fuck out of our house and don't ever come back." They died before I could apologize.

My parents tried too, but I drove them away just the same. I couldn't stand their tears. I guess, more than anything, they were just a constant reminder of my brother. He understood, though; gave me distance. Didn't try to force his way back into my life. He knew where I was. Still, I couldn't look at him or my mother and father without being back in that waiting room.

At this point, all I had left were Jax and Mike. They were closer than family. We had met when we were just kids, but had taken very different paths later in life. Chosen different ethos, different understandings of the world. We voted for different presidents. We had no business still being together and yet, through everything, we kept each other from complete collapse. We comforted each other and held each other up. They were the only people I wanted to be around.

The three of us sat, too many empties to count, laughing and relaxing in the shade.

"I'm sorry I never joined up with you guys," I said.

"You didn't miss much," Mike said.

"Yeah man, it's not what you think," Jax said.

"I sit here, getting wasted. Thinking about my life, everything I didn't do. How empty it all is. I can't look back on one goddman thing and think how I made the world a better place. Just fucking nothing, it's all just nothing. Kat was my one positive contribution to this world," I stopped, feeling tears pushing their way past the edges of my beard. Mike looked off into the yard, his stare more off into nothing than anything into particular.

"A lot of guys think just like that when they join. But being in the Army is basically sitting around doing stupid shit for like 90% of the time. Then you're in the action for a brief minute. Maybe you kill someone. Maybe your buddy does. Maybe your buddy dies. Maybe you do. Either way you get fucking hooked on that shit. That combat high. Feeling so close to death makes you hyper aware of what life is. It's not about changing the world. It's about feeling alive," Mike said.

"Yeah, why do you think so many of us come back and suck start a shotgun?" Jax asked.

I shrugged, spilling a little beer in the process.

"They do it because they either can't live with the things they have done or they can't get back to it," Jax said.

"You guys ever think about that? Think about that way out?" I asked.

"Fuck no," Mike said. I chuckled.

"I had my moments," Jax said.

"Like watching a buddy die?" I asked.

83

"No, not quite. I mean in the moment it's pure adrenaline and training. Your hands are flying over the guy. You're snapping open pens and throwing quick clot or doing compressions while stabilizing him. It's all very mechanical. If the guy dies. The last thing you want to do is quit. You just snap back to the next target," Jax said.

"So what, you miss that?" I asked "Hard to wake up and flip burgers having been through that?"

"Fuck you," Jax said in an exaggerated drawl. "I'm in school right now, what else am I supposed to do?" Mike and I laughed.

"Nothing wrong with fast food work, man," I said. "Someone has to make my lunch. I get paid way too much to be bothered with meal preparation."

Jax extended two very firm and very animated middle fingers. We all laughed, taking the edge out of the conversation. That's what made this all so therapeutic. We could take any terrible, unbearable moment and work in a dick joke; suddenly the world didn't seem so bad.

"Do you even work anymore? Every time I text you to hang out, I always get a 'yes'. It's like your one of those goddamn kids Jax goes to school with," Mike said.

"Fuck, man, I don't want to talk about work," I said.

"Must be nice to do absolutely nothing and still get paid," Mike said.

"Hey, no one said I wasn't the smartest guy here," I said. The conversation lulled for a few seconds so I asked, "Ok, so if it isn't the trauma of watching people die or not being able to save them, what would make you want to kill yourself?"

Jax swirled the remnants of his drink, finished it and opened a new bottle. The seemingly endless cooler of beer had definitely been reduced, but there was still more than enough for us all to pass out, which was the likely scenario.

"It starts with the nightmares," Mike said

"Like flashbacks?" I asked.

"No, you wake up, terrified. At the ready and staring into the dark," Jax said.

Mike chimed in, "At first, it's kind of weird. You come out of the initial panic, fumbling for the light. You're wondering where your buddies are, where is your rifle? Why does the room not look right? Why is everything so quiet? Your heart.is pounding; you're

85

sweating and disoriented. Then, after a few minutes you come down; wake up a little and you're like, man, that's some strange shit."

"Like you're dreaming about some generic army stuff and you wake up all freaked out?" I asked.

"No, man. It's so much worse. Maybe you're dreaming. Maybe you're not, but your mind suddenly switches on and you know, you just fucking know, there is danger. Something is there to kill you. Your weapon is missing, you're alone and it's dark and you can feel something there, trying to hurt you. You're in a full blown panic," Jax said.

"Jesus," I said.

"That's why a lot of guys sleep with a sidearm on the floor or night stand. In case that happens, they can at least grab something familiar," Jax said.

"You can imagine how easy or fun that is to sleep next to," Mike said.

"I just assumed it was your tiny dick that kept most women away," Jax said.

We all laughed, but it fell hushed quickly. Another long lull, a breeze picked up, stronger than before that helped clear the wave

86

of booze in my head.

"So you have these anxiety attacks and what, you go crazy or something?" I asked.

"Nah, those aren't so bad, after a while anyway. You learn to control them or at least minimize it," Jax said. "The lack of sleep is real bitch though."

"No joke," I said, finishing my beer and grabbing another.

"So you have these uncontrollable waking terrors, you can't sleep," Jax said. "So what do you do?"

"I guess you drink," I said.

"Bingo," Mike said.

"OK, so you're fucking drunk, then what?" I asked.

"People lie and say they drink to forget. That's bullshit. You drink to feel better. And you do for a while, you do. But at some point, you start pulling down all those carefully constructed mental barriers. You become free to explore all the deep, dark shit you locked away," Jax said. He took a long draw from his bottle and resumed. "Maybe it was the way you fucked people over before you left. Maybe it's how much of a cold-hearted bastard you are now. Now that you had time to rest, it could be the memories of all the things you saw and did while you were in. All the buddies that you lost. Maybe how, when you look at the people in your life, your best friend, your family, you can't even begin to empathize with them. There's this barrier between you and them."

Jax stopped again for a long pause. He worked his hat back and forth on his head and I expected him to continue, but he didn't.

I said, "Ok, so I get that. You get lonely, you can't forget when you were in, either good or bad. You drink, you don't sleep. I'd kill myself too."

"That's not it either," Mike said.

"Well," I said. "Fuck."

"You see, you do think about the people you've lost, what you've lost. You remember the faces, the sounds, the screams. You remember the good times. The drunken, crazy shit you got into with your buddies. It all swirls around in your head and this one question just keeps coming up. Just one." Mike finished his beer and threw the bottle out into the yard.

"Was it worth it? Did it really make goddamn difference whether I was there or not?" Jax said.

We sat silent for a moment, the warm breeze no longer

cooling us down at all. It only managed to push the wet, thick air around our faces. I walked to the edge of the porch, stood on the low concrete wall and pissed into the neighbor's yard.

"Of course it did," I said.

"How the fuck would you know?" Jax shot back.

I zipped up and returned to my seat, grabbing a fresh beer on the way.

"Look, life is a series of decisions right? We make choices that set us on a certain path. Sometimes, god or the devil or karma or just fucking bad luck fucks us over. You lose somebody or you get sick or you lose your job or whatever. This happens a fuck more often than you're told as a kid. Most of us, we spend every waking moment insulating ourselves from that shit. We work really hard, put money in the bank. We fall in love, we leave those we love because it's too hard. We are selfish, petty self-entitled pieces of shit. The sum total of all of that bullshit is nothing. None of it matters. Do you know what I spend most of my time doing at my job? Do you know what I actually get paid to do?

"I assumed it was some kind of perpetual ass-rape," Jax said.

"Fuck you," I said. Taking a large gulp of beer, I continued,

"Anyway, I manage the drama. I am goddamn emotional support for thirteen idiots. My employees are so intrinsically fucked that I have to gently remind them not treat each other like its high school. I say gentle, because if I was to actually enforce the rules, they'd complain to my boss, who is all too eager to listen. Full grown adults who spend more time with each other in the office than they do with their families. They are obligated to be together almost every fucking day of the year and they can't muster enough basic professionalism and respect to not gossip, lie, cheat or otherwise fuckover their teammates. And it's my job to massage their egos and sense of self-importance so that they'll stop all this shit long enough to pick up the goddamn phone."

"Sounds like an easy gig to me," Mike said. "You don't really do anything."

"I know!" I shouted. "That's the point! It's so totally backwards and meaningless, but I'm told 'don't complain, don't you realize how good you have it?' But all I can think is that I have been working towards this my entire life and a well-trained rock could do my job. It makes absolutely no difference what I do."

"Look man, we had plenty of screw-ups, too. It's not like the

Army is taking the best and the brightest. We had to deal with some pretty dumb shit," Jax said.

"Yeah, guy I went through basic with freaked out during a live fire exercise. We were training with a SAW, light machine gun type, and this guy wandered out onto the course. He got blasted in the gut," Mike said.

"That sucks," I said.

"Yeah, he didn't make it," Mike said.

"Oh, sorry," I said. We sat in silence again. The hum of cicadas filled the summer air as the sun began to set and, with it, some relief in the heat.

"Another guy I had, this guy actually worked for me. We get deployed, my first, and this guy is just the nicest dude you'll ever meet. Liked everybody. Didn't have any of that baggage a lot guys show up with. He was tiny too, just short and light, maybe a buck fifty. He worked really hard. Not like he had anything to prove, no, he just cared about his job and did it really well. Anyway, while we're out in the shit, I mean we were just sucking out in the desert. Hadj would plant IEDs outside our picket line at night, waiting for patrols to leave in the morning. It's hard to do your job as a goddamn pathfinder when you're catching shrapnel and HEs before you leave the goddamn gate.

If that wasn't just the shittiest way to start your day, we had this landing area for supply drops, embark, disembark, whatever. These fuckers would wait until a helicopter would arrive, especially when they spotted wounded, and start firing rockets, mortars and sniper fire into the base. The pad was on this low rock outcrop at the back and you had a pretty decent firing position from the rolling hills that faced the front of the base. Guys would run out to meet the crew and start getting blasted," Mike stopped.

He readjusted his hat, but said nothing. I almost asked him what was wrong, but thought better of it, taking the moment to enjoy the setting sun and fading light flutter between the leaves. Summers here could be beautiful, in a way. When a decent breeze picked up, even when it was warm, you could sit outside and just be.

Mike took a sip of his beer and finally resumed. "Anyway, my buddy and I fought through all that shit. He had a girl back home and they kept up pretty well while we were over there. You know, Skype when the internet worked, regular mail, whatever they could do. So we get back and he proposes, almost immediately."

92

"Shit," Jax said.

"What?" I asked.

"Only one fucking way this ends," Jax said.

"Well I was pretty sure you were going to tell me you had to deliver his medals or something. So, fuck me, I don't know," I said.

"That movie bullshit almost never happens," Jax said.

"Yeah, when we got back, guys started tellin' him things like 'Your old lady is a whore. I saw a video of her fucking two guys at once.' Just typical Army bullshit. So, you know, he's like 'Fuck you, no, I love her, we're gonna get married.' that sort of thing and these guys are like 'No man, I'm telling you she's a fucking whore.' Well, one night he finds this tape of her fucking these other two dudes, guys from our unit that didn't get deployed," Mike said.

"Did he get her?" Jax asked.

Mike held up three fingers while smiling.

"He got all three?" Jax asked.

"Yep," Mike said.

"I don't get it," I said "He did what to all three?"

"Fucked them over pretty good with a .45," Mike said.

"Jesus," I said. "So he, what, murdered all of them?"

93

"Yeah, man, he got all three. He got 25 years for it too," Mike said.

"Look, I don't know what the average murder sentence goes for these days, but that seems pretty low for a triple homicide," I said.

"Only reason he got that much is because he was high as fuck on cocaine when he did it," Mike said.

"Yeah, the Army takes infidelity pretty seriously since senseless shit like this happens pretty frequently. It's actually a crime in the military to cheat on your spouse. With this being a crime of passion after a recent deployment, yeah, I could see 25 years," Jax said.

"Nicest guy, dedicated to the job, killed three people because some girl couldn't get her fill of dick. If that isn't the stupid fucking thing you have ever heard, I don't know what is," I said.

"So I get it; that's pretty fucked up, that whole murder story. Thank you for sharing that, just great, heartwarming stuff," Jax and Mike chuckled. "But you have to understand what kind of mindless, just awful people work for me. I had one guy who just could not stop calling the women in the office 'bitches'. I mean how hard is it to just not whisper 'bitches' every time a woman walks by your desk? One of my employees was arrested on an outstanding bench warrant when she entered a courthouse while attempting to attend her son's arraignment for burglary charges.

I had this one, oh man, this guy, he got arrested while on lunch by a fucking bounty hunter for skipping his pleading hearing. Apparently, this dumb piece of shit chose the BBQ place across the street from the bail bondsman's office. The bounty hunter was at lunch too and was lucky enough to have him stroll right in for some ribs. My employee calls me from jail. I was his one call and he starts with 'OK, the coke was not mine. I was accidentally holding it for a friend.' How the fuck do you accidentally hold 5 kilos of coke? I fired him immediately. He called a few days later to say he had been shot and it was my fault because he didn't have a job. I mean what the fuck, man?" I stopped, almost out of breath, my rant exhausting my very out of shape lungs. Mike and Jax were shaking with laughter.

"That's pretty fucking hilarious, actually," Jax said.

"Yeah, laugh it up chuckles," I said.

"Sounds like whoever hired these fuck-ups was, in fact, a

fuck-up himself," Mike said.

"I know, man, I know. We have this absolutely asinine policy of only hiring temps and then paying them very, very little. So, talk about not getting the best of the best. Interviewing is mostly separating the accidentally shitty from the willfully shitty," I said.

"Aren't you constantly hiring all the time?" Mike asked.

"Yep all the time," I said.

"And management, says to suck a dick? Or what?" Mike asked.

"Pretty much. I don't even try to bring this up anymore. Every time I have asked or provided less insane alternatives, all I get is a very polite 'fuck off.'"

"Aren't your customers pissed off all the time having to deal with these people?" Jax asked.

"Don't even get me started on the goddamn customers. I had one particularly crotchety old fuck accuse me of being a part of the Westboro Baptist Church just because I said my office was in Kansas,"

"Fuck that guy," Jax said.

"Yeah, but it's that type of shit all the time. People are stupid.
96

I am convinced most couldn't correctly sign their name, let alone fill out proper paperwork, even when that is all that stands between them a large check."

"Listen," Jax said. "I'd come unglued if I had to deal with one of your employees."

I shook my head, "Not employees...temps; for legal purposes. And sure, sometimes people get mad because my gal or guy followed their natural inclination to be an idiot. Most of the time though, we aren't the ones to screw anything up. The customers either ignored our instructions, ignored our direction, just decided they knew best, or are illiterate, and then get super pissed at us for telling them they screwed up.

I had this old lady call me in tears with her agent on the phone demanding a rental car. We had towed her legally inoperable vehicle without her permission and now she had no car left to drive. Mind you she didn't work, just needed it to get around. I should also mention she never paid for the fucking rental car coverage either. Just thought she was entitled to it for some goddamn reason. As I am calmly explaining all of this and apologizing for having the car towed without her permission her agent, mister big dick, cuts me off

97

and demands that I authorize a rental for her. Literally screaming and stammering over me 'You better get this done, John, John, just make it happen, John we all know what the right thing is to do here. John I will get your manager involved, this will not end well for you.' This guy was an agent of the same company as me! We were supposed to be on the same team and he is absolutely fucking me over. He knew he didn't sell her the right coverage and now she had a loss and I was the bad guy.

So anyway, I keep explaining I can't provide something she didn't pay for, ect. I don't raise my voice, I don't point out how irrational the two of them are. I am poised and articulate and empathetic. Eventually, after going around and around in circles, I get a manager to take the call and I get off the line. I check on this dumpster fire a few days later and the manager tells me we did have permission from the actual owner, the husband of this crazy bitch, to tow the car. He had just forgotten to tell her. All that energy, all that brain power and patience, just exhausted into entropy for no reason. This agent was prepared to climb over my body, contribute to the financial ruin of the company, just so he could save face with this one customer, just so he could hedge just a little bit of profit, the rest of the world be damned, and it turns out the whole argument was meaningless!" I was out of breath again, man did I need to get in shape. Mike and Jax laughed under their breath as I finished off a bottle of beer.

"I had to manage money for a few my guys. They were fully trained soldiers, assigned the most advanced and lethal military hardware available and they weren't trusted with credit cards. They would get these crazy high interest rates and really long lines of credit and just buy all kinds of dumb shit. One guy used his card at 45% interest as a down payment on his $50,000 truck which was also financed on an 18% loan," Mike said.

"Yeah I saw that too. Trained killers; expected and relied upon to watch your back and they don't have the personal management skills of a teenager. A lot of them were, too. Just kids; fresh out of high school, ready to change the world and kill some bad guys. Honestly, I spent more time checking dude's dicks for gonorrhea than fighting hadj. You flip rocks from one side to the other. Its pointless man. I didn't accomplishing anything over there," Jax said.

Mike added, "I didn't mind humping ammo and shit up

mountains. You know? Like combat, that's pretty fucking awesome. But yeah, I didn't do shit for the locals. I didn't win any hearts and minds. I spent a lot of time babysitting a bunch of highs school dropouts, who drove drunk every day. And it was my fucking mess too when they got busted or pissed hot on a drug check. And the people you work for, I mean my staff sergeant was a good guy, but fucking command? The officers? Those guys are the biggest fucking assholes. They couldn't do fucking shit."

"I don't know. I just...," I took a moment and breathed, "I just have a hard time not wanting to die. I mean I look back on all that I have, right now, in this moment, the summation of my life and I can't shake that nagging thought in my head that I wasted it. I went to college. I got married. I had a family. I did everything I was supposed to and it's just so fucking empty. I desperately want to point to something, anything in my life and say, 'that made a difference.' Some kind of good in my life. Something, that isn't me being a selfish bastard. I hate myself. I do, really, I hate myself and everything I am and everything I have become. I can't find any good. I just want to die and go to hell and at least start making up for this fucking wasted life of mine," I said.

"Jesus, man," Jax said, "What the fuck?"

"I don't know...I just don't fucking know anymore," I said. I reached for a fresh beer and grabbed empty space. Peering into the cooler – it was empty. I stumbled into the house and returned with a bottle of bourbon. I pulled the cork out and threw it into yard.

"This is a $100 bottle of bourbon and I don't have anything to keep it fresh. We need to finish this fucking thing," I said.

Mike went into the house and came back with three empty highball glasses. He set them down on the porch table while I poured. I thought I would start with a sip, but found myself drinking the sweet and aggressive whiskey in gulps. I set the glass down, belching and feeling the putrid mix of beer and liquor tumbling in my stomach. Mike and Jax had taken a similar approach to their glasses and were slamming them down on the table as well. I refilled everyone's glass and we settled back in for a more civilized approach to our booze.

"You asked why I thought about putting a gun in my mouth. It's not the death, it's not pain or the loneliness or things I did while I was in. It's this sharp, almost uncontrollable thought: that it really didn't mean a goddamn thing," Jax said.

I considered this and, I'll admit, my initial reaction was anger. It was so obvious to me that the things they both did would echo throughout the whole world. How could he ever wonder what his sacrifice had meant? It was me, I was the one with the fucking stupid and pathetic life. But then, the longer I spent on this; sipping my bourbon and feeling the dark fingers of sleep reach up from my stomach and pull down my eye-lids, I started to understand. Coming back home, having been through war and everything else, it was over now. There wasn't any other mission to go on and the world was just as fucked as ever.

"You...feel the same way, Mike?" I asked.

Mike took a long moment, swirling the alcohol in his glass and taking metered sips.

"I don't know. I loved being a badass, but I don't mind being home either. I guess, maybe, you just adjust to your circumstances and try to find happiness. That's not to say I don't think about joining back up every day. It was nice, having purpose, even if that didn't last longer than the moment I was in it," Mike said.

Chapter 4

Aleela opened her eyes as pain arced through her arm like a broken power line whipping violently along the ground. The acrid smell of burnt flesh floated in the air as the buzz of electricity hummed nearby. She tried to move, to run away, but couldn't more than rolling over onto her side. Her legs and arms tied together with barbed wire; the more she struggled, the more the sharp metal dug into the flesh of her calves and wrists.

"Good morning, girl," she strained her neck in all directions, trying to find the source; the voice seemingly disembodied. She wondered if she really heard it; she tried to focus her eyes in the dim room. Her sore joints and muscles crying out as she moved; her throat was so dry it burnt. Light poked in through holes in the broken walls of wherever she was.

"Let me go!" she screamed; trying to kick free, instead tearing more skin off of her legs.

"Quiet!" the voice commanded.

Searing pain in her back; stabbed by something that radiated fire through her entire body and caused her muscles to seize.

"Jesus, help me!" Aleela shrieked once the pain and paralysis faded. She again tried to kick and squirm away.

With a rough tug, a hand pulled her back and flipped her over; the force nearly ripping her shoulders out of place. A man with blue eyes and light hair smiled as he leered over her. He wore a light, gray suit and white button down shirt that was open at the top, revealing an inch of throat and chest.

"I am going to break a rib every time you struggle," he said, not breaking his smile. "Do you understand?"

Aleela tried to slow her breathing, unable to brush the tears from her cheeks. She considered whether she could reach his nose with her teeth, but decided he was out of lunging distance. She shook her head 'yes', deciding to rest for the moment.

"Good," he said.

"What do you want?" Aleela asked, her voice horse and dry.

"That, I think you already know," he moved away and held his hands behind his back. "I want to make money by selling your body." There was a plate of fruit on a small table set in the corner. He plucked an apple and took a bite. "I think people will pay a good price. I certainly hope so, for your sake."

He set the apple down, quietly chewing the pulp, and moved closer. She tried to push herself away, but he caught the wire wrapped around her ankles with his shoe and pulled. He held a long, black tube of metal that sparked at the end. Digging it into her stomach, her whole body contorted and froze. Her whole world was agony that coursed through every muscle in her body. She felt urine run down her thighs.

"Normally, I wouldn't bother with some bitch pulled off the street; we get so many. But the men were talking about all the trouble they went through to get you" he said.

Aleela tried to talk, but her mouth was completely dry and she had trouble commanding her lips and tongue. She stammered sounds, but nothing resembling words came out. "I was curious what such a difficult young woman looked like. If I had been there, I probably would have just put a bullet in your brain. But, I believe everything happens for a reason. I guess I'm religious like that. Looking at you now, I see why they kept you in one piece. I'm glad they had more patience. You are very beautiful."

Aleela started to feel control returning to her muscles, but it was uncoordinated and produced jerky, broken movements.

"P...pl...please...," she was able to sound out with great difficulty.

"You are probably wondering who I am, where you are for that matter, and when you can leave. First, and this is the most important because I want you to really understand this, you can never, ever go home" he said.

Aleela laid still for a moment and stared into the man's eyes. A smile still on his lips. She knew he was just trying to scare her, to break her, and it was working.

"I heard what happened to your brother," he took another bite of his apple. "He didn't have to die, Aleela. You're here now, with me, just like you would have been if you had just listened to your Uncle. Elim, I think was your brother's name? He could have gone on to live his life, happy and healthy. But you…you had to fight, to resist and now he's dead. That is, unmistakably, your fault" he said.

"Fuck you" she forced out.

"Now, let's be honest with ourselves, your brother was very stupid, no doubt about that. I mean, from what I understand, your uncle is a dangerous man. Trying to cut him with a pocket knife? How absurd. Of course his biggest mistake was believing you loved him" he said.

Aleela felt hate grow inside. This gave her strength where none had existed. Very slowly and deliberately, she pulled her left wrist, testing the give in the barbed wire. It dug deep into the meat between the bones in her wrist, so she stopped and began pulling with her right, hoping to it find room to move through the wire.

"You're selfish. All you cared about was yourself, so you dragged out the inevitable. I mean, you could have saved your brother's life, it would have been so easy." He stopped for a moment and knelt down, "Take a look around, Aleela, I own you. There is nothing that is ever going to change that. What happened to your brother - look at what the consequences are for disobedience. If you defy me, there will be more" he said.

Aleela, despite the pain and cutting in her hands, pulled on the wire, deciding that she might be able to free herself if the barbs cut completely through her flesh.

"As for your uncle, he certainly doesn't want you back. And in case you think I'm speaking out of turn, I did offer to sell you back, at a small profit of course. He declined. He doesn't want anything to do with you. You are a piece of property that he has no use for. Think about that for a moment. Your own father's brother, your own flesh and blood, doesn't care or love you even the slightest. Is that a place you really want to go back to? You'd have to look your brother's murderer in the eye every day. That, I can assure you, is a greater pain than you'll ever experience here. Besides, if he was willing to sell you to me, who else might he do? Who else might offer the right price? And if you didn't go home, where else would you go? This is not a caring world. The things that will happen to you out there…" he looked past her and trailed off.

The metal cut deep into her palm, snagging on bone. She slowly moved it back and forth, the pain unimaginable; using every ounce of strength not to cry out.

"Now this might seem a little ironic given your current situation," he chuckled to himself, "but here, I can keep you safe. This is my home and I like to keep it clean and comfortable. You'll be treated well, I promise. You will have everything you want. All the ice cream and cakes you could dream of. You will have friends, so many other young girls, just like you. No one will touch you except our guests. You'll have your own guard to watch you and make sure you are safe every night. Doesn't that sound nice? Think of all the pretty dresses you'll get to wear. Aleela, I will buy you all the clothes you could possibly want," he said.

She stopped for a moment. Exhaustion and pain and blood oozing out of her like oil from the ground.

"I am going to be honest with you, Aleela. I don't care about you as a person. I don't care that you are young or that you are a girl. I could not care less that you are an orphan or that you watched your brother die. I don't give a fuck about any of that. The things I have done in my life many would consider abhorrent. When I get to hell, the devil will have a drink waiting. So there is no morality to play with me. No conscience to appeal to. What I do care about, what always gets my attention, is making money and that is a very good thing for you because I can't make money on a dead girl. You and I can be partners in a very successful business, one that constantly requires new stock, though. As you can imagine, the girls get too old, they get sick or maybe they decide to run away and I have to purchase new ones at great cost to me. The fatter, the happier the healthier you are, the more money I can make. The easier you make my life, the easier I will make yours. Aleela, this is important. I know you are trying to get you hand out of the wire," he said.

She froze, a shot of panic through her stomach like ice water.

Her chest heaved as she sucked in huge breaths. She felt the impulse to kick and did so, although without any real effect; her legs bleeding from fresh gashes.

"Let me go" she spat, her lips now fully under her control.

"Aleela, all those cuts are going to cost me money. I'd very much like it if you stopped." Josef dug his cattle prod into Aleela's stomach. "I get it. You're scared; terrified probably." She again contorted and twisted as the volts spanned through her like fingers through hair. "The thing you have to understand, I don't give a fuck about you. I own you. You are a fucking piece of meat and I am going squeeze every last penny I can from you. If you help me be rich, I will make your life very pleasant. When you're all used up, I will personally strangle the life out of you." Josef raised a boot and brought it down hard on her stomach. She felt ribs split as he put all of his weight on her side. She tried to cry, breathe deep, but she couldn't. It felt like dying. The oxygen had left her lungs and it wouldn't return no matter how hard she tried to inhale.

It's said that a person drowning will often push their rescuer down below the water. Not just as a vehicle to escape, but out of spite. The human spirit is vindictive. Aleela, desperate to free herself

110

and do violence to her tormentor, thrashed around wildly; her brain pumping huge amounts of adrenaline into her nervous system. She kicked with all her strength, but was still caught in the wire. Her vision narrowed, her brain screaming for air. She raised both legs up off the floor and caught Josef in the groin with her feet. The barbs on her ankles catching his pants and slicing through thigh muscle.

"Bitch!" Josef yelped. He crumpled to his knees, holding his crotch. Several men rushed the room and found him lying next to Aleela; both doubled in pain. Blackness crept in around her eyes as she desperately tried to take a breath. She fought for consciousness. Just as she was about to pass out, her stomach finally loosened and her lungs pulled in air. She coughed and gasped, streaks of lightning running up and down her spine and side as splintered bones ground against each other.

Those in the room were puzzled by the scene. Their employer and hostage lying next to each other in agony. After some discussion, they picked Josef up by his shoulders and dragged him outside. They found a chair in the shade and gingerly sat him on it. They stood around waiting for orders as he regained his composure.

"Fucking bitch" he muttered.

He examined his testicles, relieved that they were still intact. A man with a baseball cap gave him a bottle of water and a white bundle of gauze, "What do you want us to do with her?" he asked.

"What?" he asked, distracted by his weeping wounds. "Give me a minute."

"Do you want us to kill her?" Baseball Cap asked, pulling a large pistol from his waist band.

Josef looked at the man and shouted sternly, "Give me a fucking minute, alright?"

"Sure, boss," Baseball Cap said.

He retreated to a group of armed men, rifles slung over the shoulders, all whispering quietly to each other. Josef waited for the aching in his crotch to subside before taking the time to deeply examine his cuts. Blood caked his inner thighs and the fat was ripped and raw. He used the water to wash what he could, but every drop stung and burned. He waited in the heat, gauze pushed gingerly into the wounds to slow the bleeding.

He took his time, moving deliberately; trying to avoid any chance of moving the cuts. He wrapped the white cloth around and around his thigh. Once cleaned and bandaged, he limped back into a

112

large and well-furnished home that dominated the compound. High walls surrounded it and several other buildings on the acreage. A handful of vehicles and oil drums were set up as a makeshift fuel depot in a distant corner. Opposite of the house were barracks for the men. Between them and the main home were dormitories for about thirty young girls. The property was well kept and quiet.

Aleela was able to control the aching in her side by taking deliberate, short breaths. It required a tremendous amount of concentration, as she fought off another blackout; her body demanding relief from pain and stress and fear. She burst into tears and exasperation. Renewed shocks of pain as she convulsed from crying. She tried to stop, but couldn't control herself any more. Her mind, overwhelmed with pain and grief shut off.

Chapter 5

Have you ever woken up, completely disoriented, unsure of where you are, so hung over you prayed for death? That happens to me pretty regularly, but there was one day in particular that stands out in my mind. I don't really remember anything from the night before, but I do recall waking up in the doorway of a church. My guess is that I drank more than usual, wandered out of the house, was a generally shitty person and then settled in what appeared, to my drunken eyes, to be a nicely covered sleeping hole. Pretty likely that's true, but who knows?

Now, I have never been a religious man; especially at that point in my life. When I wasn't ruining what was left of my marriage or breaking my mother's heart or drinking my weight in cheap liquor, I was unconscious. Those were pretty much my modes of operation. It had been almost a year since Kat had died. Sephie had moved out. She was tired of my bullshit and who could blame her. I heard she had quit her job and was taking up cupcakes. Or was it regular cakes? I never could figure that out.

I had started back to work fairly regularly, only because booze is expensive and putting off my boss was getting harder and harder; his cosmic patience starting to wear thin. My routine was to drink when I woke in the morning; have a few beers to stave off the thundering headache from the night before. Since I was in the office every day, I kept little flasks hidden around my desk and would spend hours sneaking mouthfuls of whiskey. When the day was done, Mike and Jax would find their way over and we'd drink until we passed out.

The church I found myself in that morning was not close to my home or the nearest bar or liquor store. It wasn't on my way home from work and it wasn't near the two restaurants I ate at. I have no idea why on that particular day, after a long shift at work, my inebriated brain thought a long walk to the other side of town made sense, but I rarely reason with this part of myself.

I was more confused than usual when I awoke. I must have slept in a side entrance, one out of the way for the parishioners because I'm sure they would have thrown my sorry ass out, if I had been noticed. No need for a drunken bum disturbing their worship. I reasoned that it was Sunday if only because the building was filled

115

with people and they were singing.

I think there's some kind of inherent shame in passing out drunk in public, because even in my less than presentable state, I felt guilty for having used their comfy stair case as bedding/bathroom and then just leaving, without at least saying "thank you." The building was made of cured limestone and was, architecturally, quite beautiful. Had I believed, even a little bit, this would be the type of church to attend. The only redeeming part of religion is the art. No one can deny the beauty of stained glass windows in the morning light. You ever been to Saint-Chapelle in Paris at dawn? That will move even the most cold-hearted bastard to tears. I don't understand why anyone would subject themselves to the stupid and mundane rules of faith without at least going to an aesthetically beautiful church. Why meet in the basement of an old supermarket and believe you're going to burn in hell for all eternity if you didn't stop masturbating? I could probably give up masturbating to sit and admire the works of the ancients; probably.

I think it's the ritual for most. The mysticism of it all. You sit and watch archaic rites supersede the physical world and you can't help but feel connected to something so much larger and more important than yourself. That's the key; that feeling of interconnected meaning. At our core, we humans know that we are all worthless, selfish assholes. That momentary link to something good, whether by communion or prayers to Mecca or meditation under a goddman bohdi tree, we tap into that ideal of perfection and forgiveness and love; that human craving for love.

There I sat, a filthy vagrant with a conscience; worried that passing out at God's doorstep would somehow be the last straw that ignited my damnation. So I went inside; what else was I do? I'd like to say that I snuck into the last pew and sat quietly with what little dignity I had left, but no, that would be a lie. I assumed the heavy door was hinged to slowly close, but instead slammed behind me and made a cacophonous rattle that reverberated off the walls. The closest section of audience turned to see what caused the noise and were expectedly disappointed to see me under the open arches of the sanctuary. I tried to apologize, stumbled over my words and awkwardly skipped to an open pew that was quickly vacated by few others also sitting there.

I was still a little drunk, so I slumped back into the seat and took in my surroundings. The interior matched the exterior's décor;

soft white stone and colored glass. Each window depicted a story from the Bible; a bronze plaque at the bottom, thanking whoever donated the small fortune to pay for its creation. There was a large altar flanked by candles and priests muttering incantations or spells; whatever it is they do during a service. The parishioners were a majority of elderly, although I did see a few squirming children and commiserated with them. I couldn't sit through a full service as a grown man, I couldn't imagine trying with the attention span of a four year old. I felt my stomach flip as was common occurrence in my mornings. I let out a small belch, covering my mouth and then braced myself for the wave of nausea that followed.

Say what you will about alcoholism and its effects on those around you, no one suffers more than the alcoholic. You begin each day with a clear understanding of your own weakness and failure, despite the brain damage created the night before. And your body, indignant at the pleasure your mind received the night before, wreaks such an awful revenge that you curse yourself and swear never to drink again. That is of course until that tug, the bony fingers of booze pulling on your subconscious. Your anxiety balloons and all you can think about, the only thing that will comfort you, the only thing in the whole world that you really need is a drink. And, like all proper addictions, when you finally give in, it is everything you knew it would be; it takes you in a warm, furry embrace and loves you.

However, I was at that stage of sobriety that pain and regret were sitting on either shoulder taking turns driving nails into my head with what felt like a cannon. I started to think moving inside was a mistake and I should have stayed on the stairs. That nausea wave passed and I felt a little better. It's a weird sensation, when I get like that, like my body can't decide to be sick or not. I cycle through wanting to vomit, to feeling fine, to vomit again, over and over until the hangover passes.

The singing stopped, which was nice as the quiet helped soothe the splitting pain in my skull. The congregation focused their direction of one of the fancier dressed clergy. He produced a small stack of papers and a Bible and sat them on the lectern in front of him. "If this guy is fucking loud...," I thought.

"Good morning," the priest boomed from his microphone.

"Goddamn it," I rubbed my temples in an attempt to calm the ringing in my brain. I had seen someone do this on TV once and mimicked the motions, hoping it would help. It didn't.

"My homily this morning is a little different than what you are probably used to. I was moved by God to share with you something…something we should all be aware of; something we should collectively take a stand against. What I share with you today is physical proof of the devil and his existence in this world; something that clearly shows Satan and his demons at work," he said. I snorted a laugh and drew the ire of several parishioners. "You see, this week I watched the national news; not something I do often, it was more of coincidence. Just flipping through channels and this story caught my eye," he said.

Sure, can't find decent masturbatory material so you have to keep checking around.

"There on my television where pictures; pictures of little girls. Some like those in our very own Sunday school. The very definition of innocence. Bright shining faces, full of hope and life and love. And as they scrolled across the screen I started to catch bits of the report. These girls, they were missing. Stolen from their homes. Grieving mothers, shrieking into the camera, begging for help in a language I couldn't understand; except for their pain. That

120

is a universal tongue we all recognize. My heart went out to those poor, heathen women. Desperate for the embrace of our lord and savior."

"Jesus Christ," I thought, annoyed.

"Jesus Christ," he continued. "But it wasn't just that these girls were missing, not just that their mothers wanted them home. No, they were taken and they were sold." Something about this caught my attention and I began to focus. Something about that word, sold, it clenched my stomach into knots.

"They were bartered, like cattle, into the hands of evil, terrible men. The type of filth that are so far from God's mercy they are hopelessly lost; destined for the deepest, most agonizing pits of the inferno. Men who would prostitute children for money," he said.

The crowd was visibly uncomfortable. Some shifted in their seats; some looking down to ensure they didn't lock eyes with the priest and somehow feel responsible. Those words hung heavy on my heart. I had this thought about what I would do if Kat were still alive, like she never died, and someone tried to hurt her, take her away from me. How I would make them hurt. It was a fantasy, obviously, Kat was dead, I knew that, but I still role played the protective father in my mind.

"Fathers, brothers, uncles, giving up whatever slender hope they had for salvation. Pittling away their hopes for eternity; a mockery of our holy covenant, they enter into an abortion of baptism with Lucifer, the Evil One, bathing in the blood of their daughters, sisters and nieces. They abdicate their humanity for something as base as money. Children deflowered and irreversibly broken by the sins of those they trusted most. And those that would have these children; those that seek out and pay for this type of abomination, they're rich Europeans. Too much money to live in decency. No, instead they commit this cardinal sin. As Jesus said 'those that word harm one of these little ones, it would be better for a mill stone to be tied around their neck and thrown into the sea.' This...this is the great cause of our generation," he paused for a minute. I wasn't close enough to see if he was crying, but I could hear that twinge of emotion in his voice that men often make when feeling betrays them. I'll admit, I was moved. He was so passionate, so convicted of his own righteous platitude. It was hard not to be caught up in his charisma. Those who had their heads down quickly raised them, perhaps curious to see if he would completely break down.

"I want to tell you the story of one young girl. Her mother died, at a very young age; she being married under somewhat questionable circumstances herself. Her brothers left home to seek gainful employment and support their wretched, drunken father. Alone with his only daughter, this devil of a man committed terrible acts upon her...repeatedly. She attended school, though, through all of this. She was a student at one of our academies in eastern Africa. That's how I found her and learned of her trials. From all accounts, she kept up a strong spirit, working hard during the day and did reasonably well in her studies. Her dream was to go to America to study engineering. She wanted to build bridges in her home country so that business and success and life could flow across the land she loved.

Now, after losing his job due to his alcoholism and what I can assume was an overarching corruption in his nature, her father turned this girl onto the street. She was raped over and over and over. Her body ravaged, but most importantly, her soul quenched by the sins of others. I met her in our hospital. I'm sure you all remember my recent trip and let me say how proud I am of our congregation and the generous donations that continue to improve

123

lives in impoverished parts of our world. Anyway, to continue, disease wrecked her young frame. She told me all about her hopes and dreams and her love for this church. She was happy and grateful, not showing a hint of revenge or resentment.

She told me all of this with just days to live; our doctors having done everything they could for her. I blessed her and took her confession. What brings me to tears and causes my heart to burn in my chest; not just the suffering of this girl, not just the disgusting perversions of this world, but the fact that she was so faithful. She kept saying how she knew that God would heal her; that she had to live so that she could help her people. She died, believing in that hope until the moment she could not draw another breath. Her father, he disappeared. I'm sure sensing that even the maligned sense of justice in his country would awaken and pursue him. He fled in the night and has, for all our efforts in aiding the authorities there, escaped his just punishment. She died alone, without family, broken and sick and woeful, but happy and grateful for the love of Christ, our savior."

I looked around; many were wiping away tears from their eyes.

"Our blessed Father spoke of his hatred of Moloch and the Baals. That he detested them; that they defiled the very ground on which their shadow fell on. These are the false gods that he sent Samson and David and Samuel and Daniel to rid the world of. He commanded the saintly of old to tear down these bastard sons brick by brick. These human traffickers, as they are called, such a euphemism for enslaving children to fulfill the sexual decadence of broken men; they are the pagans of our age. They are the Baals that must be burnt to ash and covered over with salt and dust. They are the devils cast into pigs. Let us not forget them in our prayers; that the Lord our God may strike them down like the burning sinners of Sodom and Gomorrah."

He was shouting and breathing heavily between words. I was enthralled. I had never heard anyone in my life talk with such conviction. My mind drifted onto Kat. Her bright, happy face filling my mind's eye. I thought about all the times I had hugged and kissed her; felt her hold tight onto my clothes and bury her head in my chest. All the good of her completely consumed my attention. It was overwhelming. I could almost feel the warmth of her body wrapped in her favorite blanket and laid on my lap in a delivery room. Then, all of that was swept away, my mind flinging these happy images into the recesses of my consciousness. I imagined her crying; lost and alone and in danger. That panic you feel when reliving some trauma, it crept into the muscles in my neck and worked its way into my skull and face. I felt her in pain. I felt her being hurt by someone else. I felt her being raped.

I leaned over and vomited. The homily stopped as the entire congregation turned to watch my anxiety attack. I recovered; realizing that every eye was on me. I muttered something not like words, more like throaty grunts. I picked myself up, stepping over the pooled liquid on the ground and walked out. I don't know if they were too shocked to say anything, or I was just so focused on leaving that I didn't hear any of them shouting after me, but as far I as know, the entire group silently watched me slink back into the shadows and out of their lives.

Outside, I felt a warm gust of wind and breathed deeply in relief; stumbling to my knees. I coughed and vomited again, this time mostly bile. There wasn't anything else to do but sit back and hang my head in my hands. A crack of thunder overhead. I looked up into the sky, hoping it was only a passing cloud. Instead, rain poured down in a deluge of a thunderstorm.

"Goddamnit!" I shouted, "What the fuck do you want from me? Haven't you taken everything already? Have I anything left for you to squeeze out?" I screamed and at nothing in particular. I'd like to say I had some momentary connection to the divine, but in reality, I think I was just talking to myself. My self-loathing had become sentient and was often my only companion. I sat letting the rain pelt me with indifference. I had become nothing. I was the stinking mud I sat sinking into.

I felt a chill run through my spine. Not something created from the freezing rain, but radiating out. Those images of Kat, everything that had permeated my mind, they came back, but in a different context. I could see the men hurting her. I felt their lust and greed and hubris and enjoyment. The priest's words filled my head as all this passed through me like lighting. A hate so real, so palpable, sparked to life in my heart. It scared the shit out of me. It was a split in personality. The old John had broken into two pieces. One was a damaged man, devoid of any meaning and real love in his life. The other…well, the other was a force of raw, burning hell. I swore in that rain and muck and isolation that I would kill every single one of those bastards; every single person who hurt those children or I would draw my last breath trying. This oath stopped the tremors in my hands. I managed to stand. Picking a direction, I started walking.

I can only assume that this entire episode is fondly remembered as the stupidest day in the history of that church. What they saw was a filthy and obviously hung over man stumble into the middle of their service, scatter several families by his stench, vomit and then stumble outside to shout nonsense at the sky in the rain. Although with all the crazy shit these people are into, maybe I was just an annoying footnote.

I walked about seven miles until I happened on my car, parked under a tree in a public park. It had been ticketed and was likely to be towed had I not found it. Luckily, I hadn't hit anything, or at least it there weren't any visible impact marks or smeared blood. I found the keys in the ignition, drunk me was again, a complete asshole. The engine fluttered to life and I pulled onto the street. I dug my cellphone out of the console and had just enough battery for a quick call. The dial rang three or four times and then:

"What the hell, John?" Jax said sleepily. "Its way too fucking early on a Sunday, man."

"Wake up asshole, it's time to go get breakfast," I said.

"Fuck you," he muttered.

"Common, twenty minutes, I'll meet you at the usual spot," I said.

"Fine," Jax hung up.

I dialed again, my phone beeping in my ear that it was about to die.

"Heelllo?" Mike said.

"Breakfast?" I asked.

"Fuck yeah, man," Mike said. "I want some fucking waffles and hash browns."

"Are you still hammered?" I asked.

"Uhh, yeah, a little, I think," he said. "Never stopped drinking."

"Jesus, alright, I'm on my way over, be ready and don't pass out," I said.

"Don't worry man, I'm still working on this bottle of, what the fuck is this...absinthe? Holy shit, I am fucked," Mike said.

"Put that shit down and brew some coffee, I'll be over soon,"

I said.

It was about a twenty minute drive to Mike's place. My phone had died, so I had it plugged into a dash outlet and was letting it charge. I found Mike sitting in a rocking chair on his front porch in shorts, sandals, sun glasses, no shirt, an enormous travel mug of coffee and what appeared to be several used condoms scattered around.

"Go get a shirt, asshole," I snapped.

He looked around at his arms and bare chest, "Oh, right," he muttered. He set the mug down and stumbled back inside. I waited, annoyed, for several minutes before he came back out. Admittedly he had complied, but had put on a red and white Che Guevara shirt.

"Every day with this shit, you know?" I said.

"Hey, I am wearing it ironically," he said.

We got in my car and got about a block down the road from his house when the car started chiming.

"Is your car gonna bitch at me until I put on my seat belt?" Mike asked.

"Yes, Mike," I said. "As all cars do."

He never wore his seat belt and it bugged the hell out of me. I

130

asked him about it once and he told me that a buddy of his burned to death when his humvee got hit with an RPG. The vehicle flipped and he couldn't undo his restraint in time. Mike was in the vehicle ahead and immediately started taking fire once the convoy stopped. By the time he could move, it was too late. Pinned in cover, he had to listen to his friend scream. I didn't blame him for the sentiment, but it was still super annoying to drive around with the ding!, ding!, ding!

When we arrived at the local Waffle House, there were several customers eating, all looking thoroughly drunk from the night before, greedily swallowing hash browns, eggs and orange juice. Jax had gotten a table and was nursing a cup of steaming coffee. His hat pulled down over his brow and dark, puffy circles clinging under his eyes.

"Well, what was so goddamn important?" Jax asked.

Mike and I sat in the booth across from him. Flopping clumsily into his spot, Mike knocked the table with his knee rocking liquid out of Jax's cup.

"Is he still drunk?" Jax asked.

"Go fist yourself. You look like you have hepatitis," Mike said.

131

"Oh yeah, which one?" Jax asked.

"All of them," Mike said.

Facing me Jax said, "You and your buddy here are a couple of bastards."

"Look just order some food. Jesus, it's like having children again," I said.

Jax raised a menu and I found mine. We poured over it, placed our orders and sat in silence. There was so much I wanted to say, but could not find the words; not without sounding crazy. I wanted to spill my mind, describe in detail my epiphany. I almost did once, but brought coffee to my lips mid-sentence, burning my tongue. Mike and Jax were content now that we were here and food was coming, so I let the quiet hang over us. I stared out the window at the cars on the highway. The food came and we ate quickly, our stomachs craving heavy fat and grease to quench the burn of congealed whiskey and beer. As we worked on our meals, I felt anxiety working its way through my gut. I would have to give an explanation, some reason why I had dragged all of us here. And saying I had a craving for waffles was only half true. The plates were cleared and we sat half dazed in our syrup and carbohydrate

132

euphoria.

"Guys, I...I went to church today," I said; losing concentration long enough to let my subconscious take over.

"What?" Mike asked.

"Yeah, man. If all of this was because you found Jesus this morning, I am going to be pissed." Jax said. "You're paying for breakfast, too."

"What? No, I mean, I don't think so? Whatever, that's not what I mean," I said.

"Dude, you seem really fucked up. How much did you have to drink last night?" Mike asked, his mouth muffled by the piece of pie he had ordered for some reason.

"A lot. Look, that doesn't matter. None of this really means a goddamn thing," I said.

"I don't disagree with you, man. You're still not making any sense, though," Jax said.

"What I'm trying to say is...," I said.

"Yeah," Mike said, talking through pastry.

Jax and I looked at him, waiting for him to continue, but he didn't.

"Look, can, I please say what I came here to say?" I asked.

"No one's stopping you," Jax said.

"I went to church today and I heard this guy," I said.

"He's called a priest," Mike said.

"Motherfucker...anyway, this priest was talking about these children in Africa. He said that they get sold into slavery by their parents and uncles or whatever. They get pimped out to these rich fuckers who bang these little kids" I said.

"That's fucked up," Jax said.

"Yeah, what the hell?" Mike asked. "I am trying to finish my pie in peace here."

"I want to kill them…kill them all," I said.

Not surprisingly, this brought an awkward lull to the conversation. I don't know if this actually happened or if it was all in my imagination, but it felt like the entire restaurant had gone completely silent and everyone was staring at me. It had been that kind of a day.

After several seconds Mike asked, "What?"

"I want to hurt them. I want to torture them and listen to them scream and then I want to murder them," I said.

134

"You don't mean that," Jax said, dismissively. The look on his face made my blood boil; brushing me off like loose dog hair.

"It's the only thing I want in this world. I need to watch them suffer and then die," I said.

"You're such a pussy, you know that? What you ride in like a hero and shoot a bunch of bad guys? Then what? You think playing soldier and savior will change a thing in your life. The only thing you will accomplish is add the faces of the people you hurt to your nightmares and I'm not just talking about these pimp assholes," Jax said.

"No, you're not hearing me. I don't want to just kill them. It's not about just shooting a gun and swinging a big dick. I want to be the last thing these fuckers see when they take their last breath. I had this whole experience this morning. It's like my calling, or something. My whole life has been leading up to this moment. I didn't have a chance to save Kat. I wasn't there to help here. I sat helplessly waiting for her to die. It's not going to be like that for those girls. I won't sit idly by, squirming uncomfortably in my seat and doing nothing like the people in that church. I am going to actually do something and it will matter to those children," I said.

135

"So, what, your daughter dies and now you're the goddamn angel of death? Get out of here. You're just another pathetic, delusional scumbag who thinks pain and despair will solve anything," Jax said.

"I don't care what you think about this. I am not asking for your permission. I am not asking for forgiveness. I am telling you what I am going to do. I have nothing left in my life. I have lost everything. If there is even a little bit of good I can put into the world by putting down some sex trafficker, then I am going to do that or die trying," I said. We sat in silence for a long while. Jax shaking his head, looked out the window.

"Listen you…you are going to get yourself killed and hurt a lot of people," Jax said.

"Fuck you," I said.

"Just listen, alright? Jesus. You're are the sorriest looking soldier of fortune I have ever seen and you will definitely die before you do any of this avenging shit you dreamed up," Jax said.

"If you're not going to help me, just leave me alone," I said.

"Goddamnit, can I please finish my sentence before you open your fucking mouth," Jax said. "Man, you are an uppity motherfucker."

"Alright, well, say it then," I said.

"You are going to fail and fail so fucking hard you're going to end up on YouTube. Look, I love you enough not to watch you shoot yourself on accident. What you're talking about, it's not a matter of buying a firearm, walking to your nearest child brothel and blasting someone. It's going to take time and planning and intel. You need money and connections. How do you plan on working all this out? You think you can walk through customs in Africa and they'll be totally fine with you importing weapons?"

"Look, man, I don't have all the details...," I said.

"You don't even know how to start, dumbass," Jax said, clearly frustrated. We sat in silence; neither considering relenting.

"I got a buddy who works black ops shit in Nairobi," Mike said between mouthfuls.

"What?" I asked.

"Yeah, buddy of mine is stationed with a CIA detail in Kenya. He can probably make a few connections," Mike said.

"You're full of shit," Jax said.

"Fine, whatever, but if you want to kill a bunch of skinny

137

child fuckers, he's probably your guy," Mike said.

"So does that mean you're in?" I asked.

"I mean, I just assumed...," Mike said.

I looked at Jax and said, "I need you with us."

"You're going to die," Jax said.

"Fine, but…," I couldn't get the worlds out before Jax cut me off.

"That's why...that's why I am going to help you. Even though I know it is going to end so, so badly for all of us. I'd rather die doing something this utterly stupid than die from liver failure or my gun in my mouth. But we are going to run this the right way and that starts with getting you into some kind of shape other than fat," Jax said.

"We are going to fucking smoke you," Mike said.

Chapter 6

In what was becoming a terrifying new normal, Aleela awoke in unfamiliar surroundings and debilitating pain throughout her body. She was prone, the ground soft. It took a moment for her synapses to fully fire and the interim had that dizzying, disorienting feeling of having no memory of the previous several hours; days maybe? She perceived low lights and hushed whispers. White sheets and pillows - she was in a bed, her head propped up. When she tried to sit, her right arm stuck; caught in something metal. Turning her head, she saw that her wrist was handcuffed to the bed frame. Panic set in again as she scanned the room for other people.

"Help," she tried to scream, but the words choked in her dry throat.

"Take it easy, girl. There's no need to hurt yourself anymore."

She turned her head and saw a middle aged, dark skinned man sitting next to her reading a book. He put the paperback down and stared into her eyes. Aleela burst into tears and tried to claw her hand free from the handcuffs. Uncle leaned forward with his powerful hands, reaching for her neck,

"Easy, easy, you're going to break your wrist. Josef is spending a fortune on a doctor to patch you up. You hurt yourself any more, he is going to put you down like a wounded animal," he said.

She turned her head, still sobbing and took in the man's features. He was too young, his hair too short – eyes too auburn, it wasn't Uncle. No, this was someone new she didn't recognize. Tears continued to flow; if she was trapped and a man was hanging over her bed, it could only mean he was there to hurt her.

"Please," she sobbed, "please don't touch me, please don't hurt me," she said.

The man chuckled, "I'm not here to sleep with you, girl."

Aleela slowed her breathing, "Well? What do you want with me?"

"You are a commodity, an investment. As long as you are healthy and the men pay and pay well, you are worth protecting," he said.

"You're here to protect me?" she asked; confusion oozing out of each syllable.

"I'm here to make sure a client doesn't damage Josef's product or fail to pay for services," he leaned back in his chair and raised the book back to his eyes.

Aleela laid her head down and wiped the tears from her eyes with her free hand; using her shirt to dab her face. She laid in silence, not sure what the next moment would bring. She scanned the quiet room and saw four other empty beds, each with a matching night stand, next to and across from her own. There were voices coming from somewhere else in the building, but she couldn't pin the sound's location.

"I'm thirsty," she said.

"They'll be here with food in an hour, you can wait," he said

"I need to go to the bathroom," she said.

"You can hold it," he said.

"What? You want me to pee the bed? How long do you think before I get sick doing something like that? Is that good for Josef's investment?" she asked.

The man sighed heavily and set his book on the night stand. He walked to the side where Aleela's hand was cuffed and undid the

141

lock. She sat up rubbing her wrist. He turned to walk back to his seat, "bathroom is over there," pointing to a curtain drawn around a corner of the room.

She stood, turned toward the open door and pushed as hard as she could towards the exit. As soon as she planted weight on her left leg, she collapsed, pain exploding in her stomach and chest.

"Now that, was a very stupid thing to do," the man said. He walked over to the shivering child, picked her up and placed her back in the bed. "Your ribs are broken in three different places. You aren't running anywhere for a while." He grabbed her hand, but she pulled away. "I was told how clever you were and how hard it was for them to catch you. I trust you learned from this?"

Aleela turned her head away from him.

"You try that again and I'll break your toes. Not something the clients need, but it will hurt like hell and make it impossible for you to move. You understand?" he asked. His voice was calm, but stern, like a patient father. "Don't be stupid."

Aleela continued to ignore him. He grabbed her chin and roughly forced her to look him in the eyes.

"You get me, girl?" he asked. She shook her head "yes". He

returned to his seat and resumed reading. She lay still, the ache in her side subsiding the longer she didn't move. Time passed, she wasn't sure how long. Her body begged for sleep, but the fear of what might happen if she were to close her eyes kept adrenaline and other chemicals pulsing through her, making it impossible to relax. She knew when exhaustion settled in, she would pass out, but for now, being awake was everything, as there was no guarantee she would wake up.

"I'm hungry," she said. The man sat there, indifferent. "I said, I'm hungry. I don't even remember the last time I ate."

The man looked at this wrist watch and then continued reading.

"Hey. I'm hungry," Aleela said loudly. At this, the door was thrown open, and a man walked in with a sandwich, oranges and a glass of water on a tray. He offered this to Aleela and she snatched them and ate greedily. She finished and laid back onto her pillow, drinking the water in one long gulp. Her stomach felt sore, but full and the feeling sent shivers of relief down her spine. She studied the man sitting next to her. He wore a button down shirt that was open at the top and jeans. His boots looked expensive and complimented a

143

serious looking wristwatch.

"What's your name?" she asked.

"Duma," the man said.

"What a stupid name,"Aleela said. The man did not respond.

"What are you reading?" she asked.

"The Inferno," Duma replied.

"I've heard of that in school. It was a requirement for the next grade," Aleela said. The man did not reply, so Aleela asked, "What is it about?"

"Hell," Duma said.

"Ha!"Aleela spat.

"Is there something funny about that?" he asked.

"Funny is not the word I would use. I think it's fantastic. I hope everything you read about comes true. I hope that book haunts your dreams," she said.

"Hmm," Duma smirked.

"Are you...are you afraid of what will happen when you die? Doesn't your conscience scream inside of you?" Aleela asked.

Duma looked over his book at Aleela for a moment and then continued reading.

"That was a silly thing to say," Duma said.

"Silly? Do you see just a little girl lying here? I am a hollowed out shell. I watched my uncle snap my brother's neck with his bare hands. I have been kidnapped. I am going to be sold as a slave. My mother and father and grandmother are dead. There is nothing silly in me, not anymore," she said.

Duma chuckled to himself but did not respond.

"Is this funny to you?" she asked.

"You think you're the only one to have a hard life?" he asked. "Does that somehow make you special? Should I feel bad for you just because you are now a slave?"

"How can you even ask that? Why don't you help me? Just let me go and I'll never tell anybody. I swear it," she said.

"I get paid too much to help you," he said.

The silence fell over them again and Aleela fidgeted with her bed sheets. Her mind working on the layout of the room, the position of the windows, analyzing opportunities in her surroundings. She noted several things: 1. the room she was in was on the ground floor. 2. There were a lot men in the compound. Between those she could hear in adjoining rooms and those she could see out the windows.

This was a large and complicated property. The pain in her side had dulled, but was a constant reminder of her limitations. Scaling a wall was out of the question, at least until she healed and she did not know how long that would take. She had no access to food or water beyond what they brought her and, most importantly, she had no idea where she was or where she would go. One thought did creep into her mind, something she actually had control over– she could break her water glass and slit her throat with a shard. Killing herself would deprive them of their property and likely make them very angry…but beyond that she wasn't sure. Death had been so close to her the last couple of days, she had considered giving into it, but every time she got close, that vitriol hate welled up inside of her. The need to cause pain in others; it pushed her back from the edge.

"What's your favorite part so far?" Aleela asked.

"I thought you didn't care?" Duma said.

"I'm bored," she said.

"This book, it's not about what you like. It's poetry. It's about what moves you. That being said, the seventh circle has always been something I have enjoyed," Duma said.

"Why is that?" Aleela said.

"It's the circle where thieves are sent," Duma said.

"Isn't there a place for pimps?" Aleela said, "I would think there would be a special place for people like you."

"You are clever...I am not a pimp, though," Duma said.

Aleela laughed, "How are you not?"

"For what I do and how much I get paid, I am a thief," Duma chuckled, pleased with his quip.

"Is that it?" Aleela said.

"I have taken much more precious things than just money," Duma said.

"The innocence of young children, like me?" Aleela said.

"No, nothing so common," Duma said.

"If it matters, I consider it something very precious," Aleela said.

"It doesn't," Duma said.

"Then what?" Aleela asked, annoyed that the conversation had run in circles.

"When you take another man's life, you are stealing from god. You take only what he can give. That seems fairly important to me," Duma said.

147

Aleela considered what he was implying and wondered how little motivation it would take for him to strangle her to death. "Have you killed many?" Aleela asked more out of disgust than curiosity.

"Enough," Duma said.

Aleela considered pestering Duma with more questions, but was afraid he might answer them with honesty. She had sufficient suffering in her own life without the burden of knowing what others had done. She turned from one side to the other trying to find a comfortable position.

"Can I read that after you?" Aleela asked.

Duma looked over the book, "What use would you have with a book like this?"

"Just because I am to be a whore doesn't mean I can't continue to read, does it?" Aleela asked. "I was supposed to return school soon."

Duma was silent and continued to read. Aleela waited for a response, but when she got none, she rolled onto her side away from him. The book bounced next to her as Duma left the room, locking the door behind him. She picked it up and, propping herself up with pillows, began reading.

Chapter 7

I'll admit, I was shocked to see Sephie's car in my driveway. It was about 10 in the morning and I had just quit my job. My plan, whatever you want to call it, suicide mission, was all I could think about. It consumed my whole world. The last thing I needed was to worry about gainful employment. Also, it was best for everyone for me to just move on. They would replace me and trade stories about the guy whose daughter died, and eventually forget about me altogether and that would be good.

Judging by the surprise in Sephie's eyes when I opened the door, she was not expecting me home. There were a few boxes with clothes and pictures around the living room; looked like she was packing. When she had moved out, it was more like she just stopped coming home. Had I been a better person, I might have noticed sooner, her drifting away, but I got comfortable being alone, and didn't notice until she was gone. She hadn't taken any of her belongings. I'm sure some things to wear and makeup, that sort of thing. But for the most part, her closet was full and her possessions untouched since the last time she had used them.

"I guess you needed to get some of your stuff?" I asked.

"Jesus, John, you scared the shit out of me," she said.

"Sorry, I uh, just got off of work," I said.

"It's like 10:30, what are doing off of work?" she asked.

"I quit," I said.

"Oh," she said.

"Yeah," I said.

"Me too," she said. "I'm moving again. Need to actually take stuff with me."

"Oh, where are you moving?" I asked.

She didn't answer; instead kept packing. She went upstairs and I set my office supplies on the kitchen counter. I opened a beer and sat down at the island stool. I noticed a nearby box full of things from the living room. I began pulling out pictures, mostly of Kat, and drawings she had done. This sort of experience happened pretty often now. I would go through some drawer and discover half a dozen things of hers. I would love every inch of whatever it was, maybe weep over it and then, when I was good and drunk, burn it in the fireplace. I couldn't handle having them around anymore.

Sephie came back downstairs and I asked, "Hey, do you want to have a beer with me?"

"I better not, I'm meeting friends later," she said, continuing to pack.

"Oh, ok," I said. After a moment, "I mean, it sounds like I might not ever see you again. It's just one beer, right?" I asked.

"I'm not here to hang out, John. I just want to pack and go," she said.

"Yeah...I get it...I guess," I said. I sipped my beer and looked over the picture in my hand. Sephie stopped and looked me up and down, probably taking pity on me.

"You know what? Sure, one beer, why not?" she said.

"Alright," I said; practically skipping to the fridge. I opened a beer and placed it in her hand. We both sat down at our kitchen table.

"What are you doing with all of her old pictures?" Sephie asked.

"I'm taking one last look and then burning them," I answered, terrified at her reaction; honesty having taken me by surprise.

"Good," she said; waves of relief rolled over me.

152

"So, what have you been up to?" I asked.

I very much wanted to seem together for some reason, which was stupid since the beer I was drinking was just beginning to help calm the tremors in my hand.

"Well, I was working up until a few days ago. Like 16 hours a day, just full tilt on whatever I could do. I had a breakdown, oh, a week ago. Just lost it in a manager's office. It started with screaming and ended with hysterical crying. I think. I kind of blocked it all out from embarrassment," she said.

"Ah, yes, I'm familiar with that," I said. She looked at me quizzically. "The blackouts I mean." I smiled slightly in an attempt to diffuse the awkwardness and failed.

"Yeah…after that, it seemed like a good idea to move on. I'm sure they were going to walk me out if I didn't. They probably felt sorry enough to give me a chance to quit," she said.

"Bastards," I said.

"Yeah," she said.

We both sipped our beers in relative silence. The hum of an elderly neighbor mowing drifted in through the walls. The day was bright with that crisp feeling that fall brings, even though the

153

temperature would be well within what most would consider warm.

"What about you?" she asked.

"I'm doing fine, I guess. Drinking less," I said, which was utter bullshit. If anything I was consuming more, but no reason to bring that up.

"You look like shit," she said.

"Been sleeping better too," This was technically true, only because I was consistently blacking out, which I guess is a kind of sleep. I would not recommend it as a form of rest, though.

"So, why quit?" she asked.

"That, well, Mike and Jax and I...we have a side project. I wanted to spend more time focusing on that. More of a passion, I guess," I said.

"Oh, well, what's that?" I said.

"What's what?" I asked, a twinge of panic in my gut. I did not have an answer for this.

"Your passion," Sephie said.

"Oh, that, uhh...," the words kind of died in my mouth. Sephie stared into my eyes, eventually raising her eyebrows and tilting her head to say "I'm waiting."

154

"Booze," I stammered.

"Booze?" she asked confused again.

"Yeah, we want to open...a distillery?" I found myself saying.

"You're cutting back on drinking, but want to open up a distillery?" she asked.

"Yeah, well, I can't drink all of our product. The point is to make money, you know?" I said.

Sephie stared at me and then shrugged her shoulders, "Alright, I guess."

"Yeah...yeah of course. I need to be careful, you know, it's going to be so good, I don't want to lose out on...all...the...profit."

"You already said that," she said.

"I just wanted to make it clear how concerned with the profits I am," I said.

Sephie abandoned this conversation and resumed drinking her beer. I was relieved.

"So are you going to tell me where you are moving?" I asked. Sephie sat silent and I got the impression she was afraid to tell me. "I'm not going to chase after you, Sephie. I have no illusions about us. We're done. There's no coming back from where we are. I know that. You moving is absolutely the best thing for you and I am happy," I said.

"Seattle," she said.

"Oh, that seems nice. Kind of rainy though isn't it? Gloomy all the time?" I asked.

"I guess," she said.

"It just doesn't seem like you. I remember you complaining about an afternoon shower, let alone months of drizzle," I said.

"First of all, that afternoon shower was a tornado that ripped the roof off of our house," she said.

I jumped in, "And you always hated when it was cloudy for like more than a day…"

She cut me off, "I'm moving there with someone, John."

"Like a roommate or something?" I asked.

"No, like a man. I met someone," she said. This did not hurt as much as I thought it would. I had anticipated this for a while now and I guess my mind had just gotten used to it. I expected to be burning with jealousy, but it was just kind of a dull calm; disappointing, really.

156

"Does he have a big dick?" I asked.

"Jesus, John, really?" she asked.

"I feel like that's a fair question," I said.

She stared at me for a moment, I think in disbelief, before adding, "It's big enough."

"So it's a baby penis?" I asked.

"Not everything is about dick size, you know?" she quipped.

"Maybe not for everyone, but definitely for you. If I remember correctly, it was, in fact, my gigantic cock that first intrigued you," I said.

"God, why do you have to be such an asshole?" she said, chuckling under her breath, which brought another wave of relief. I hadn't heard her laugh in a long, long time.

"Seriously, though, this guy, is he like a good person or whatever?" I asked.

"He's taking care of me," she said.

"Does he have a job? I asked?

"Do you?" she returned.

"Right, good point," I said.

"I'm not a child, John. I'm not looking to make all the same mistakes I did with us. He's a good man who cares about me," she said.

"Do you love him?" I asked.

This took her back. I could tell by the way the words hung over her like the shade of our relationship.

She said, "Yes," and meant it; just something about her body language.

"Do you love him more than me?" I asked.

"John...," she didn't finish her thought, but I knew what she meant.

"Well, I'm glad you're happy, I guess. I don't really know what I want anymore. It kind of sucks, but then I don't really have to fight myself anymore. I just exist, kind of," I said.

"I've spent, the last almost two years, trying to find some reason to live. I mean, I thought about killing myself, but in the way you consider what you want for dinner. It was on a list, I mean a literal list I made, of choices I could make. Isn't that crazy? Who does that?" she asked.

"I did," I said, "Well, I didn't make an actual list or anything; that would be crazy. But I did think...I do think about it a lot." She pulled out a faded and worn piece of paper. The fold lines beginning to tear from use and wear. "You are nuts," I said.

"Whatever. It helped. It helped a lot actually. I added to the list when I thought of things. I struck out others when I decided against them and then wrote them back in. I'll let you guess how many times 'drowning myself' is crossed and re-written," she said.

"What is it with women and drowning themselves? I mean what a fucking terrible way to die. There are literally thousands of better ways," I said.

"I don't know, there's something poetic about it," she said.

"You know what else is poetic? Snorting so much cocaine off of a hooker's ass that your heart explodes. Like a fucking rock star," I said; she laughed.

"Anyway, I got to the point where I had no room left to put suicide back on. I took it as a sign from, the universe. I decided that was it, I wouldn't kill myself. I had to find something else," she said.

"You didn't just like add another piece of paper?" I asked.

"Wow," she said.

"What? I'm sorry. I'm just thinking logically here; didn't actually mean that. I never...I mean maybe when I was really angry, but that was just the booze...I mean, no I never wanted, I never want that. I love you, I love you with my whole heart," I said crazily. I think saying those words out loud, it was like reminding me of a name I had forgotten long ago. I felt something. I felt not what I was used to.

"I know," she said. "I...do still love you. I do. I just...," she said.

"You just want to fuck tiny dicks?" I asked. She laughed, I felt like I had done something good.

"God, you are so annoying," she said.

"Look, if this guy, whoever he is, if he makes you happy; if he makes you feel like not drowning yourself, and I don't? Then fuck me. Get as far away from me as possible.
Run and don't ever come back, don't call, don't look at my Facebook. Just let me be and you be happy. I couldn't....I can't be the reason you have that list," I said. She sipped her beer, then threw it back and finished it.

"Can I have another?" she asked.

"Uh, yeah, of course, let me...," I practically leaped out of my seat to get a beer out of the fridge. Anything to keep her here for just a little bit longer. She was smiling at me when I sat back down and my heart fluttered.

"What?" I asked.

"I liked that, what was that, a pirouette?" she asked.

"What?" I repeated, genuinely confused.

"I didn't realize you had been taking ballet classes. Do Mike and Jax spot you while you flutter around?" she asked.

"Um, no," I said; we laughed.

We sat staring at our drinks, suddenly aware of how well this was going; we hadn't screamed at each other for minutes now and it was obvious we were entering new territory.

"So, how are your parents?" she asked, breaking the silence.

"I...I don't know, actually. I should probably call them, or something. I really haven't talked with them for a while," I said.

"Yeah," she said. I started to get nervous, fearing our conversation had run its course, she would leave and I would never see her again.

"So you have a job lined up in Portland?" I asked.

"Seattle," she said, "and no, not yet."

"I thought you were being responsible. Not like you to just

161

up and move half way across the country without a solid thing lined up," I said.

"He has a job," she said.

"Oh yeah, what, does he own a bunch of coffee shops or something?" I asked.

"Yeah, actually," she said.

"Oh," I said.

"He makes pretty good money," she said. I wasn't sure what to say.

Sephie picked up on this and asked, "What about this distillery? Are you really going to do that? With Mike and Jax?"

"Oh, yeah, that's totally something that's real...I mean that's happening. We are definitely doing that," I said. Beads of sweat started forming on my brow. Lying to Sephie, for some reason, made me feel guilty.

"You seem kind of conflicted," she said. "Nervous about quitting?"

"No, not at all. Going to the office every day, it's the emptiest thing I can imagine. I never felt fulfilled there, but it put money in our pockets and it's not like I had anything better to do.

But after Kat, the money, the work, it just made me angry. Watching those around me live a normal, boring life; nothing ever really changing, just corporate bullshit piled on top of paperwork. I feel frustrated just thinking about it," I said.

"So, what, working, being away from us, it was good when we were all together, when we could have spent time together, but now, its meaningless, when everything is broken and you have nothing else going on?" she asked.

I was surprised by this. Sephie had always had the more demanding job. It was one of the things that really attracted me to her, how ambitious and driven she was.

I said, "Look, this isn't some veiled attack on you. I don't have anything left throw in your face...I know you would have been home every night and never missed a thing if you had known...what would happen," I said, finishing my beer. I thought about grabbing another or ten and drinking them all consecutively, but something tugged on my sense of modesty and I decided against it. Sephie watched me, I think expecting me to dive into the booze.

"I don't know what to say to that, John," she said.

"I'm not looking for anything. I just wanted you to know. I

understand why you are doing what you are doing. I know that none of this was supposed to happen and we are irreparably broken and I know that means we both have to live the rest of our lives this way," I said.

"What is that supposed to mean? 'Live our lives this way.' Are you quoting something?" she asked.

"Huh? No, I'm trying to be sensitive. This isn't easy for me," I said.

"I'm leaving, not because I am broken, but because I am finding a way to be fixed. John, I still cry every single day. I hate it, and I know it will never leave me, the agony of her being gone. But I choose to live. I choose not to feel despair and it may seem impossible, but it is working. This isn't the end," she said.

And there she was, that bullheaded woman that I fell in love with.

"How can you believe such bullshit?" I asked.

"Because I feel it. I'm happy when I'm with Doug," she said.

"His name is Doug?" I asked.

"Yeah, and?" she asked, suddenly aware that she had given away too much information.

"Nothing, that's just a bitch name, is all. Just a terrible name," I said.

"What? What's wrong with the name Doug?" she asked.

"I had a boss named Doug once. That guy was a dick; just the worst. Now I hate everyone named Doug, just categorically," I said.

"That's absurd," she said.

"It makes perfect sense. Everybody does that; name association it's a real thing. Google it. I have every right to hate all Dougs. In fact, it would be un-American for me not to," I said.

"You're telling me, if the doctor had been named Doug and he saved Kat's life, you would have still hated him?" she asked.

"Absolutely. I would have respected the hell out of him, been grateful even, but hated him, down to the stupid shoes that I'm sure he wore," I said.

"You're full of it," she said.

"Eh, whatever," I said.

"Oh, shoot," she said, "I think the doctor's name was Doug."

"That motherfucker," I said. .

We both laughed.

"This distillery thing, that's not exactly what we're doing," I

165

said. She looked at me, still smiling, but letting it fade.

"What do you mean?" she asked.

"I can't tell you," I said.

"Why not?" she asked, a bit of alarm in her voice.

"It's complicated," I said.

"I told you all of my secrets; com'mon, you owe me," she said, playfully slapping my shoulder.

"All I can say is, we are going to do something really good. Something that will change...that will make my life have meaning again," I said.

"There you go with cryptic messages again. Why can't you just say what you mean? Who talks like this in real life?" she asked.

"I'm not trying to be a dick, it's just, this is really important, but I'm afraid...," I trailed off and went to sip my beer, realized I didn't have one and just folded my hands in front of me.

"You're afraid I'll try to stop you...John what are you thinking about doing? You're not going to hurt anyone, are you? Please promise me you won't hurt anybody," she pleaded. I was a little surprised how quickly she jumped to that.

"Wow, you must think I am just a terrible person," I said,

trying to act casual. I leaned back and locked my hands behind my head and smiled. In my mind I thought "relaxed." However, judging by Sephie's reaction, I probably looked psychotic.

"Promise me, John," she said, still visibly concerned

"Alright, fine, I promise. I am not going to hurt people," This lie came much easier and with none of the guilt I expected. She shook her head in agreement, although hesitantly.

"Find something to make you happy; fight for it. Please, don't just drink yourself to death," she said.

"Sephie, you have to believe me, this thing that we are going to do. It's all I think about. It's the most important thing in...it, really, really is going to change the world, OK. Do you believe me?" I asked.

She looked at me, her eyes running up and down my ragged features and with a lot of trepidation in her voice, she whispered, "Yes."

Chapter 8

"What have you been doing, girl?" Duma asked.

Aleela stepped into her dorm from the hot sun. It was comfortably furnished; a T.V. sat in the corner, there was a couch and coffee table. Rows of beds with nightstands between them. She shared the space with half a dozen other girls. There wasn't much room, but it was clean and comfortable; an acceptable place to sleep at night. She was alone, except for Duma, who sat with his feet on the coffee table, reading; most of the children played in the garden during the day.

"I went for a walk," she said.

"What do you mean, you went for a walk?" he asked.

"Just that, Duma. I went for a walk along the wall," she answered, sitting in front of a small mirror. She studied her reflection and the bruises on her face and neck. Her ribs had mended enough to relieve the sharp sting each time she breathed, but anything too strenuous would bleed over into a dull ache in her side.

"I told you to wait," Duma said over his book. "You are not

allowed outside without me," He clenched his teeth, visibly frustrated by Aleela's disobedience; she smiled.

"I'm old enough to walk around without an escort," Aleela said. "What could possibly happen? Could I be kidnapped?"

"I have no doubt you would escape if your ribs were fully healed," Duma said.

"Ha! And where would I go? You all have made it very clear how worthless and alone I am. What difference does it make?" Aleela asked.

"You are my responsibility. I forbid you from walking alone. You understand?" Duma demanded.

"Maybe I will kill myself? Slit my throat on one of the disgusting perverts that comes to this place. Do you think he would like that?" Aleela asked, not looking away from the mirror. Duma stood and in a quick blur had his hand around her throat. His fingers dug into her skin and she felt her airway being squeezed. She turned her head.

"Now you listen to me. I will kill you myself and throw your body outside the wall before I let you do that," he said, grinding his teeth again. "Do you understand?"

She whispered, straining through the pressure on her neck, "You're hurting me."

Her words hung in the air. He looked at his hand and then Aleela's face and slowly let go. She coughed, breathed in deeply; coughed again. She steadied herself on the back of the chair, rubbing her throat.

"You're going to damage your product if you keep throttling me like that," she said.

"Do you think this is a game, girl?" he yelled.

"I keep getting asked that," Aleela said.

"What?" Duma asked.

"I don't think you are very good at your job," she said, returning to her reflection. "Look at these bruises I am going to have."

She defiantly avoided his eyes crouching in the corner of her mirror.

Duma studied her, "You are going to die in this place, Aleela," he said in a low, almost whisper. She stopped for a moment and turned her head just slightly.

"I know," she said.

She stood and moved deliberately towards the door.

"Where are you going now?" Duma asked.

"Out again, it's stuffy in here," Aleela said.

"I am coming with you, then," he said.

"Whatever you would like," she said.

She walked back out into the heat. There were men milling around, some cleaning rifles, others napping in the shade. As the industry was driven by the setting sun, the days were often calm and quiet, almost eerily so. Aleela walked along the shade of trees planted near the walls, the limbs cut deliberately short and high to discourage anyone from using them to climb. Duma followed a short enough distance that he could wrestle her down, had she attempted to run away, but gave her enough room to feel like he couldn't.

"Why don't you go play with the other children?" Duma asked. "Why are you always by yourself? You have been here for weeks and all the others are together. There are toys and treats; just go play," Duma said.

"I am not looking for friends here," Aleela said.

"It makes it easier, all of this. Life can be good for you, if you make it so," Duma said.

171

Aleela kept walking.

"You could be dead in the street, or nearly there. Not fed, no dry bed. It could be much, much worse," Duma said.

She turned and shouted, "Why do you even care? How could this possibly be good? I am a slave. I am a whore." She waited for a response, but Duma just stared at her; she kept walking.

"Have you ever slept naked and hungry in the gutter? Have you even ever gone without a meal? I know that letting men have their way with you, it scares you, but after a while, you get used to it, maybe even enjoy it. You could have a nice, easy life here without having to worry about your food or bed or anything," Duma said.

"I would rather starve to death; I would rather die in a fire than have this...this life," she said.

"My family died that way," Duma said. "Starving."

Aleela stopped again, the breeze blowing dust gently around them.

"Good," Aleela said.

"I had two sons, just babies, and a wife. We lived in Mogadishu," Duma said. "They were good people and I was a good father."

"Did you watch them die?" she asked.

"Yes, he said.

"And you did nothing to help them?" she asked.

He was still for a moment, before slowly walking to Aleela. He looked her in her eyes, his face an inch away. She stiffened her body, waiting for him to do something, anything, but he remained motionless. After a tense few seconds, he smiled slightly and turned away. Aleela was about to resume walking, when he spun, catching her cheek with his elbow, knocking her hard off her feet.

He stood over her, and in a calm, but hateful tone said, "Don't you ever speak of them again." Aleela watched from the dust as his chest heaved with exasperated breaths. She dabbed the blood trickling from her nose with her hand. Her face was tender and starting to swell around her eye. "Get up," Duma's voice aggressive, but fading.

He held out his hand, but she knocked it aside with her own and stood. She dusted herself off and started toward the dorms. The chirps of insects could be heard through the hot, blowing wind. Duma walked to a nearby barracks and returned with a wet rag and water, catching up with Aleela.

"Please take these," he said. "Clean yourself up.

She didn't stop, so he kept her pace with his hands held outstretched. They walked this way to the point of embarrassment for Duma. He grabbed her roughly and forced her to stop, forcing the rag and cup into her hands. Taking a few steps back, he lit a cigarette. Aleela looked at what she held and let them fall to the ground, the water spilling. Duma watched and shook his head.

"Why...why are you so difficult? Why can't you just keep your mouth shut and do as you are told?" Duma said. He threw his cigarette on the ground and forced another out of his pack. "You are forcing me to smoke these, you know that?"

"I hear cancer is excruciating," Aleela said quietly.

Duma looked at her and then his cigarette and took a long draw. He puffed the smoke out of his lips and watched the wind carry it to where Aleela stood. "Good. Maybe I can take you with me."

Aleela continued to the dorm as Duma followed closely. Even in early evening, drunk men stumbled around the main yard. A few stopped and jeered at her; asking for a price from Duma and trying to haggle – never wanting to pay full price. He would be polite and joke with them, but would never actually make arrangements for them to have her. They stopped at her quarters. The door stood open; the sounds of sex wafting out. Aleela turned her head and looked at Duma. Her eyes conveyed a disgust and fear that knotted her stomach so tight, she thought it would burst.

"I...I can't," she stammered out.

"Can't what?" Duma said. A small smile curled across his face. He laughed at her and hate boiled up in Aleela. "You're not well enough yet for that. I'm afraid your ribs would break again."

A wave of relief crashed over Aleela followed by a sudden return of anxiety and she considered how long she could fake her injury.

"I need to get my book," he said motioning for her to follow. She remained; her feet firmly rooted to their spot. Duma opened the door, looked her over and said, "Alright, wait here, but do...not...move." He looked her over again and stepped inside.

Being outside and alone made the night suddenly cold and lonely. The sounds of debauchery and deprivation and desperation clung to the air as groups of men drank and laughed around the house. A large bonfire had been lit that drew many revelers. Couches

175

and other furniture had been dragged outside so that the guests could sit comfortably in the yard.

Aleela, desperately wanted to find Duma, but was too scared to go inside the dorm; afraid of what might happen. She thought about what to do, how to stay out of sight, when a branch snapped behind her and she spun to face it; sending a crack of lightning through her. She scanned the darkness, unable to perceive anything. She pleaded with herself that it was her imagination; trying to suppress that natural fear of the dark, when something darted out from the behind the house. A small, dark animal sprinted past Aleela. The shock of sudden movement, of actually seeing a physical manifestation of her fear, froze every muscle in her body; except for her mind which was screaming.

She watched as the thing, whatever it was, darted from cover to cover and then behind another building. Her brain tried to refine what her eyes had seen. It was an odd creature, running on two legs, and its hair was long, but uniform, almost cloth like. She squinted into the dim distance and it finally dawned on her terrified mind that it wasn't, in fact, some wild animal, but a small child. Her mind shifted quickly, now concerned about such a young girl being all alone in the dark of the yard.

The shadow stopped behind a small wooden shed near the corner of the compound. Aleela followed and rounded the same corner, her heart pounding in her chest. Where she expected to find the small girl, was instead the backside of a utility shed. She leaned around the far corner, in case the girl had kept going, but again she was alone and had a clear sight to the next hiding spot that was more than a few yards away. No one could have moved that fast. She retraced her steps to the back of shed and stopped. Looking for a door or some other way to hide. There was a nagging pull in the back of her consciousness that she had imagined the entire thing, but she pushed it aside.

Aleela searched every dark, shadowy place she could find around the shed, but found nothing. She was about to leave when the faintest sound floated up from the ground. On her hands and knees, Aleela could see that the base of the shed had been pulled away and a very small and very scared pair of eyes pierced through.

"What are you doing?" Aleela asked.

"Hiding," the girl said.

Aleela thought for a brief moment, "Can I join you?" she

asked.

"No, this is my spot," the girl said.

"Please," Aleela begged, "please let me in."

"No!" the girl said sharply, clearly frightened.

Aleela leaned back on her legs, an ache growing in her neck and lower back as she leaned over.

"What's your name?" Aleela asked.

"Hawa," the girl said.

"That's a pretty name," Aleela said. It was hard to tell in the dark, but the girl seemed to be years younger. She had dark skin and longing, exhausted eyes. He face was slightly bony, as if she hadn't eaten in several days, but her voice was sweet.

"How did you get away?" Aleela said.

"Emile had too much to drink," Hawa said.

"Is that the man who watches you?" Aleela asked. Hawa shook her head, but did not speak.

"How did you find this place?" Aleela asked.

"The first time I ran away, someone else had pulled the board away, but no one was in here. I come here every time he drinks wine," Hawa answered. "What's your name?"

178

"Aleela," said.

"I saw you, when they brought you in. I saw what you did to Josef. Everyone did," Hawa said.

"Was that the white man with the blond hair?" Aleela asked.

"Yes," Hawa said.

"I don't remember much...from that day," Aleela said.

"I was so happy. We all were," Hawa said.

"How long have you been here?" Aleela asked, shifting her weight again to take pressure of her legs.

Hawa stretched out her hands and began counting her fingers. The bones in her arms were thin and protruding. There were numerous deep scars. "Two years," she said. Aleela began to cry. The thought of being there for that long, it was overwhelming.

"Shh, please, oh, please don't cry, someone will hear you," Hawa pleaded, but Aleela, couldn't restrain the ruin that ran in her like a river.

"I'm sorry, please don't cry. Shh, please," Hawa said.

"Sorry, sorry, I'm not trying to cry, I just...," Aleela stopped, unable to put her despair into words.

Hawa cowered in the dark, damp crawl space under the shed.

"I'm sorry, I didn't mean to scare you," Aleela said.

"It's O.K., please just be quiet now," Hawa said. Aleela looked over her face and took in the deep lines and sharp cuts of Hawa's features.

"When was the last time you ate?" Aleela asked.

"Few days ago, I think," Hawa said.

"Doesn't the man who watches you bring you food? Or take you to the kitchen?" Aleela asked.

"What? What man? I am with all the other girls. They all watch us," Hawa said. "We eat when there is enough after the others. They don't want us to get fat because no one likes fat girls."

"Doesn't someone watch you? Like Duma?" Aleela said.

"No one like Duma cares about me," Hawa said.

"Duma doesn't care about me," Aleela said, "It's his job. He tries to keep me from running away."

"No one follows me around. Duma brings you food sometimes?" Hawa asked, seemingly confused. "You're the only one. You're special."

"Why? Why would I be special?" Aleela asked.

"I don't know, no one does," Hawa said.

Aleela thought about this, putting her hand in her dress pocket. She felt the crust of bread she had left over from lunch. Offering it to Hawa, she said, "Please take this. I'll get more."

Hawa looked at the food and then at Aleela and then snatched it out of her hand. "I'll get more," Aleela repeated.

"Hey! What the hell are you doing?" Duma yelled.

Hawa pushed herself back into the shadows. Aleela breathed deeply and turned her head.

"I'm playing in the dirt. I got bored waiting," she said.

"Who is there with you?" Duma demanded.

"No one," Aleela said.

"Don't lie to me Aleela. I heard you talking," Duma said, grabbing her by the arm and yanking her roughly to her feet.

"I was talking to myself. There's no one else," Aleela said, walking passed Duma toward the dorm.

"Wait!" Duma demanded. Aleela kept walking. "I said wait, goddamnit," Duma caught Aleela by her arm and dragged her back to the shed. Bending down he peered into the opening at the baseboard. Duma squeezed her arm tightly; no chance to run away. The throbbing in her ears from the blood pounding through them was almost deafening. Duma would find Hawa, and then what? Would she be hit more? Would Hawa? Aleela stammered a few syllables, trying to distract Duma, but couldn't find any words. He looked in for a long, long moment.

"Come on," Duma said, standing up.

He let go of her and walked to the dorms. Aleela followed, looking over shoulder for any sign of Hawa, but saw none.

Chapter 9

"Yeah, well, you're an asshole," I said, completely out of breath.

"Does it look like a give a fuck?" Mike shouted, as I pushed myself up from the floor.

"I banged your mom," I said.

Mike put his boot down roughly between my shoulder blades.

"Keep going; twenty more," he said.

I struggled against the added weight; the muscles in my arms and chest screaming for oxygen.

"I...always...hated...you," I grunted between gasps.

"Good, hate will make you strong," Mike said. He checked his phone; swiping through menus to quick electronic chirps. He was dressed in sturdy jeans and a short sleeved t-shirt. His hat pulled down over his brow. I pushed through a handful more push-ups before my arms gave out and I crumpled to the floor. Mike glanced at me over his phone, "You're not done yet."

"Fuck you; that was twenty," I said.

"Well, since half of those were the weakest goddamn pushups anyone has ever done, you get ten more," he said.

"Unless you come down here and move my arms for me, I'm not doing another fucking thing," I said, finally able to slow my breathing.

Mike put his phone back into his pocket and screamed "Give me ten more fucking push-ups or I will curb stomp your fucking face. You think this is hard? You know what will be easy? Getting me killed in some hajj infested hell hole. Get the fuck up and keep going."

"Alright...alright," I stammered.

Somehow, I managed to put my hands under my chest; my arms basically numb. With every ounce of strength in my body, I forced myself up, working against the weight of Mike's boot which had found itself on my back once again.

"One," Mike screamed in my ear. "Two." I struggled to lift myself and with each attempt the pain in my muscles exploded. I tried to ignore it, to think about anything other than what was happening; trying to distract my mind, but all I could think about was how much it hurt and how much I hated it. Finally, with the very

184

last bit of energy I could muster, I finished the last push-up and collapsed.

"Good, John, good, that was really something," Mike said. I lay on my stomach, unable to move. "Really, I thought you were finished, but you showed a lot of heart. Of course that's the women's workout routine...," The words trailed off as I outstretched both middle fingers from my lifeless arms.

"Jesus, Mike, what the hell have you guys been doing?" Jax asked, walking to our position. He was wearing jeans with a thick, heavy belt holding a pistol holster. We had been staying at a small farm owned by his family. It was a place of solace for all of us; the quiet, rolling hills offering peace when there was little to be found. Even as kids, we would camp and pretend to be real men roughing it in the wilderness. We thought it would be a relatively inexpensive place to practice everything we needed to: survival, shooting, physical exercise. But what really drew me to that place was the connection to my childhood. I don't know, something about coming home before leaving forever.

Anyway, Jax had made a run into town to get supplies and left Mike in charge of my fitness. I was, to put it kindly, out of shape. They were both working hard to ensure I wouldn't just die immediately of exhaustion and being fat as soon we left the States. Mike really enjoyed this part of my training. He also and liked to be an extra special cock sucker when given the chance.

"What? It's arm and chest day," Mike said.

"He looks like he's fucking dead," Jax said.

I just moaned and continued to lay on the ground, the feeling starting to return to my arms.

"He was being a pussy about it, so I started smoking the shit out of him," Mike said.

Jax stared hard at Mike, "If you blow out his heart, it will be pretty fucking hard to..."

I stirred, trying to sit up. Mike shrugged his shoulders and sat on a nearby rock. Pulling out a small granola bar, he started carefully unwrapping it.

"I'm so fucking thirsty," I said. I sat with head between my knees. The hot air leaching the moisture in buckets from my body. A water bottle fell between my legs. I grabbed it and began inhaling as quickly as my mouth and lungs could draw in the liquid.

"You better slow down. That's gotta last the day," Jax said.

I coughed out, "What?"

"You're not getting another bottle. You better make it last," Mike said.

"What?" I asked. "Why?"

"You never know if you'll find water in the field and filtering it takes forever," Jax said.

"You gotta learn to pace yourself. Conserve what you got. Tactical and operational advantages are what keep you alive. Being all dehydrated or stopping every 30 minutes to filter piss poor water, that will get you killed," Mike said.

"They really teach you that or are you just fucking with me again?" I asked.

I placed the bottle on the ground and stared at them. It took every ounce of self-control not to finish it. Mike and Jax returned my stare with silence. I stood, shakily. "Alright then, if that's what it takes."

"You got a long way to go," Mike said.

"Yeah? No shit," I said. "What's next?"

"Basic weapons training," Jax said.

We moved to a nearby makeshift range. A plastic folding table was covered in black gunmetal, boxes of ammunition, rags and targets. At the end of the lane was a wooden pallet standing upright and braced with cinder blocks. A target with concentric circles was stapled in the middle.

"Today, you're going to learn how to field strip, clean, reassemble and fire a .45 semi-automatic 1911 model pistol."

"Jesus, you're starting him with a .45?" Mike asked.

"Yeah, that seems a little big for my first time," I said.

"That's what she said," Mike said.

"Fuckin...alright, look, yes it is a large caliber. However it has a tremendous amount of stopping power. If you can master this sidearm, then anything else you might actually carry will seem much more manageable. Besides, we might actually be using these in the field and I am not taking a bunch of limp dick 9mm," Jax said.

"Fair enough," Mike said.

Jax stood next to me and presented the weapon. The slide was locked back, revealing the mechanical innards. He handed me an empty magazine. "Slide the magazine in till in clicks." I pushed it in and felt it click into place. "Alright, press the slide release." I used my thumb to push down on small round button right above the handle grips. The magazine fell out.

"That'd be the wrong one, there," Mike said.

"Go fist yourself," I snapped back.

"Look, this is the slide release," Jax pointed to a small rectangular lever near the base of the slide. I pushed it and the top half of the gun shot forward.

"Now, pull it back until it locks into place," Jax said. With more effort than I'd like to admit, I pulled the slide until it locked again.

"This is called the action," he said pointing to the slide. "This is the frame and trigger. This particular pistol also has a safety. Two things to remember with that. Black is boring and red is dead." He pushed the safety button demonstrating the function. "Rounds are fed from the magazine into the chamber. When the action has been charged and trigger pulled, the firing pin strikes the igniting charge on the back of the round, igniting the black powder inside the casing. The pressure from this reaction propels the bullet out of the barrel." He held up a brass round from a nearby box.

"This is really important, so pay attention," Mike said. "Don't ever put your finger on the trigger until you are ready to shoot and don't point that fucking thing at anything you don't want dead."

189

"Alright, give it a try," Jax said.

I felt like a little more instruction was needed before setting me loose with such a powerful tool, but what can I say? I am a man from the Midwest. I was born with a hard-on for guns; I just never got around to learning how to shoot earlier. I took the magazine, now loaded with a few rounds and the pistol. Following the instructions barked by Jax, I slammed the magazine into the handle of the pistol and felt it click securely into place. I then very carefully pushed the slide release and jumped a little when it slammed shut. Mike and Jax took a collective step back.

I raised the pistol, gripping it as tight as possible in my right hand and cupping it with my left. I had seen every shooter ever in every modern movie hold a gun this way so it just felt normal. I raised the sights and focused on the target at the end of lane. I applied pressure to the trigger and waited and waited and waited. It was nerve wracking, anticipating the powerful bang. I squeezed to the point of feeling ridiculous I turned my head to ask if I was doing something wrong and Mike and Jax were shaking heads at me. I lowered the pistol and noticed the safety was still in the "black" position.

"Oh, look I..." Mike and Jax both cut me off before I could finish; swearing things I dare not repeat. The muzzle had apparently drifted over them as I examined the safety pistol. I immediately pointed it towards the target and pushed in the safety. "Sorry" I said sheepishly.

I raised the pistol again and expected a long trigger pull but instead, before I was ready, there was sharp report; the gun almost jumping out of my hand with the force.

"Fuck, man, holy shit, that was loud," I turned my head and saw Mike and Jax both wearing earphones. "Oh, haha, very funny assholes. Thanks for the heads up."

"Why are you shouting?" Mike asked.

"Fuck you!" I said, the ringing in my ears almost deafening.

Mike handed me a pair of ear protection and yelled, "Also, shooting 101, eyes and ears. You're already wearing glasses so you got your eyes covered. Always wear ear protection, too. Especially in the field. We'll be buying radio headsets; wear them. Always. There's nothing fun about tinnitus."

After what felt like too long, the throbbing in my head subsided and I convinced myself I could hear, although I had this
191

paranoid feeling that I had lost something even from that one round. The remaining rounds in the magazine were squeezed off without any of the bullshit of the first, but I still didn't manage to hit the target.

Jax stood next to me and took the pistol from my hand, "You load each round one at a time. Use the back of jacket to push the lever down." I watched him insert the first two and then I finished loading. "Alright, this time I want you to square your shoulders and legs. Bend your knees a little but not so much that it's uncomfortable. Remember, you're battling physics. The propellant in the casing pushes the bullet down the barrel. All that force is pushing back on you – your hands, your arms. This causes the muzzle to jump each time you fire. You want to compensate for all of that by leaning into the pistol; use your weight as a counter balance."

I took this stance and Jax walked around me, inspecting my posture. He used his leg to kick my feet farther apart and squared my shoulders with his hands, "Now, pick a spot on the target. Once you got it, focus entirely on the front sight. Line it up with the back. When you're ready, hold your breath and squeeze the trigger; do not jerk it."

I picked my spot, lined up the site, held my breath and just lightly kept pressure on the trigger and bang! The pistol discharged. This time, however, I could feel the difference. It pulled in my hand, but not uncontrollably. I found myself in the same starting position. I lowered the weapon and scoured the target. I was about an inch off from where I had aimed.

"Hey, not terrible," Mike said.

"Not bad, not bad at all," I said.

"Do it again and then get cocky, asshole," Mike said.

I returned to my stance and fired off several more rounds. The grouping was all over the target, "I guess I got lucky?" I asked, dropping the magazine and plugging new rounds into it.

"It's all about repetition; muscle memory. You're gonna need a lot more range time," Jax said.

I must have shot a thousand rounds that day and by the time we were done, my hands ached, by shoulder muscles burned and I was absolutely sick of the burnt waft of gunpowder. They had left the range before me to set up tents and a fire going. I sat down next to it. This was the first time all day I had decided to actually sit rather than just collapse from exhaustion. By the time I got back, Jax and Mike were eating from pouches of dehydrated food they had cooked with boiled water. The thermos sat over the fire. I fetched it and poured it into my own bag – macaroni and cheese.

"This is probably the most disgusting shit I will ever eat, but I am so fucking hungry. It smells delicious," I said.

I had to wait for the food to cook. If I reopened the bag too soon after pouring in the water, it would release all the heat and I would end up eating very tough food. The pangs in my stomach were almost unbearable, though. I thought about sucking on the uncooked pasta; anything would be preferable to waiting.

"It's actually not that bad," Jax said.

"Well, the teriyaki is, in fact, terrible," Mike said.

"So what's on the agenda for tomorrow?" I asked.

"Leg day, bro," Mike said. "You are gonna get smoked."

"Five mile march in full gear," Jax said.

"Sounds fun," I said. They continued to eat while I sat, my gut churning with anticipation. The silence was unbearable; the sounds of my stomach eating itself over the crackle of burning wood My mind was too worn down to think of anything coherent to talk about so I just said the first thing I thought about. "So Mike, how come you never settled down with anyone?"

Mike looked at me while chewing, clearly annoyed at the question and that I was interrupting his meal. I let the silence hang rather than pursue a conversation, but after a moment he shrugged and said, "Just prefer not to get continuously fucked over, I guess."

"I thought you and that chick, what was her name? Kelsey? Kelley? Whatever, I thought you two might work out. You seemed happy," I said. The timer went off and I greedily ripped open the pouch and shoveled scalding noodles into my mouth. "Holy fuck," I gasped; muffled by the food trying to burn through the roof of my mouth.

"Yeah, we were happy for a while," Mike said.

"What, it just stop being fun, or something?" Jax asked.

"I dunno, man. Things just got stale after a while. I think she was really into the whole 'hero' complex. You know, fuck a soldier, everyone thinks you're a saint. That shit or whatever," Mike said. His voice trailed off, almost like he was remembering something. I took this as a sign this woman had meant something to him. Mike had a long list of conquests. None had appeared to be too serious.

"That was it? Like, she realized you were an asshole and the magic

195

died?" Jax asked.

"I don't know. She just got quiet after a while. Then she left," Mike said. "What about that bitch, oh, who was it, oh yeah, your wife?" Mike asked. I thought he meant me, but before I could answer Jax said, "Listen, she was a perfectly respectable lady, until she was a complete whore who banged everyone who had a dick and some that didn't."

"She ever say why?" I asked.

"Because she likes dick, I guess," Jax said, returning to his meal.

We sat in silence for a moment. Although it was still painful to eat, I was able to choke down my food. It actually was pretty good.

"She was spoiled. She lived her whole life without ever having to give to another person. When I was deployed, it was easy. She wrote letters, took pictures; told everyone on Facebook how much she loved me. We didn't actually have to be together. She could tell everyone we were together, live her own life and not actually have to deal with me as a person. When I came home, I was too much work. She just gave up," Jax said.

"What?" I asked.

"The reason Brittany left: she just walked away. I don't think it was laziness. It think she made a deliberate decision that being with me was harder than she wanted in a relationship. I'll be the first to admit I am fucked. I have no illusions about who I am; combat makes that real fucking obvious. For someone like her, comfort and routine are god. She just wanted to get hammered with her friends, eat shitty food and feel loved by someone, anyone, who didn't push her too much.

When I was in, it was so easy. She would be at some party, make a big deal when I called, you know, let the whole goddamn place know she needed to answer. Then she would be super sweet, listen to all my shit. Wouldn't be long, I'd need to get back to work and she'd get back to her booze. " Jax said.

"I had no idea it was like that," I said.
Silence fell again. The fire crackled and despite the ache in my joints and muscles, I felt relaxed. I took a pot of coffee sitting next to the fire and poured a cup for myself.

"It's a shitty thing man...what happened," Mike said.

"Yep, sure was," Jax said. "The worst part was, I didn't mind all that much. I knew she was fucking around. I knew she didn't really love me anymore. Broken as I am, I still felt, you know? But, at the end of the day, all I really fucking cared about was having someone to talk to. Someone who was willing to listen."

"And someone to bang," Mike said.

"Shit...," Jax said.

"I tell you guys that Sephie met someone else?" I asked.

"No shit?" Mike said.

"Yeah, she's moving to Seattle or something. She packed all her stuff. She's gone," I said.

"Dude, I'm sorry," Mike said.

"No, no it's alright; really. It's for the best. I mean with what we are going to do, this...this is really for the best," I had a hard time finishing this. There was an odd pain in my chest; not physical so much as emotional.

"That doesn't make it any easier," Jax said.

"Yeah, I mean, it is pretty shitty, but what did I expect was going to happen? She can't live the rest of her life orbiting the sphere of my misery. I knew we were done the second Kat died. I wouldn't ever function again in a way that resembled normal. She's different.

She has more than just the people around her. She is a unique, strong individual who has purpose and meaning. That's the fundamental difference. I am parasite. She is a cure," I took a long draw from my coffee and admired the night sky. So bright, even in pitch black, the stars, they were something. That's what you get when you are far enough from all the light pollution of a city; beauty and space and immense expanse.

"I think I'll find someone," Mike said.

"Oh yeah, why's that?" Jax asked.

"We'll, for one, I'm not completely fucked like you two bastards," Mike said.

"Fair enough," I said. We all laughed.

"Really though, I think being warped is not limited to the male gender. There are plenty of chicks out there that are just as twisted as us. I've met some. It's just a matter of timing, you know? We're all just drifting. Sometimes, you get real lucky and find yourself loving someone who actually matters," Mike said.

"Wow," I said.

"What?" Mike asked.

"That's the stupidest shit I have ever heard," I said.

"Fuck you," Mike said, raising his cup of water. He refused to drink coffee because he is a fucking communist.

Chapter 10

"Hawa, why are you hiding over there?" Aleela asked.

"Josef is here today," she pointed to a well-dressed man, standing in the large doorway to the main house, giving orders to those around him.

"I thought he was here every day," Aleela said. She knelt down next to Hawa who was crouched next to stacks of sand bags and wooden pallets.

"Who are you talking to?" Duma asked. He sat in the shade of a nearby tree. He was reading and sipping from a tin mug. The day was hot, as usual, and most of the girls were napping in the cool of their bunks. Aleela hated being in there. The acts committed inside had a heavy warmth that turned her stomach. She spent her time outside. A few men, following Josef's orders, were unloading large boxes, probably food, into the nearby main house.

"Nobody, just myself," Aleela said. Hawa crouched in fear.

"Girl, I think the sun and heat are starting to get to you," Duma said. He took a drink from his mug and then threw a water bottle to Aleela. "Drink," he commanded.

Aleela caught the bottle and took a long draw. She turned and offered the bottle to Hawa who took small sips while looking around.

"Aren't you hot out here?" Hawa asked.

"It's not so bad. The breeze is nice," Aleela said. It was, in fact, whipping sand and burned exposed skin. "Aren't you?"

"No, I'm used to it. I lived in the desert. It got really hot there, not just warm, like here," Hawa said.

"This is only warm?" Aleela asked.

"Yeah, you get used to it," Hawa took another sip. "Is Duma still watching you all the time?"

"He's right over there. He'll see you for sure if you stand up," Aleela said, taking the water bottle back.

"I am going to try and run away, Aleela," Hawa said. Aleela choked on water.

"You alright?" Duma asked, not looking up from his book.

"Yes," Aleela choked out, working hard to suppress her cough.

"In a couple of days. I'm going to sneak over the fence,"

202

Hawa said.

"Hawa, are you crazy? Where will you go? What if someone sees you?" Aleela said.

"I have to Aleela, I have too. Emile will be here in a few days. He always comes back at the end of the month. I can't," her voice trailed, "I can't do it again. If I don't leave, I am going to kill myself," Hawa said.

"Look, if you leave here at night, you will be killing yourself. You have no way of knowing where you are going. No idea of the land or what is really out there," Aleela said. She tried hard not to raise her voice.

"It can't be worse than this place," Hawa said; drawing in the dirt.

"You don't even have any food or water. You'll starve," Aleela said, placing her hand on her shoulder.

"I saved up some. I've been keeping my meals. I have plenty to get me into town," Hawa said. "I know you're worried, but I promise, I'll be OK. I just need to get over the wall."

"This is crazy. What will you even do when you get to town?" Aleela said.

"Tell the police, of course," Hawa said. Aleela felt the betrayal and anger of her own abduction as she remembered.

"Believe me, they won't help. They probably come here on the weekends. They'll promise to save you and then dump you right back here. There is no place to go. You have to listen. I can take care of you. I can make sure you are safe. Out there, you'll die and there will be nothing I can do."

"How? How can you help?" Hawa pleaded. Her eyes were hopeful. She wanted nothing more than to believe.

"I...," Aleela thought for a moment. "I don't know. " Hawa's face fell with such weight and such force that Aleela's heart tore.

"You can't do anything. No one can. I know you're worried about me leaving, but anything, anything would be better than staying here another night. I don't want to die alone out there, but, but...," Hawa's words died away.

"We can figure something out. There has to be a way to keep you hidden. What about under the shed. "Aleela asked.

"They boarded it back up after the other night," Hawa said. Aleela felt guilt coiling around her mind. Her stupid curiosity had jeopardized Hawa's safety and exposed her to terrible things.

"Look, if I can find a place for you, will you at least consider not leaving? Staying here is awful, but leaving will mean death or worse," Aleela said.

"You only say death is worse because you haven't been with anyone yet. Duma hasn't made you. It won't take long for you to feel this way. If you had done what I have done, you wouldn't try to stop me," Hawa said.

"I am not going to make it easy for them. They will have to kill me," Aleela said.

"I thought that too, when I first got here and for a while I fought them. Then I got hungry. I got cold and thirsty and I kept telling myself I will die, I will die and then they will never have me. But, watching the other girls eat and drink and have new clothes...I gave up. But I don't want food or water or a new dress anymore. I don't want to die, but I cannot let another man touch me. I want to live. I want to be happy. I want to leave and not let them take me anymore. "

"But running away in the night, that's suicide. They will take everything from you," Aleela said.

"Do you know why Duma hasn't forced you yet? Hawa

asked.

"Because I'm not well yet," Aleela said.

"So? Do you know how many girls here have broken bones? This is not a comfortable place. The men are rough, even the ones who aren't paying. Do you think they care about if you are in pain?" Hawa asked.

"I haven't seen any other girls with casts or bandages," Aleela said.

"How many of them do you know or even talk to?" Hawa asked.

"I don't know," Aleela said.

"Ask Duma sometime. Ask him why you are so well taken care of," Hawa said.

"What? Aleela asked. "My bones are broken, my family is dead. I am slave here. How am I taken care of at all?"

"We all are lost and broken, but are also forced to do terrible things," Hawa said.

They sat in silence, the frustration hanging between them.

"Why don't you come with me?" Hawa asked, she became animated and Aleela motioned for her to be quiet. "Please, Aleela, please. Come with me. We can run away together, tonight. You will be with me and keep me safe," Hawa said.

Aleela felt a twinge of pain in her ribs, she winced.

"I can't Hawa, I don't think I could even raise my arms above my head," Aleela said

"I thought you are getting better?" Hawa asked.

"I am, but I can't scale a wall and rough if it in the bush. I can't take care of you out there," Aleela said. She crossed her arms and scowled at Hawa, "This is nonsense. You cannot go. I forbid it. You understand?"

"Please don't be mad, Aleela, I'm sorry. I didn't mean it. I won't go. I promise, I won't," Hawa tugged on Aleela's skirt. She stood, the wind blowing dust around her ankles, covering her feet. There was a calming silence during the day. The truths of the dark hidden in the quiet.

"Hawa, you must keep your promise that you won't go. I'm not mad at you. I'm...," Aleela said.

"It's this place. I know," Hawa said.

"What do you mean?" Aleela asked.

"It makes you crazy. You start thinking things you'd never

think; doing things you'd never do. I've eaten garbage. I've slept in the dirt. It just breaks you," Hawa said.

"No, that's not going to happen to me," Aleela said.

Hawa laughed, "What makes you special? You think I didn't feel that way?"

"I know, Hawa. But *I am* going to see this place torn down brick from brick. I think the devil took me when my brother died. All I can think about is tearing these men to pieces. It consumes me. I haven't figured out how yet, but it will happen. This isn't something they can stop or take from me. It's who I am," Aleela said.

Hawa started to speak, but closed her mouth. They stood in silence again.

"Alright, Aleela, I'll stay. You must find a place for me to hide though. I can't go through another night," Hawa said.

Aleela left Hawa in the shade behind the pallets and walked slowly toward Duma. He eyed her carefully over his book.

"What, girl?" he asked.

"I'm hungry," she said.

"And? We don't eat till later," he said.

"Now, Duma. I feel faint. I think I'm sick," Aleela said.

Aleela walked to where Duma was sitting and he grabbed her chin with his thumb and finger. He peered into her eyes and moved her head around, inspecting her ears, nose and neck, "I knew it. I told those bloody doctors you needed antibiotics longer," he released her head. "Come on, girl. Let's go."

She took a step and stumbled to the ground, "I can't. I'm too weak," she said.

Duma looked at her on the ground, helped her up and sat her in his chair. "Don't move," he said sharply. "I mean it, do *not* move."

Aleela nodded and watched Duma walk into the kitchen of the main house. As soon as he turned the corner. She exploded out of her chair. Sprinting to Hawa, she said, "I'm going to find you another spot. I'll come by and let you know when it's safe. Hawa said, "OK, don't take too long. Duma will be very angry if you are gone."

"Don't worry about him. Just wait for me to get back," Aleela said.

She sprinted to the old shed where she had met Hawa that first night. She used her hand to scoop the dirt away from the new skirting screwed in place. Digging deep enough, she put her hand under the metal and pulled. It dug deep into her flesh, cutting her palms, but it didn't move at all. She wanted to scream, mostly in frustration, but bit her lip instead. Letting go, she leaned back and kicked it with all her strength, the metal clanging with the effort. Out of breath, she stopped and examined what process she had made. The skirting was bent slightly, but was no closer to being loosened.

Tears crept into the corners of her eyes, but she wiped them away quickly and stood. Walking to the door of the shed, she picked up a heavy rock and knocked the door handle off. Her heart stopped as she heard Duma's voice carrying on the wind. She leaned around the corner and saw him talking with another man. The two were laughing and involved in their conversation.

Stepping inside, the walls were lined with tools. She grabbed a crow bar and ran outside. She jammed the heavy claw into a small gap between the skirting and wood frame. With all her strength, she pushed the lever. The metal screamed in protest, but gave slightly. She stopped and reapplied pressured. The pain in her ribs was unbearable; tears flowed freely down her cheek. With a sudden *pop!* the screws ripped from the wood. There was now enough play for a small child to climb under. Throwing the crow bar in the dirt under the shed, she pushed the skirting back to make its sabotage less obvious. She closed the door, which no longer latched, but was otherwise intact. She ran, each step compressing fractured bone. There was a large tree and a stack of wooden pallets between her and where Duma was standing. She heard his conversation end; he would see the empty chair any moment. She pushed herself, kicking up dust. She threw herself into the seat, just as Duma came around the corner.

Duma looked her over. She was sweaty and breathing heavily, "Jesus, you look terrible. How do you feel?"

"Awful," she said.

"Let's get you to the infirmary," he said. "Josef is going to be furious."

Chapter 11

"You're awful at this," Mike said. He watched as I assembled my rifle. We sat in the dirt. This was supposed to get me comfortable in field stripping and cleaning, but in reality it was just a pain in my ass.

"Well, your constant criticism doesn't help," I said, fumbling with the bolt and spring, trying to compress them back into the breach. I got frustrated, pushing too hard; sending them flying out of my hand. Catching the fleshy part of the palm of my hand, the breech tore an inch long gash. Blood oozed out. "Fuck," I said, throwing the rifle pieces to the ground.

"Pick it up. You're going to have to re-clean every piece. All that dirt and shit is going to gunk up the spring and firing mechanism," Mike said.

"Fuck you, asshole. It's fine. Give me a goddamn bandage for my fucking hand," I spat.

Mike, without any verbal response, reached into his field jacket and tossed me a gauze pad and tape. I bandaged my hand, which was my first break since sunrise. I hadn't eaten all day and my water ration had been cut in half. I was on a jagged edge.

I'd be dragged out of bed at 3 A. M., marched five miles; carrying 100 pounds of gear on 500 calories from the previous day. I had this cadence in my head, fuck this, I'm fucking done. Every step, I would repeat this to myself, but then when I was about to just collapse, my foot moved one more time. Mike and Jax would run ahead and behind me so that I was never last. Their constant footsteps kept pushing me and pushing me to take just one more step.

Every moment I wasn't shooting, or fashioning a shelter, or cooking an MRE, I thought about how much of a fool I was. The entire plan was insane. What could it possibly accomplish besides my untimely death? More than that, what really made me a truly terrible person, I was jeopardizing Mike and Jax's lives, too. This, looking back now, is completely unforgivable. I'll be going to hell for many, many reasons, but this...this alone buys me a spot in the special section for people who take up two parking spaces in a crowded lot and eat all of the banana flavored runts out of a box.

Cutting my hand though, sitting in the mud, cold, exhausted and starving, I started to cry. I'm not ashamed to admit that. Being

213

through that fucking mess, any man would. It wasn't just the physical toll that the last month had taken. No, it was more so the mental flogging of just constantly failing. I was flailing around, trying to play soldier and wasting everyone's time. Not only that, but I knew that once I did give up, I truly had nothing but mediocrity and failure as companions. No good man turns his back on those around them. You push yourself to your limits and then however many needed steps beyond for the man next to you. Quitting would have been pissing on that idea. I would be alone, wallowing in shame and just waiting for the courage to blow my brains out.

So, there I was, tears rolling down my cheeks as I put pressure on my hand. I wrapped it up tight. Mike stood, placed his hand on my shoulder and whispered in my ear something that I will never, ever repeat. All I can say is that, it was the only thing that could have gotten me back on my feet. It gave me enough to stand up; to put one foot in front of the other.

I found myself gathering the pieces of the rifle. I used cotton cloth to wipe away the greasy mess that caked the bolt, spring, and everything else that comprises the moving parts of a firearm. I applied new oil and carefully and deliberately reassembled the

214

weapon. I slapped the magazine in place and rolled onto my stomach. I crawled about 50 yards to a downed tree. Very slowly, I peaked over the bark. Three dummy targets were staked another 100 yards away. I raised the rifle and sighted their heads. I squeezed off three quick shots and struck each one with precision. I dropped the magazine and recharged the weapon. I fired three more times and hit each target. I released the magazine, pulled the bolt to make sure the chamber was cleared and safetied the rifle.

Mike from behind me said, "Good job."

Tears came again. I don't know how long we were out, but it was dark when we made it to camp. I sat down and used my pack as a cushion to sit against in front of the fire. Jax had taken the truck and set up a fire so that we could rest on arrival. The chill in the air was sharp. My coat and thermals blocked most of it, but my fingers and face were red. Warmth and light poured into me as the flames whipped around in rough pit of stone.

Had I not been exhausted and starving, it would have been a perfect night for camping. I set my water near the fire and waited for it to boil. Jax and Mike did the same and we sat in a quiet tiredness that crept into all of us.

"He did well today," Mike said.

"Oh, yeah?" Jax asked.

"I was pinging targets from 100 yards," I said, smiling. I felt a sense of pride I had never felt before in my life.

"Fuck yeah, bud. That's outstanding," Jax said.

"Won't be long now," Mike said.

That realization, the epiphany that we would soon be leaving; I think it hit us all with more force than any of us expected.

"Jesus, we really going to do this?" Jax asked.

"Absolutely," Mike said without hesitation.

"Look, I know you both have put a tremendous amount of time and work into the last couple of months with me. I don't want to seem ungrateful, but we don't have to do this," I said. I felt guilty evening mentioning this, but I felt like it was essential they had every opportunity to stop...that I had every opportunity. We sat, watching the fire dance, all of us contemplating how to answer.

"I'm in," Mike said.

"Why?" I asked.

"Ever see a man shot in the gut?" he asked.

"Uh, no," I said.

216

"They just scream and roll around on the ground. It takes fucking forever for someone to die that way. You have a lot of time to watch what you did. I mean, not as awful as actually getting blasted, but it sticks with you. I've had a lot of time to ask myself some really fucking terrifying questions. And, well, I don't have any answers. None I'm willing to say out loud. This, what we're doing right now, it just makes sense. No questions to ask, no guilt, no fucking desperate attempts to rationalize it. No, fuck all of that. This...this is a good thing," Mike said. He leaned on his back and stared into the sky.

"What about you?" I asked looking at Jax.

"The three of us, this is all I have in this life. I'll be damned if I let you guys go alone. I mean, I'm not gonna let school and certainly not some service job be what holds me here," he said.

"What about Brittany?" I asked.

"She made her choice a long time ago," he said.

"And you?" Jax asked.

I took some time. I didn't want to go through the same bullshit as before. I wanted to be genuine. "I want to say it's because it's the right thing to do, but I'm not going lie. I know, in my heart, I just want to make as many other people as possible feel like I do when I wake up every morning. I want to cause heartache and suffering. In my own twisted morality, it's OK to do this, somehow; to the pimp assholes, I mean. They deserve this; why shouldn't I be the one to deliver it?"

Mike and Jax were silent, both avoiding making eye contact. I wondered if this would be the moment they walked away; realizing just how far I had fallen. I didn't blame them. I knew, hearing the words come out of my mouth, I deserved to be alone.

"Glad to see we have the moral high ground in all of this," Mike said.

"Fuck, at least we're together," I said.

Jax produced a bottle of bourbon from his pack, "We haven't had a drop in months. I say we make a night of it."

"Man, do I need a drink," I said.

He popped the cork and we each took a moment to enjoy the ritual. We breathed in the dark, sweet burnt sugar that wafted out of the bottle. We measured its color on the fire and finally poured enough fingers to actually feel something. That first sip, it was like being born again. That smooth burn that rolls over your lips and into your throat. I know it sounds like I have a problem and I'm not going to argue with you, but damn, is it hard to fight something like that. It doesn't take long either for that warmth to bellow up from your soul and into your hands, feet and finally into your mind; you're set free from all the anxiety and pain and responsibility of sobriety.

The rest of the evening was really quiet. We were tired and had talked enough; letting the waves of alcohol crash over. In the morning, the coffee was outstanding and my oats were probably the best breakfast I have ever had. There's something about being separated from the world that makes you really appreciate food.

After that day, things came easier. I still hated every second of being cold and tired and hungry, but it didn't slow me down; not like before. I could move quicker; run farther than ever before in my life. Fear didn't have a hold on me anymore. A normal person gets worn down and says "my body is telling me it's time to stop," and that's OK. But now, when I got fatigued and my stomach churned from hunger and my muscles screamed for relief, my response was, "Fuck you body. I'm in control," and I'd keep going. Also, my pants were almost comically oversized because of the weight I had lost.

I got really accurate with a rifle, too. I didn't hesitate now, that was the thing. I'd line up a shot and just take it, like my body remembered shooting straight.

I don't remember how long exactly, we were out there. Time has a way of just floating when you're stretched beyond whatever limits you thought existed.

There was was one morning, though. Jax woke me up roughly; kicking my rucksack and saying something like, "get up asshole." It's a bit hazy. I was being tested; an opportunity to put together everything I learned and prove I could really function in their world.

This was something we had practiced a dozen times in pieces. I would fail, and start over, and fail again. Over and over until finally getting it; then moving on to the next part only to fail again.

Now, it was time to execute as a unit; we were pack hunters designed to take down much larger prey. We packed up our gear and set out; marching 25 miles with 100 lbs of gear to take a mock objective. Don't ask where Mike and Jax came up with this plan or whose land we were trespassing on. I can only assume that, with what we were carrying, most countries would have considered us an act of open rebellion.

We hiked for the better part of the day without stopping. Despite feeling like I could take on anything when we started, by then, I could barely move. "Fuck my legs are tired," I gutted out as we ascended a small hill. My legs were so numb, it was painful; the nerves burning with each step. Leave it to the human body to be somehow both feeling and unfeeling at the same time.

"I know, man. Just keep putting one leg in front of the other," Jax said.

"When I felt like this on our ruck marches, I would pick someone else who was sucking worse than me and just keep telling myself, 'I'm better than that fucker', over and over," Mike said.

"Well, that doesn't fucking help me, asshole. It's just us," I said.

"Oh, right," Mike said.

"Motherfucker...," I squeezed out under the heavy work of my lungs.

"Double time," Jax called out.

"Fuck you, asshole," Mike and I grunted in unison.

Somehow, and to this day I have no idea how, I mustered

enough energy and strength to push myself faster. The pace was brutal and every iota of reason in me demanded I stop, but the illogical part of my brain was on overload; completely overwhelming any normal decision making process. The illogical side had pushed me this far and just kept taunting me: you're going to fail; just give up like you always do. Mike's advice rang in my mind, but it was the new me, the determined, purposeful John that saw the old me lagging behind and I kept saying I'm better than that asshole. It worked. I kept up with Mike and Jax and the last few miles melted as we closed in our rally point.

Jax gave the command to stop and we all three took a knee simultaneously. We caught our breath, forming a triangle with our backs to each other; our rifles pointed out. We got all of thirty seconds to rest before we were moving again in formation towards an incline and wooded grove. We entered and kept cover behind trees. We continuously scanned the area for "threats", leapfrogging so that no one person was moving without the two others covering his movement.

Mike made a hand gesture ordering me to take point and lead the group. I read my wrist map and compass and confirmed our heading. As we moved up the hill, we stopped at a large formation of rocks. I motioned for a full stop while I looked over the top. I climbed a few feet and leaned my rifle over the edge. I got my eyes over the boulder and saw a scarecrow, pinned with a target and toy gun, about 20 yards down range. I alerted Mike and John of a threat and confirmed I would engage, all with very deliberate hand signals. It was screaming in sign language. They took defensive positions to cover me. I squeezed the trigger in three successive movements. The suppressor muffled the report into a fwap, fwap, fwap. The dummy took all three rounds square in the chest and exploded into atomized straw and paper.

"Holy shit," I blurted out; confused, not expecting the target to disintegrate.

"Shut up motherfucker," Jax said muffling his voice, "I loaded them with strike charges so we would know when we got a kill shot."

"Ohh, that's pretty cool," I said.

"Yeah," Mike said.

"Shut the fuck up. Keep operational silence, motherfuckers," Jax said, his annoyance tempered with the pride he took in his range course design.

I pulled myself completely over the rocks and motioned down to them to advance. I had taken a knee scanning the trees ahead as Mike and Jax completed their climb. We moved ahead as before, moving one at a time to cover each other's advance. Jax and Mike eyed additional targets and took them down with relative ease as we moved. Each straw man atomizing when hit.

We finally made the top of the ridge and there at the top, on a small plateau, was a "fort". Basically logs piled into a vague pyramid shape with several scarecrow men guarding it.

"Alright, this is it. Plant the charge without getting caught. I put trip flares around at different points. If you hit one, you're dead and we gotta do this all over," Jax said.

"Fuck that," I said.

"Better get your shit squared away then," Mike said.

"We'll provide cover. Once the first set of guards goes down start moving," Jax said.

Mike placed a live semtex charge in my hands and it was fucking terrifying. I had practiced assembling and "detonating" dummy charges for weeks, but this was my first real one. It was absolutely overwhelming. There wasn't much explosive, about the size of small apple, but then a thumbnail sized piece would turn a car into molten tinder. I placed it into my cargo pocket and started crawling towards the structure. Sporadic grass provided just enough cover to make it difficult to see more than a few feet. Jax and Mike's rifles rang out fwap, fwap, fwap, fwap and the line of dummies closest to me exploded.

I started crawling. The gravel and rock dug into my elbows and knees and made every inch a battle. I kept my breathing as minimal as possible and concentrated on my next movement. I noticed a few flare traps after I had moved by and considered myself incredibly lucky I hadn't take a different path. As I moved, it seemed as though the fort remained just as far away. It was incredibly frustrating. Pushing through the dirt, I kept my eyes focused on the first line of logs as a directional marker. It would have been easy to get off course my just moving in the direction my hands pulled me.

I put my elbow and forearm on something tense. I intended to push on, hitting a stiff branch or bush, but my training, I think, pulled from the recesses of my mind, caused me to stop and really contemplate what I was doing. The thin nylon line came into focus

225

briefly and I realized I was resting on a flare line. Fuck , I thought. Except, it was more like, fuuuuuuuck!, extra emphasis on that.

I lifted my arm as slowly as I possibly could and followed the line back to its origin. Dug into the ground about a foot away, three inches of metallic tube protruded. The nylon ran around a pin that sat about an inch from the base. It rattled around and started to slip. In a fit of panic, I swatted at the flare, somehow managing to push the pin back into its housing, knocking the tube sideways in the process. It would have definitely started a forest fire had it ignited.

I held my breath, waiting for it to burst in a shower of white phosphorous. Nothing happened. I considered digging the tube back down, buy decided against it. With about as little confidence in the nylon and pin as a man can have, I moved on, but with renewed purpose and determination. I was a few yards from the base of the structure now, progress appearing slower than it actually was, and a few more fwaps rang out; scarecrows about a yard ahead erupted. I crawled and crawled, diligently testing each handful of dirt, testing for anything that could be a flare line.

My hands and knees and elbows ached from the hours of hiking and the grind of dirt and rocks against my skin. Even through

226

my clothes, the meat was chewed raw. My lungs burned as I pushed with fatigued muscles. Finally, I reached the structure and retrieved the plastic explosive from my pocket. I pushed in two detonation pins, nearly touching two wires that would have splattered me over the hill in a fine vapor. I attached a radio transmitter to the pins and switched it on. The confirmation light blinked steadily and I took this as proof the package was in working order. I set it into the base of the fort as far as I could and started my slow crawl back.

As long as it took to crawl to the fort, it felt twice as long going back. I tried to trace my exact route out, following the crease left in the grass, but even in the minutes after I had passed, the wind seemed to have swept it all back into place. My heart was pounding with adrenaline and I had to push everything out of my mind except for focusing on moving one handful of dirt at a time, ensuring I didn't hit a flare, not this close to being done.

I came across the flare line that nearly ended my mission and extended a very firm and defiant middle finger as I crawled by. When I finally made it back to Jax and Mike's position, they had gotten bored and were checking their phones for Facebook and text messages because the internet is fucking everywhere these days.

227

They refocused when I produced the detonator. I detected just a hint of fear in their eyes, like maybe I had kept the thing in my pocket and would kill us all. They watched as I switched on the small device; all the lights going green, meaning it was armed.

I whispered to the men beside me, "fire in the hole" and pressed the trigger. We all buried our heads behind the rocks and dirt at the expectation of the intense explosion. We held our breaths, wrapping are arms around our chests; trying to protect ourselves from the enormous shockwave that could loosen bowels. Instead, nothing. I squeezed the trigger again. Nothing. I took out the batteries and put them back in, let the device cycle through its connectivity protocol, pushed the trigger. Nothing.

"Way to fuck this up John," Mike said.

"Fuck you, I did everything the way you taught me to," I said. The frustration and fatigue worked through my body like electricity.

"You attach both pins?" Jax asked.

"Yes, you fucking bastard, and I checked the transponder and everything read green," I said, standing up.

"Well, something went wrong," Mike said.

228

"Pack it up, assholes. We're starting over," Jax said.

"No fucking way," I said.

"Yeah, no way," Mike said. "I'm not doing that shit again because John fucked up."

"You're the one who's been carrying it all day," I said. "I bet it got ruined in your pocket."

"Fuck you," Mike shouted. "How the hell does that happen?"

"That's enough," Jax said. "We run it again, and again and again, until we get it right. Either of you to got a problem with that and I will personally fuck up your world."

"Bring the heat, you small dick bastard," Mike said.

"That's big talk for such a whiny bitch," Jax said.

He was inches from Mike's face. The height difference would normally make a man retreat, but Mike could hold his own against pretty much anyone.

"Oh wait, I forgot to switch off the safety," the words left my mouth only to have the absolute shit knocked out of me. The shockwave was like nothing I had ever experienced. The logs and debris that had made the fort ceased to be. All three of us were knocked on our asses.

As the smoke cleared, Mike stammered, "holy...holy shit, John."

We stood, our ears ringing and equilibrium completely fucked; taking in the substantial crater we had just blasted into the hill. There were a few small fires, but for the most part, the explosion had pushed out all the usable oxygen in the area. Splintered pieces of oak hung in air like snow. It was an incredible sight. I switched off the detonator and placed it back into my vest; my mind clicking through boot up menus, trying to switch back on.

We called it after that. Packing up the rest of our gear, we headed back to town with renewed purpose, albeit a range of hearing problems. We went to a diner for our first real meal since heading out into the bumble. Ordering a range of fried foods and carb heavy sides, we started into the dirty business of eating. We tore through that spread like killer whales tearing through baby seals. It was entirely satisfying. We ate in silence, partly from fatigue, partly from tinnitus.

We crashed at Jax's house after gorging ourselves on fast food. I'll never forget the feeling of sleeping in a real bed after months of passing out on the ground from exhaustion. The warm embrace of sheets and blankets and a climate controlled house were things I had always taken for granted until now. Being out there, with Mike and Jax, that's something I'll take with me forever. It's a part of who I am now. That man forged out there, that's the better version of me.

Chapter 12

Aleela was happy to leave the makeshift infirmary at the compound. It stunk of disease and filth; the fresh air of the courtyard made her feel clean. Her "sickness" lasted for a few days, which gave her time away from her dorm, the nightly guests and all the terrible things that could happen. She desperately wanted to check on Hawa while confined to the hospital, but couldn't without exposing her lie. Aleela kept telling herself that Hawa was safe and it was unlikely anyone would bother to check the metal skirting behind the shed. But, there was no way to know for sure. A few older women attended her in the infirmary. They didn't seem to have any formal medical training though; their treatment consisted of alternating cool washcloths on her forehead. They also didn't talk, even once.

Aleela had tried several times to start up a conversation, try to gleam some kind of update on what was going on outside, but they always ignored her. It was some time before she realized they were deaf. It's hard to overhear the secrets of your employer when you can't hear at all.

There was one other girl in the small ward, but she was perpetually unconscious. Aleela asked what was wrong with her, but Duma brushed her off abruptly and she didn't bring it up again.

It was late afternoon when Duma came to take Aleela back to her dorm. The day was hot; dust kicked up every time the dry breeze passed through the compound. They took a slow walk through the yard and sat outside in the building's shade. Aleela pried Duma with questions; hoping to annoy him enough he would leave and she could search for Hawa, but he stubbornly ignored her.

"I don't understand why you have to be so rude. I'm only asking what we were having for lunch," Aleela said.

"You'll eat what you're given, girl," Duma shot back.

Without his usual book, he just stared off into the haze in silence. A group of girls played with a soccer ball towards the back of the compound. A few guards stood around lazily watching.

"We both know that's not how this works," Aleela said.

"Girl, I will hit you if you don't shut up," Duma said.

Aleela leaned away from him. Duma's threats were often sarcastic, even playful, but this was a different tone. He avoided her
233

eyes as she searched him; they sat like this for a long moment. Aleela looking for motive in his face.

After a few minutes she asked, "What's wrong, Duma?"

"Nothing, leave me be," Duma said.

Aleela moved closer to Duma and placed her hand on his shoulder, "I can tell something is wrong. Just talk with me."

Duma threw her hand off violently, "Leave me alone."

Dust blew around their feet, whipping into short lived whirls.

"Please Duma," she said. "You're scaring me." She didn't really fear his silence, but was more curious than anything. She had not seen him act like this for all the time she had been there. He liked to talk, to tease her. She wondered what had warped his usual personality.

More silence and then, "Nothing, I'm just tired. Been a long couple of days." He turned to her and smiled, but it was so forced and void of emotion, that it unnerved Aleela.

"Oh...are you not sleeping?" she asked.

"Yeah, something like that," he said.

"I'm a great listener. Just tell me, I can help," she said, searching for anything in his facial features. They remained bland

and roughly cut, like a jagged stone.

"I lied to you, Aleela," Duma said.

"Oh?" she asked. "When?" Aleela's stomach turned to ice. She wasn't sure what Duma meant by this, but it certainly could not be good for her.

"I didn't have two sons, I had two daughters. They were a lot of trouble, just like you. They were always causing mischief and I swear I spent more time apologizing to our neighbors...," he trailed off, his voice cracking slightly. "They were beautiful. The oldest was the smartest child I have ever seen. She would have gone to a university; would have done great things. And the youngest, she was so, so beautiful. She had a smile like, like a red morning sky. It melted my heart and no matter how angry I would get with her, she would grin at me with so much mischief in her eyes, I couldn't help but love her more." A tear ran down Duma's eyes. What could it possibly all mean?

"Oh, well, that's not a big lie," Aleela said. "They sound wonderful."

Duma flashed a genuine smile mixed with a hint of pain.

"The day al-Shabaab razed my village, I was at work in town.
235

We got word from our supervisor that people had been killed and taken. I ran back, didn't wait for the bus, I ran with the hate of the devil. I ran and ran and ran and when I got there, there was almost nothing left. The army had sent two soldiers to assess the damage, but left soon after hearing reports that the militia could return before long." Duma, took a moment and wiped the tears from his eyes. They were large and heavy and flowed freely.

"I found my home and it was still smoldering. There was nothing left inside and I my heart pounded, I remember that, it pounded in my ears. I looked everywhere for my family. There were bodies everywhere. Some burnt beyond recognition. Young, old, it didn't matter. They were all torn to pieces. When I found my family, they had been mostly piled together in a clearing just outside the row of huts we lived in. There they were, huddled together. My wife, she had held them close, shielded them with her body, but those rifle rounds tear through flesh. Have you ever seen what that type of bullet does to a man?" Duma asked looking at Aleela with wide eyes.

"No...," Aleela said, not sure what else to say.

"It's devastating. She did her best, but they went through her like paper. My girls, they were broken, bloody pulps. I wailed like a child and held their ravaged bodies. When they finally pulled me off of them my clothes were completely soaked with their blood. I left the next day, looking for revenge. I tracked a few al-Shabaab to a campsite not far from our village. A raiding outpost used to sneak in and out of nearby towns. They were just kids, not more than 16 or 17. I waited for them to fall asleep," Duma pulled out a large, wicked looking knife from his belt. "I used this to cut the throats of the oldest. I tied the youngest to a rock and peeled the skin off his face; while he was still alive. I still hear his screams, echoing in the dark. The look on his face before he died, just that wide open stare; no eye lids to cover the pupils. I left him like that for the others to find. I left my soul out there. I was so angry and so full of hate. All I wanted was for them to feel the way I did." He turned to Aleela, "I did terrible things, Aleela. Things that will never leave me. I will carry them with me into my death and, if there is any justice, into hell after," Duma said, wiping ears away. "I wandered after that night. Left everything; my job, what was left of my family, my home.

I didn't want to live, but was too much of a coward to kill

myself. I even put a gun in my mouth. Hoping my finger would just flinch and it be over, but I couldn't push myself across that line. It was too much somehow.

So, I took every dangerous job I could find; hoping I would die. First it was salvage jobs on the coast, diving into wrecked ships. Then it was construction on high rise buildings; walking the steel with no harness. Then I started stealing, burglarizing homes. That turned into selling drugs and then killing for money – then just killing. I even tried joining the pirates that murdered my family. They wouldn't have me though. Apparently my reputation was too much. That's how I ended up here. This was the last place anyone would have me. It's been easy, over the years. No one asks questions when one of the guests gets rough with a girl and then goes missing. No family members to worry about; no one cares about the type of men who visit this place. I don't care what happens to these girls either. There all dead either way," Duma stopped, letting the wind brush across his cheeks.

"Why are you telling me this?" Aleela asked.

"I have to let something awful happen tonight," Duma said.

"What are you talking about?" Aleela said, putting her hand

238

on his arm, trying to make eye contact with him; to look into his mind. She waited for him to speak, but he rolled his shoulder, pulling away. He walked quietly into the main house, leaving her alone.

Aleela was shaken, sitting alone in the dust. Duma had never spoke so openly to her and clearly he was disturbed by whatever was planned. She wanted to follow him; press him for answers, but she was not allowed in the house he seemed in no mood to talk further, anyway. So, she decided to take advantage of her solitude and look for Hawa. Starting in the courtyard, which was partly filled with girls and men milling around, she asked different groups of children. None of whom had seen Hawa. They all gave Aleela short, uninterested answers; like they were eager for her to leave. She checked the shed and, the skirting was still in place, but no sign of her friend. Aleela completed a full lap around the wall and found herself back under the shade where she had started. She sat and ran her hands over face then put her head between her knees. Startled by the dirt kicked up around her and the sudden shadow falling her head, she looked up.

"Did you hear?" Hawa asked.

"Where have you been?" Aleela asked, "I have been worried sick about you?"

"I've been here. Haven't left...yet," Hawa sat down next to her. "How was the hospital?"

"It was fine. I'm so sorry I didn't check up on you, they wouldn't let me out for any reason," Aleela said.

"I'm OK. I can take care of myself," Hawa said.

"Hawa, please, I'm sorry," Aleela said, guilt welling up once again.

"No, really it's OK. You fixed my spot and I have been safe," Hawa said.

"Oh, thank god. You were all I could think about," Aleela said, wrapping her arm around Hawa's shoulder and pulling her closer.

"So, did you hear?" Hawa asked.

"Hear what?" Aleeela asked.

"Apparently, Josef heard about Duma keeping you out of the rooms at night, keeping the men away. I heard he told Duma to make you go to bed with someone or he'll kill him," Hawa said.

"Where did you hear that?" Aleela asked.

"All the girls are talking about it. I guess Duma and Josef got into a very loud fight while you were in the infirmary. Josef had no idea that you hadn't been with the men regularly," Hawa said.

"What does that mean, Hawa? What's going to happen?" Aleela asked.

She held onto Hawa so tight, she felt her push away some to relieve the pressure on her small frame.

"You'll be sent out with the other girls for sure tonight. No one says no to Josef. He'll kill Duma for sure," Hawa said.

"No, I don't believe it. He's kept me safe all this time, why would he give in now?" Aleela asked.

"Because it's your life or his and no man is going to sacrifice himself for us," Hawa said.

"No, no I can't...I can't, Duma won't do it. He'll hide me, he'll trick the other men like he always does," Aleela said.

"Not this time, Josef will be out in the rooms tonight to make sure. You must have hurt him badly when you first got here, because he has it out for you, or that's what I've heard," Hawa said.

They sat in silence, the shade moved slowly as the sun made its way across the sky.

241

"Duma is a good man, he is, somehow, deep down, he is and I just know he won't let that happen," Aleela said.

"Please, Aleela, please come hide with me tonight. I'll meet you at the back of the shed when the gates first open, we'll be safe. We can be together and no one will find us," Hawa pleaded.

"Hawa, I can't. You know I can't. If I'm gone, they'll hurt Duma and if something happens to him now, I won't survive," Aleela said.

"What are you saying Aleela, why do you care? Duma has held you here for months and will be there tonight to help another man have his way with you. He is evil. You can only save yourself."

"What if Duma dies, then who will keep me safe?" Aleela asked.

"You are the one who has kept yourself alive this long, not Duma, not anybody else. If you start putting others before you, if you trust any man here, you will only suffer more. Please, please come hide with me," Hawa said.

"Hawa, I can't. Even if you are right and my suffering really is that important to Josef, they won't stop at Duma. They will tear this place apart looking for me and I can't risk you getting hurt. I

242

would rather die than let that happen," Aleela said.

"We can still run away. There is still time," Hawa said.

"Please don't. We both know I can't. My bones are still healing," Aleela said.

Hawa stood, "Are they? Or is that what you are telling yourself because you are scared."

Aleela didn't respond.

"I saw the most beautiful butterfly today. It bounced on the wind and danced and whirled. I smiled so big, it almost hurt just watching it," Hawa said, walking away.

As the sun went down, Aleela found herself alone again. The doors to the compound swung open. Torches were lit and long strings of white garden lights were powered. Men came stumbling in, holding each other up; laughing. Some of the more tenured girls looked them over; trying to find the best clients. This was part of their survival strategy - find someone who was in a good mood. This often meant presents, drinks, food; gentler treatment – and if they were really lucky, someone who passed out early. The girls that waited generally had the most violent customers.

The noise from the party picked up as music started and more guests arrived. Aleela stayed in the shadow of her dorm; watching as young girls had their innocence stolen over and over. Every time the crowd pushed towards her she felt the electricity of fear pulse up and down her spine. She wished to just be forgotten, to turn to dust and ride the breeze into nothingness. What felt like hours passed and fatigue set in; sleep sitting heavy on her eyes. She wondered how long it was until light. She sat on the ground when Duma, clearly drunk, stumbled out of the crowd toward her.

"Get up, girl. It's time," Duma stuttered.

"No," Aleela said firmly.

"Girl, get up. Do you want to die?" Duma said.

He towered over her as she stared off into the night sky.

"No," she said.

He grabbed her roughly by the hair and pulled her up. She fought and screamed, but he was overpowering. He dragged Aleela, kicking and flailing, in front of a group of men who all laughed at her.

Banging open the door to her dorm, he threw her roughly on a bed. There were several others already engaged and paid no attention to the loud entrance. Aleela shot up, ready to run when

Duma turned his back to lock the door. He caught her with a swift fist to her cheek that sent her stumbling back. A tall, lanky man, who had been sitting in the corner drinking some kind of dark alcohol that stank like lighter fluid, swallowed the remaining liquid in his glass and set it on a nearby end table. He stood and unbuckled his pants and removed his shirt.

Aleela dazed from the blow, couldn't orient herself to the room. She tried to sit up, but was held down by Duma. He stood at the head of the bed and leaned over her, holding her arms and chest down. She screamed as the man slid her panties off. She wrenched her body sidewise as hard as she could and felt her ribs crack in protest. Pain exploded in her body. She didn't really notice the point where the man entered her, but she suddenly realized he was on top of her and pushing. She opened her eyes and screamed again, her voice dying as it became horse from the exhaustive effort.

Duma's face, only inches from her's, was a blank casket of skin stretched over bone. She made eye contact with him, desperately trying to reach him, but when she finally connected, she realized he was completely empty.

Chapter 13

I was good and drunk when I knocked on my brother's door. Well, drunk enough, I guess. I had driven there, parking haphazardly on the curb; more in his lawn than on the street and yes, I am a piece of shit for driving, but let's be honest, I wasn't going to win any awards for my morality. My hands trembled as I knocked and not just from dehydration. I was scared. I needed the booze just to leave the house; to just even things out in my mind. Doing something like this sober – it was impossible for me.   The look on his face was absolutely priceless, though. It was a weird mix of shock, pain, relief and fear all mixed together in this confused, broken scowl. What a stroke patient might look like right as that blood clot stops the flow of oxygen to the brain.

"What are you doing here, John?" Virgil asked, pulling the door shut behind him as he stepped out onto the stoop.

"Kind of a dick move," I said, nodding to the door.

"I'm just not sure I want you in my house," he said, looking me up and down "You smell like a distillery."

"Sorry, I, uh, had a few drinks after work," I said.

"It's 2 in the afternoon. And did you drive here?" he asked, judging my parking job.

"Yeah, but I'm fine. Look, its awkward enough being here do we have to do this on the front porch?" I asked, imagining disapproving looks from the neighbors.

He hesitated, unsure of why I had come, not sure of me.

"Please, Virgil," I said, softly.

Another moment and then, "Yeah, sure," He reached for the knob, stopped, turned around and asked, "You're not here to kill me, are you?" I felt like he was completely serious; his brow still furrowed; a nervous smile on his lips. Maybe it was everything I had been through the last few months, but I loved it. That look of weariful expectation. I laughed, which likely did nothing to ease his mind, slapped him on the back and said, "Open the goddamn door."

He led me into the small living room and offered me a seat on his couch. He took an overstuffed recliner, noticeably closer to the exits, which I felt was kind of rude.

"Can I get you something?" he asked.

"Sure, I'll take a beer," I said.

"Sorry, I don't have any," he said.

"Oh, well a whiskey then," I said.

"Don't have any of that, either," he said.

"Any booze at all?" I asked.

"John, are you sure drinking right now is a good idea?" he asked; glasses hanging loosely on his nose; his hair swept aside. Well-manicured stubble on his cheeks. He leaned forward in his chair and his look changed. It wasn't apprehension now, but pity. The initial shock of my visit having worn off; now able to really look at me. I hated it. More than anything, that expression of "he's broken beyond repair." I knew what I was. I didn't need to be reminded by every single person I met. You're forced, for the rest of your life, into a predefined space – you buried a child and that's the sum total of who you are.

"Look, Virgil, I'm gonna be honest with you, I've already been drinking pretty hard already today. It was really, really fucking hard to come over here. Let's not have the 'you shouldn't drink so much' talk right now, alright? Let's save that for another day. Let's try and make this work, okay?" I asked.

He stared at me for a moment, stood, walked into the kitchen and came back with an opened, half empty bottle of red wine and a coffee mug.

"Thank you," I said, pouring a glass. I took a hearty gulp and leaned back into the couch. His home was nice. Similar to mine in age and style, but decorated with the Spartan aesthetics of an attractive, unmarried man. There were a few pictures on top of a piano; one of Kat. Did he realize it was there? Did he leave it out intentionally? How does live with himself? Where all things I might have thought about, if I hadn't become fixated on a large collection of vinyl records. I found myself reading the labels and experiencing old memories the way only music can conjure them. I'm not sure how much time had passed, but I had nearly finished my glass when I noticed Virgil was waiting patiently for me to speak. I remained silent, just looking at him stupidly.

Finally, he shrugged as to say "So...?"

"So what?" I asked, out loud.

He closed his eyes and rubbed his eyes with his thumb and forefinger, "Why are you here, John?"

"I wanted to say goodbye," I said. He shifted in his chair slightly, glancing at the door.

"Jesus, man, just relax. I'm leaving the country," I said. "For a little while."

"Oh," he said. "Where are you going?" he asked.

"Africa," I said, sipping on the wine, "This is shit wine, man."

"It's like two weeks old. I hardly ever drink," he said.

"Oh," I said, taking another sip.

The conversation effectively died as I concentrated on pushing the stale liquid past my lips.

A long pause and then, "Why Africa?" Virgil asked.

"I have a little project I'm pursuing," I said.

"Cool," he said. We sat in silence for another awkward lull. "So, what's your project?

"I'm going with Mike and Jax," I said. "We're going to kill a bunch of child pimps."

"What?" Virgil was visibly confused, leaning forward in his chair; again looking over his glasses.

"You look like Dad," I said.

"Was that a joke?" he asked, still unable to process my statement.

"You definitely got all of his features. You're tall, too. Just like Dad. You hear from them much?" I asked.

"No, not really. I talk with Mom every once in a while. I haven't talked with Dad since my birthday," he said.

"Right, your birthday. Uh, happy birthday, I guess," I said.

"Thanks," he said. The silence started to linger so he asked, "How's Sephie?

"She left me for someone else," I said.

"I'm sor…," he tried to say.

"Yeah, moving to Seattle. It's only a little fucked, though. I think she is going to be happy; I hope she is," I said.

Virgil shifted in his seat and leaned back.

"I really am sorry, John," He said, "She was a good woman. I know you loved her."

"Yeah, man, you know I did. I did love her. But that was a lifetime ago. Things just couldn't be put back together after Kat died," I stopped and glimpsed at him. I wasn't sure what to expect. He looked at me; waiting for me to continue "We talked though, got to say goodbye; work through some things."

"That's good," he said.

"Yeah, you know, I'm doing okay. Apart from the alcoholism

and unemployment, but I really am doing better with that too, believe it or not. It's just times like these, it gets really hard to talk while sober," I said.

"So, is that why you're here? Just to share all your issues with me?" he asked. This caught me off guard.

"What?" I asked.

"You show up almost more than two years after she died, without so much as an email all that time," he said. "Do you remember what the last thing you said to me was?

I shook my head "no," sipping the last of my wine. I poured myself a fresh glass.

"That you'd never forgive me," he said. "Not something you forget."

"I'm not sure I said...even if I did, give me a break, you just killed my daughter," I snapped, sitting up. I felt warmth pulsating in my face.

"Yes, I did. I did kill Kat. You know what, screw you. I'm not some race car, stunt driver. I had no way of knowing the car would roll. She was buckled. I wasn't speeding. I did everything I could have. It was an accident; one mistake. My whole life is ruined because of that one, quick moment. I can't sleep at night because every time I close my eyes, that day plays over and over in my mind. I always hear the screaming. It never goes away," he said.

"Oh, just one fucking mistake, was it? You shattered my existence. Not just mine, but Sephie's our parents. My little girl died, Virgil," I lifted my hand; my fingers trembling. "I got the fucking shakes, you asshole. I can't sleep without seeing Kat's face in my dreams. I wake up fucking sobbing every day. I lost my wife. I lost my career. You took everything from me," I screamed.

"You weren't the only one to lose somebody that day you fucking selfish prick," he yelled.

"Oh, yeah, what could that possibly be?" I asked.

"I lost my whole fucking family. I lost my only niece. I have to live every goddman day for the rest of my life knowing I'm responsible; reliving that crash every moment my mind loses focus on anything else. My only brother hates me. Talking to dad on my birthday was the first time in months. He hates me almost as much as you. And mom, she is absolutely dependent on me. I cook her meals, drive her to all of her appointments. I do her laundry; clean her house. I pay her bills and manage her finances. All of that, and she

253

hasn't said more than five words to me, all this time." Tears formed at the corner of his eyes. "Do you have any idea how hard it is to be utterly alone? To have your own mother hate you? You know what? I lost my job, too. I just got out of the psyche ward. I was hospitalized, John, for months. Spending day after day, trying to find a way to die."

"Well, what? Sympathy? Is that what you're asking for? You think I owe you that? Should I feel bad that this hasn't been easy for you?" I asked.

He took a moment, "No. You don't owe me anything."

This surprised me, "What?"

"I'm not asking for your sympathy...or your forgiveness," he said.

"What do you want then?" I asked.

"I just want you to know that you're not alone in all of this," he said. "I can't imagine what it's like to be father. To lose a child. I probably won't ever have a family. I don't think I could ever put myself in a position where I could hurt so badly again. I did love her, though. I loved her as much as anyone ever could have that wasn't her parent and it has been hell every second of every day since."

254

"What do you want me to say?" I asked.

"Nothing...I didn't mean to get so angry. I just...these are things I needed to say to you for a long time and it all came out at once. You can't imagine the things that people have said to my face. The terrible things they have called me," he said.

"Oh, I can imagine. I'm sure I've said most of them," I said.

"You deserve to, though. You deserve to hate me. All these other people, though. Friends and family who are completely blind to all the pain and suffering I've carried since that moment. It's been more than I can take more often than not." He rolled up his sleeves and showed the deep scars running across his wrists.

"Jesus, Virgil," I said.

"This was just the first time," he said.

"Fuck," I said.

"Yeah," he said.

"How many times?" I asked. He stared at me and tilted his head. "Oh, sorry, is that like, a sensitive subject?" I asked.

"Five times," he said.

"Holy fuck. How are you still alive?" I asked.

He thought about this for a long moment and then said,

"Honestly, I think I'm meant to suffer a lot more before I die."

"That's really fucked up, man," I said.

These words hung in the air and I weighed each one. I did feel a small sliver of happiness. Not so much that he tried to kill himself, but that he hurt as much as me. I had felt for a long time that he had gotten off easy. However, I had to admit that he had been through something even I thought was excessive.

"I don't deserve to just die; no. Something much, much worse," he said, turning to look into the next room.

"Alright, I'm gonna stop you right there. I'm not saying you weren't punished like you deserved, but you didn't earn a lifetime of perpetual misery either," I said.

"I don't understand," he said.

I took a long draw on the wine and put the mug down, "Look, I'm never going to say out loud what you really want me to say. I'm never going to forgive you. I can't. You don't deserve it."

"Don't do this, John," he said, water welling in his eyes.

"Just shut up a minute and let me finish," I said; taking a deep breath. "There may come a point in your life where you're able to move on and you need to know, that it's ok. Find whatever is left

256

that makes you happy. Don't let me be the reason. Don't become me."

He burst into tears.

I wasn't quite sure what to do, so I just poured more wine into my cup. This went on longer than, I would have liked, but I guess it was cathartic. I got more drunk and when he finally calmed down a little, I asked, "Want a drink?"

"No," he said dabbing tears with his sleeve. "I really don't drink."

"I was serious before," I said.

"About what?" he asked.

"About going to Africa," I said.

He stared at me, "But you're not planning on killing anyone?"

"No," I said. "I absolutely am."

"John, come on. That doesn't even make sense. What's the point?" he asked.

"I'm serious," I said. "We're leaving tomorrow."

"You three are planning on flying to a random country in Africa and killing pimps?" he asked.

"Well, not random. I know where we're flying. And child

pimps, not just pimps," I said.

That same look of confusion from before, "Does that mean pimps who traffic children or children that are pimps?" he asked.

"I...," I hadn't thought of it that way. "The first one; fuck, I hope Mike and Jax realize that. Anyway, I'm not here to discuss the details with you. I'm here to say goodbye," I said.

"What does that mean?" he asked.

"It just means goodbye. That's it," I said, sipping my fresh glass of wine.

"John, I mean what are you thinking?" he asked, hanging his head in his hands.

"Yeah, I know, right?" I said.

"How is this even possible? I mean you can't just show up in...," he said.

"Kenya," I said, finishing his thought.

"Yeah, you can't just show up in Kenya and start shooting people. You know how utterly insane that sounds, right?" he asked. He was sitting on the edge of his seat; hands gripping the arms of the chair.

"Yep, I know," I said.

"What? How can you possibly say that? This is the most asinine thing I have ever heard. I mean how did you even come up with something so stupid? I feel like this is some elaborate joke you drunkenly dreamed up just to mess with me," he said.

"Look, you're not some saint who can tell me what's wrong or right. You're a murderer," I said, spitting flecks of wine out while I talked. This derailed the conversation into total silence. I immediately felt guilty, but shrugged it off.; something I was really getting good at. Virgil stared off into the other room again, he was very consciously trying to hold back more tears. "Look, I...I didn't mean that," I said quietly.

"I have spent every day since Kat died running from medication and suicide. I have fought demons you wouldn't even understand. My life is completely shattered. But I have started to heal and I know, if I know one god damn thing, it's that what you are talking about is wrong," he said, trembling.

I fought off the initial reaction to lash out. I actually I thought about what I wanted to say and said calmly, "I have to do this."

"No, John, no you don't. You're sick; it's in your mind and its bending you to what it wants. You need help," he said.

"And what does it want?" I asked, while sipping my wine.

"It wants you, John. It want's all of you. It wants to consume you and burn you up until there is nothing left. It will make you its plaything for as long as you follow it and then take you, completely," he said. "I'm only saying this because I was right there, I was right where you are now and it almost, John, listen to me, it almost won."

"You seem to be doing OK for a guy that tried to kill himself five times," I said

"I'm not, not at all. Every day is agony; nothing is easy," he said.

"If you're so miserable, how do you keep going?" I asked.

"I found something bigger than me," he said.

I thought about this and said, "I don't understand."

"Look, I'm not saying I had a vision, or some kind of religious experience. But something happened. It was while I was...the last time I tried. Anyway, I was laying there in more pain than I thought possible for a person to experience. I was sure I had died; gone to hell, but I kept passing out, escaping it for a few moments at a time. You can't have relief and be in hell...it never stops there," he said. The look in his eye was terrifying. "So in this moment, in this complete deconstruction of my physical being, my mind wandered into a haze. I felt something while I was there; that place between death and life. I reached out to whatever it was and, you know what I felt, John?" he asked.

"No," I said.

"I felt love, John. Not just the sappy emotion that wells up and dies, but the kind created by a lifetime of being with someone who loves you. It was like what I felt when I was with Kat. It was something transcendent. It touched me and when I came to, I had something I thought lost forever," he said. He became silent and just grinned looking out into space.

I managed a large swallow of wine, "What was it?"

"Hope," he said.

"You sound pretty fucked," I said.

"What?" he asked

"That story is utter bullshit and you know it," I said.

"You believe what you want. It's kept me level and moving forward. I don't care what anyone else thinks, especially you, John," he said, turning his attention back to me.

"Look, man, I don't mean to piss on whatever is keeping you from killing yourself. If this is what does it for you, great, whatever. You deserve to have hope. I just," I felt emotion spilling up my chest, "don't want you wake up some day be let down by something that was never there to begin with," I said.

"I don't understand how someone who is planning to murder a bunch of strangers thinks he can lecture me on belief and morality. You're motivated by the belief that your psychotic rampage is somehow good," he said.

"I told you, don't call it crazy; it's not crazy. I am giving the world, real people, a tangible good. Children, just like Kat, are being used by the worst fucking kind of people. I am not going to waste my life on meaningless shit, anymore. You want to talk about having a vision. Well I can tell you, I did have one. I saw what is happening in the world. Those fuckers deserve to die," I said.

"John...," he said.

"They're selling children for sex, Virgil," I said. "What possible reason is there not to kill them all?"

"You're going to murder people, John. Arbitrarily and by your own sense of judgment. You're an alcoholic and you've lost your family...you're life. You need help, John. How is any of this going to solve anything except bring more pain and despair into this already broken world," he said.

"I have to do this," I said.

"This isn't right John, and you know it," he said.

"It's what needs to be done," I said.

We sat in silence. Virgil wouldn't look me in the eyes anymore and after a while, I took out my phone and started checking notifications. I felt like it was probably time to leave. I tried to stand and the room spun.

"I, uhh, am actually too drunk drive," I said.

"Jesus, I'll call an Uber," Virgil said.

Chapter 14

I was late for my flight. A little too hung over to function properly. What was supposed to be a leisurely ride to the airport, followed by breakfast and the morning news, turned into a full-fledged panic attack, and some incredibly reckless driving. When I finally arrived, Mike and Jax were already through security; sitting comfortably at a small café near the gate. I managed a slow burn through a long line of other travelers checking luggage and finally made it to an open counter.

"Where are you traveling today?" the agent asked. Her fading brown hair and worn skin giving her a tired face.

"Nairobi. I have two bags to check," I said.

"OK, go ahead and check-in for your flight and I'll get your luggage tagged," she worked quickly while I messed around with the automated ticket machine. I stupidly inserted, removed, and re-inserted my credit card about a dozen times before it finally worked, displaying my name and ticket information.

"Would you like to upgrade to first class for an extra $750 on the second leg of your trip? That's a steal for such a long flight," she said.

"No, thank you, though," I knew Jax and Mike weren't able to afford the additional amount. I felt I should stay in coach out of solidarity. Even if the few extra inches on a sixteen hour flight would have been life changing.

The agent ran my card again and provided me with an updated itinerary and receipt. She wrapped stickers around the handle of my bags and instructed me to them over to a security station. Most of what I had brought was just cover. We all agreed it we would be too suspicious to only bring the few items we actually needed; tactical vests, pants and boots. So went a little overboard. Jax brought skis, a duffle bag full of stuffed animals. By the way, I have no idea where he got those. And a small suitcase. Mike brought a motorcycle helmet, two absurdly large trash bags filled with literal trash and a hiking pack with his gear. I brought two full bags of clothes I had no intention of wearing including a parka, some of Sephie's bras and an old Che Guevara shirt I bought in college. I would like to point out that once the symbol of the angsty teenager, you get really weird looks these days when you wear a Che shirt. I don't get it, but that's fashion for you.

265

This airport had two security checkpoints. The first was only for those checking baggage. You handed over your luggage to a TSA agent who processed your bag through a huge x-ray machine, swabbed for explosive residue and, assuming you passed those tests, would put it on a conveyor to waiting airline employees.

After this, you had to wait in a second line to be screened personally, along with carry-on. This process was usually fairly simple and fast, despite the multiple steps, but on busy days, or say, you have fifteen minutes before boarding, it could be maddening. I wasn't the only one either, there were nervous glances around the edges of the line, frustrated sighs. One man was talking loudly on his phone, complaining about the "piss poor service of the TSA" and that "they haven't stopped even one terrorist plot. Not even one." I thought that couldn't be right, but I was in no place to argue. As I waited to be body scanned, I heard my name from behind me. It was that weird deja vu feeling, tugging at my subconscious. I turned around and saw Sephie standing about 20 yards back. I exited the line.

"What are you doing here, Sephie?" I asked.

"John, please don't go," she said; tears welling up in her eyes.

266

"What are you talking about? I'm literally in line to my gate. I don't have time for this," I said, glancing over my shoulder at the line, which had of course grown longer. I checked my phone and realized I had exactly zero minutes before they started boarding my plane.

"Virgil told me you were leaving today. John, he told me everything. You're a fucking liar." Several passersby looked at us in mild surprise at the language.

"He's my brother," I said stumbling over my words, trying to explain myself to a stranger in the brief moment they walked by. This only seemed to make things worse.

"I can't believe you're doing this; it's insane. You are going to hurt somebody. You're gonna get yourself killed. You selfish asshole. How could you do this?" She was extremely animated; pounding her fist on my chest as she rattled the words. I realized what she really meant was how could you do this to me? Which I thought was interesting.

I straightened my legs and leaned over her, "Sephie, you are the one leaving, remember. You're the one that up and vanished one day. Didn't even leave a note, just packed your shit and left. The next thing I know, months later, you show up only to tell me you met

someone and you're moving in with him. Sephie, why are you here?"

She didn't say anything for a long moment and I thought

maybe my logic had triggered something, then, "I still love you.

Please don't go, please, I can't lose you too," she said grabbing the

back of my head and pulling me into her lips. We kissed. I pulled

away; looking into her eyes.

"What is this? I don't...I just don't understand," I said; tears

streaming down her face.

"I can't live my life without. If you die...I couldn't take the

loss. It will kill me. I want to be happy again. I want to be with you,"

she said holding onto my shirt, staring into my chest.

"I love you, too. I will always love you," I said.

She smiled looking up at me. I felt a hand on my shoulder and

turned.

"Dude, we have got to go, they are holding the plane for you.

What are you doing?" Jax said. I shifted my weight and a look of

surprise jumped across his face, "Holy shit, Sephie? Is that you?" He

turned to me. "What is she doing here?"

I tried to squeak out, "I don...," but was quickly cut off.

"He's staying with me. You...you and that other bastard and going to get him killed," Sephie said, her eyes tearing up again.

"Sephie, he is a grown man. He's made his choice. This was completely his idea. We did everything but push him towards this. Hell, the only reason I am going is try and keep him alive," Jax said.

"I can talk for myself," I said, interjecting between their mutual looks of hate. I turned to Sephie, "This is happening. Maybe if things had been different, but they aren't and this sucks, I know, but it is happening. I am leaving."

She started crying again and I felt like I had really done something wrong; a strong sense of guilt I rarely experienced these days, like when you scold a child for dropping their ice cream cone.

"He is going to be fine. I promise," Jax said.

Shot him a look that I thought could draw blood. "I don't care what you think or who you are. You know this is completely crazy and you aren't doing a thing to stop him."

Jax put his hand back on my shoulder, "John, I am getting on that plane, do whatever the fuck you want." He turned and walked back to security.

It was just us again and the silence was deafening. I searched

269

for anything to say and tried, "What about Doug, isn't he a little upset with you being here?"

"He isn't part of Kat. I need to have you in my life to keep her with me. I need you because you understand everything I have been through. Doug isn't you," she said.

"What about your new life and that whole thing with the note paper?" I asked.

"I can't..." she sobbed.

"Sephie, I have to go," I said gently.

She looked up at me, tears clouding her anger, "I hate you, John. You, bastard," she said, burring her face into my chest.

"I know, Sephie, I know," I said.

I hugged her as tightly as I could and then somehow found the strength to push her away. Her face was bright red and wet. The look on her face broke my heart. I can't say exactly what compelled me to get on that plane; something beyond this world, maybe. That's the only thing that I can think of.

I turned back one last time as I cleared security. I could hear Jax and Mike yelling at me to "hurry the fuck up," but I had to see her one last time. She stood there, looking completely pathetic, sobbing as she watched me go. A short chubby officer walked up to her and was trying to talk with her, attempting to console another weeping woman in the middle of the terminal. Now, I was pretty far from where they stood and the murmur of the crowd was loud, but I swear I heard him say "Jeez, lady, did you lose another child?"

They closed the door right after I boarded. A particularly annoyed looking agent grabbed the ticket from my hand and gave me a soft shove down the ramp. Once on the plane, I noticed Mike and Jax were already seated, but in first class, rather than coach.

"What are you motherfuckers doing up here?" I asked.

The flight attendant closest to me turned and said, "Sir, please watch your language. These retired military men deserve your respect. Please show a little courtesy and quickly move to your seat. Everyone is going to be late because of you."

I didn't have the words. Mike and Jax, those smug assholes, just smiled as I moved to my seat.

As I got settled, the engines began to whirl as the plane gently rocked backward. The world moved in reverse and I could feel the jets roar to life. I thought about Sephie, how she was all alone now. That crept like ice into my mind and I had to consciously

271

push it away. It was painful. Not so much that I was pretty sure I would die and never see her again, no, it was more that she felt that too and cared enough to cry about it. I leaned back in my seat as the plane pushed away from the earth and I wept.

Chapter 15

It is a long fucking flight to Africa, goddamn it was awful. It wasn't just the cramped conditions, shitty food and endless boredom. No, it was the intermittent clinking of glasses and chuckles of laughter floating from first class. I couldn't actually see in there, they have this curtain to separate the cabins and protect the beautiful people from the regular ones, but I knew those bastards, were having the time of their lives drinking and carrying on. Not only that, but I would catch glimpses of the flight attendants suppressing smiles as they begrudgingly serviced coach. It was a party and I wasn't invited. I'm pretty sure being stuck like that for eternity would be a suitable hell for just about anyone. There's the darkness as you fly away from the sun, the shitty food, I might have already mentioned that, and that stale, stinking recycled air. Absolute torture.

Anyway, once I realized that the Mike and Jax were having a few drinks, I got hammered. The person next to me was sleeping, so I hid how much I was drinking by ordering drinks for both us. The stewardess gave me a pretty judgey look, which is just a little hypocritical for someone whose livelihood is to service customers in a flying dick-shaped tube, but whatever. Anyway, I got way drunk. For once in my life, I let someone else do the driving and tried to ignore the ache in my joints.

I passed out at some point. I'm not sure for how long, but when I was roughly woken by the stewardess demanding I buckle my seat belt and return my tray table to its upright position, I realized we were on approach for landing. I waited for the crew to move past me and sobered up by vomiting multiple times. I don't think I really had that much, but the combination of altitude and jet lag threw my system off. I had the worst headache of my life and the sun was absolutely painful; the light bouncing around in my head like daggers. Mike and Jax were still a little drunk, as we stumbled off the plane. I guess they were able to keep their booze down.

"Well, you look like shit," Mike said.

"Yeah, well you try spending over fifteen hours with your legs forced into your chest and terrible booze to drink. You'd be rung out too, asshole," I said.

"Yeah man, all our shit was complimentary," Jax said.

"You're kidding," I said.

274

"We must have drank hundreds of dollars of those little travel sized shooters," Mike said.

"Goddamn it, I hate you," I said, even more pissed.

"Yep, fucking combat veterans," Jax said.

"Can we get out of here?" I asked.

We waited for our bags as Mike and Jax sipped on Gatorade bought from a vending machine. The airport was absolutely bustling. There were vendors, all in clean and inviting stalls, catering to thousands of passengers. The amount of activity was staggering. Businessmen and women in suits, chattering away on cell phones in a myriad of languages. Children eating McDonald's while their weary parents tried to relax before a flight. Gangs of elderly wandering together, buying souvenirs and prattling at the airport porters who were assisting them with their luggage. Streams of people riding escalators to either enter or exit the terminal.

"Wow, this place looks just like a modern airport," I said.

"You're a racist piece of shit, you know that?" Mike said.

"What? I don't know. I just thought Africa and expected a dirt landing strip and cattle or something," I said.

"You think they're going to land a trans-continental jetliner on a fucking dirt airstrip. Would fuel be transported in clay pots? Are monkeys trained to do repairs?" Mike said.

"Huh?" I asked, somewhat embarrassed.

"You're an idiot," Jax said.

"Look, it's not like if you polled all the people at the bar last night they'd know either."

"You're supposed to be an educated adult. You have a fancy degree and everything. You drag us to the other side of the world to commit international subterfuge and you don't even know what the country is like?" Mike said.

"Alright, I get it," I said.

"You better get your shit together?" Jax said. "We will absolutely die if we are not perfect in what we are about to do. We have zero room for mistakes."

"Alight, man, alright, I got it. I'll get it together," I said.

"You better. All we have is each other and we are trusting you to do your job. If you don't, we die; get it?" Jax asked.

"Yes, I got it," I said, sheepishly.

We collected our luggage and snaked our way outside. The heat was oppressive. It was surreal, the scope and scale of the skyline. We hailed a cab, negotiated a price and drove to our hotel. We saw everything you would expect for a major industrialized city. Cars, traffic, joggers, shops, commerce. It was exhilarating to be in a new and exotic land and I felt my fatigue bleed away as I soaked up everything.

When we reached our hotel, the driver eagerly helped bring our bags to the door and was somewhat taken aback when we offered U. S. currency for a tip. But, after a moment's hesitation, he accepted and smiled, thanking us. Our lodging was modest, but not a dive. Mike's contact set us up here saying that it was a regular place for international operators and we could make any other necessary contacts we needed to complete our mission.

We checked in and crashed. It might have been paranoia, but we rearranged the furniture in the room so that anyone familiar with the lay out would miss where we were sleeping, if they decided to break in and start shooting. Mike and Jax took the beds and I bunked on a cot. It was the best few hours of sleep in my life.

I awoke to Jax coming in through the door with bags of groceries. The sun was setting and I felt a slight ache in my temples as I adjusted to our new surroundings.

"I bought some food. Probably best to get a few calories in before we hit the bar tonight," Jax said setting the bags down.

"Whatd'ya get?" Mike asked.

"Deli meat, bread, Doritos; just some snack stuff. We'll need to lock down good rations before we leave," Jax said.

"Fuck, yeah. I love sandwiches," Mike said.

"You hear from your boy?" I asked.

"I emailed him about an hour ago. Should be anytime now," Mike said. He was spreading mayo and mustard over four slices of bread. He generously layered turkey on two haves and pressed them together. Opening a bag of chips, he grabbed a handful and threw them on a paper plate with his sandwiches.

"Let's go over the plan again. I want to make sure we all have everything straight," I said taking a bite out of a sandwich Mike handed to me.

"We'll meet Mike's spook tonight, he should have a lead for us on weapons. We'll need to try and ask around the hotel and find transportation and food for the trip. Where we are going is pretty remote. It's not a modern city with roads and shit. It's going to be a pretty grueling hump. Plus, we'll be in completely unfamiliar terrain

278

with who knows how many or what kinds of threats. We should be getting satellite data and a briefing on our objective, but even after that, it's going to be near impossible to do this without us all getting caught or killed " he said throwing a few chips into his mouth.

"Thanks for the fucking pep-talk," Mike said.

"Don't be stupid. What we are about to do is still just as fucked as it was when John dreamed it up in his out of body experience or whatever the fuck happened," Jax said.

"Hey, it wasn't an out of body experience," I said.

"Oh yeah?" Jax asked.

"Yeah...it was more like a vision," I said.

"Well, hell, never mind then. We're totally not fucked because it was a vision, not an out of body experience," Jax said, staring at me.

"Point taken," I said, finishing my food. "That mean you're having second thoughts?"

Jax sat in silence for a moment, "No, I guess not."

"Yeah, we're not going through this again. We're here, we'll be fucking set after tonight. This is happening," Mike said.

"We got about thirty mikes until we rendezvous with Mike's

boy," that meant 30 minutes until we meet. "He better be fucking legit, asshole. This is all riding on him," Jax said, packing gear into a backpack.

"You don't worry about that, alright? I'll handle it. When we get there, just shut the fuck up and let me do the talking. I know this guy, you don't," Mike said.

I wondered if that was really only directed towards me, but Mike didn't break eye contact with Jax during this exchange and I felt like they both knew something I didn't.

We left our hotel room and tipped one of the hotel porters to watch our room. I say tip, I'm not sure what the difference is between a tip and bribe in this context. We walked about twenty minutes to a trendy neighborhood with lots of laughter, bright lights and spicy food. We paced up and down the sidewalk taking in all the people, living their lives. It was kind of odd watching something so completely normal so far away from home. I guess I expected some kind of mysterious, foreign culture, but it was completely western in every respect. Progress waits for no man, I suppose.

I bought some street food which, to this day, was both the best barbecued steak I have ever had and also the worst decision I have ever made. The ruthless and absolute destruction of my stomach that next day was the stuff of horror stories. I thought I was going to die and prayed for it. This would be a seemingly important lesson for anyone questioning street vended meat...don't do it; just don't. It will boil your insides and cause you to shit them out.

Anyway, we killed a few minutes enjoying the sights and sounds; finally wandering into a small, but popular bar with terrible American hip-hop blaring over the house sound system. We found a suitable table in a relatively quiet corner and waited. An order of drinks was placed and I scanned the room, anticipating whoever this mysterious contact that Mike had promised. As I sipped my whiskey, I heard Jax shout, "Motherfucker!" My head swiveled around and I instinctively reached for my pistol, but grasped air, remembering I had yet to purchase one in this country.

"Good to see you too, Jax," a tall black man said standing next to our table.

"You have got to be fucking with me. Him? He is your fucking contact? I wouldn't trust this asshole to shine the shit off of my boots let alone arrange an international arms deal," Jax said slamming his drink and then the empty glass on the table.

281

"You want to keep your voice down you dumb motherfucker," the man said, taking a seat and glancing over his shoulder, "You have any fucking idea how many laws both domestic and foreign I am breaking right now."

"You didn't care about rules much when you fucked my wife!" Jax said standing up and clenching his fist.

"She wasn't your wife when I fucked her," the man said.

"Motherfurcker!" Jax lunged at the man just as Mike stood up and forced the two apart.

"Shut the fuck up, both of you, bunch of pussy ass school girls with your fucking pissing contest. Goddamnit. We have much bigger things to fuck around about without getting arrested in a fucking bar fight," Mike said, trying to restrain his voice from echoing around us.

A few patrons noticed the scuffle and stopped their conversations to watch what was sure to turn into a brawl. I sat at the table, dumbfounded, and continued sipping my whiskey. I had no idea what the fuck was going on and felt helpless to intervene.

"I am not working with this son of a bitch," Jax said angrily; signaling to the waitress for a fresh drink.

"Doesn't look like you have much of a choice. Not if you want the gear and intel. you need for this little sortie you have planned," the man said.

"I would not have gotten involved if I had known he was your contact and you know that," Jax stared at Mike.

"Obviously, that's why I didn't tell you," Mike said. "This isn't some sanctioned op. where we can pick and choose what contractor we want to work with. It's James or nothing."

Jax took a moment to calm down; swallowing his entire drink and motioning for another. He looked off into the distance as his chest heaved. His grip on the glass looked like it would crack the double old-fashioned before he had a chance to bring it back to his lips...had there been anything in it. "Fine, let's get this over with," he said.

"Fine," James said. Looking at me, "Who the hell is this?" he asked, looking me over with what felt like disgust, but I don't claim to be an expert in body language.

"I'm John," I said, extending my hand for a hand shake.

"I didn't fucking ask you," he said.

This caught me off guard because he was looking right into

my eyes. I started to understand Jax's feelings.

Mike placed his hand on my shoulder, "James, this is John. The brain trust behind this little operation. He was the one who tricked Jax and I into being involved. John, meet James. He's our in country spy, who was nice enough to arrange all the minute details, like finding a target and procuring weapons."

James stood up and threw a few bills of local currency on the table, "I'm out."

"Of course he is. The most unreliable cocksucker I've ever known," Jax said, accepting his fresh drink from the waitress.

"You watch your fucking mouth Jax, I could put you in the ground out here and no one would ever know," James said.

"You could try," Jax said.

"Easy fellas, were all friends here, right?" I said without really knowing if that was true.

"You shut the fuck up, too. I don't know you. I don't deal with people I don't know. Mike you got some balls bringing these fuckers to my bar," James said.

"Calm down, James. I know this isn't exactly what we discussed, but it's cool. Look, I trust both of these guys. John, I've

284

known my whole life. This whole thing was his idea. He has more to lose on this than anyone."

"Fuck that, I could get court marshaled. I could get killed out here," James said, still standing by the table, but more or less turned toward our group.

"You're right, I'm sorry. I broke the rules and I know it, but you can trust me, alright. You can trust me," Mike said.

James looked us over, especially me and, after a long moment, sat back down, "I don't have the merchandise you ordered."

"What?" Mike asked, a look of confusion playing across his face.

"Arrangements have been made for you to pick them up, but I wasn't able to bring them," James said.

"This is fucking great. We're supposed to just hope that your random buddy, who doesn't mind dealing with absolute strangers, won't rob us blind, or worse, leave us out in the bumble fuck to die, because what, you were too fucking lazy to bring what we contracted you for?" Jax said, shaking his head.

"There has been a lot of fucking movement here lately, alright? The militants from the north are getting bolder, making incursions further south. The government is fractured from in-fighting and corruption. The people are demanding a response, but the military is hamstrung by all the ineptitude. Things are moving toward a boiling point in one of the most stable countries in Africa. Something is going to give soon and those al-Shabab assholes are a lot more prepared than anyone is giving them credit for. If Kenya falls, it would open a gateway for an almost continent wide spread of radical Islam. We're talking full scale world war, something this continent will break from," James said.

"Jesus," I said.

James' nodded towards me; an expression of "you're a piece of shit," frozen on his face. I wanted to cut it right off his damn head. I mean I was a piece of shit, but he didn't need to remind me.

"Yeah, pray if you believe in that shit., James said.

"So, what are you doing here exactly?" I asked. "Training officers or something?"

"Officially, that's classified," James said. "Unofficially, I may be willing to sell you guns, but I'm sure as shit not going to disclose top secret U. S. government mission data to someone I just met," James said.

"Look, man, I don't know what your fucking problem is, but if you don't want to work with us, just fucking leave. We'll sort our own shit out," I said, feeling emboldened by the booze.

James laughed, sipped his drink and said, "You're going to die out here, you know that?"

"Fuck you, you know what, I don't have to deal with this shit," I stood up, but Mike grabbed my arm and pulled me down back into my seat.

"Alright, that is enough, for fuck's sake. Look, do you have what we need or not?" Mike said.

"Yeah, I got what you asked for," James said, sliding a yellow, folded envelope into Mike's hand. "I got satellite data, aerial photos, topography and transit all lined up. There's a number in there; call it. They'll text you back with a date, time and location. Let me be clear, they are professionals and will have access to all the hardware you could want or need. Don't be late. Don't fuck with these guys. They're valuable, you're not," James said.

"Thanks, James," Mike said.

James stood up and finished his drink.

"Why are you helping us?" I asked, unsure what had just

happened. There was so much anger in this group it set me on edge. They all had some collective history that had chewed them up and I just couldn't put together what was holding them back from killing each other.

"Can't argue with a chance to use a totally unknown and disconnected cell to destabilize a human trafficking network. Best part is, you'll probably all kill each other and I won't have to fill out any paperwork," James said.

"Great, I guess," I said.

James flowed back into the crowded street and Jax raised his hand, extending his middle finger as James walked away.

We took a moment to collect ourselves. The music so loud and the bass so intense that our whiskey pulsed. Looking back it was brilliant for us to meet there. We had to shout just to be heard by the man next to us. It would have been impossible to overhear any of our conversation, let alone record it as evidence. It was completely deniable should anyone come asking questions about why we were there. If anything, it was old Army buddies having a drink in a popular night club. Those CIA bastards know their art.

Paying our tab, we wandered back to our hotel. We found our

porter asleep in a chair near our door. I thought about waking him, but Mike said it was rude. We checked the room for any sign of burglary. Once satisfied we were safe, Jax placed the manila envelope on the bed and we all stared at it. It could have held anything. Maybe the critical intelligence we needed. Maybe a picture of James' dick.

As I lifted it up, Mike said, "Wait!"

"What?" I asked, confused more than ever.

"It could be an explosive," Mike said.

"You got to be fucking kidding me," Jax said.

"Is that even possible? I mean, it's just an envelope," I said.

"MK-34 postal aerosol bomb. AKA the 'letter fucker'. We used it on insurgents communicating via local mail after we shut down their cell network," Jax said.

"Yeah, could be. James is probably laughing his ass off, waiting for the explosion," Jax said.

"You guys are fucking with me," I said.

"Look, you want to blow your fucking face off, you go right ahead," Mike said, gesturing toward my hand.

"Why would James bring us all the way out here, just to kill

289

us?" I asked.

"Because we know too much," Jax said.

"What the fuck does that mean?" I asked.

"Fuck, I think I just heard it engage. Put it down," Mike said, staring at the folder, as if trying to see through the paper into the package.

"Jesus, alright," I started lowering the package.

"For fuck's sake, slow down," Jax said.

I slowed my hand to a slow crawl as I tried to return it to the bed.

"Slow the fuck down, asshole!" Mike shouted.

My movement was nearly imperceptible. Sweat poured down my brow as my gut curled into knots. After an agonizing few seconds, I finally set the paper down and just as my hand let go I heard a loud pack sound. I hit the ground and covered my head with my arms in a futile attempt to protect myself.

I lay like that for a long moment, waiting to feel the fires of hell as I descended. But the longer I laid there, the louder the snickers and muffled laughs floated around me. Raising an arm and opening one eye, I looked around. Mike and Jax were doubled over in fits. A used "champagne popper," something commonly used during indoor celebrations, discarded on the floor. Its hard plastic shell shaped like a bottle; spent confetti on the ground.

"Oh, you fucking...fucking...assholes, goddamnit. I think I shit my pants," I said, sitting up on the floor, my heart racing.

Mike and Jax continued their laughter for a good while. I just sat, quietly reserved this was how I was spending my last few days on Earth.

"You guys really suck, you know that?" I said.

Between wheezing Jax said, "A letter bomb?"

"You're a dumbass, John," Mike said.

"Look, I don't know, I'm following your lead. Why couldn't it be a bomb?" I asked.

"Because this isn't a movie," Mike said.

I brushed myself off and collected my thoughts as they calmed down. They opened the packet, no bombs or dick pics, thank god. They spread out several pictures, maps and data sets I didn't quite understand.

As we looked them over, Mike and Jax seemed to nod to each other, understanding something that was completely lost on me.

291

"What are you looking at?" I asked.

"These are topographical maps showing elevation," Jax said, pointing at a map with concentric layers of colors scattered around. "These are tables of activity. The first column is which entrance or which side targets are coming and going. Its indicated by a E,W, N, or S depending on the direction.

The second column is how many on foot; third is how many vehicles. Fourth indicates if anyone is armed. Each row is a day of the week. Damn, they must have been watching these fuckers for a while, there is a ton of data."

"Yeah a lot of skinnies and a lot of shooters," Mike said, looking at different papers.

"So, what does that mean?" I asked.

"There is going to be a firefight," Jax said, not looking away from the maps.

"There," Mike said, pointing at one of the satellite images.

"What?" I asked.

"That's where we go in," he said.

He pointed to a dark line on the map.

"Is that a wall?" I asked.

"Sure is. This place is a fortress. Got several interior buildings and a perimeter wall all the way around. There are two main entrances on the north and east sides. We'll make our incursion from the west. There's a high point just before the wall. We'll send two men over while one keeps watch. We'll keep our exfil stashed here by the road about half a click away, hump it through the jungle the rest of the way."

"That's way too fucking close, they're going to hear a fucking truck bushwacking through the middle of the night," Jax said. "We should stash the exfil here about 5 clicks out and hump it from there. It will only take one of those bastards to make us on the road and we'll be completely fucked. We aren't playing in some friendly backyard with air support and evac. options. We will be completely on our own. Look, here, there's a motor pool," Jax pointed to a black and white photo. "We can plant charges on the fuel dump and take out their pursuit options. That will draw them out to us. It will be like a shooting gallery. After that we walk out the north gate, back to the road and run like hell to the transport."

"You're not completely wrong. Look at this," Mike held up a data table so he and Jax could review together. "We should wait till

Friday, they have a ton of traffic on that road. We'll just be another car," Mike said.

"How are we going to not get caught if we're in the middle of this parade into the compound?" I asked.

"That's the beauty. These guys are tourists. They're there to fuck and leave. You think they all know each other? No, fuck that. These guys are just random dudes all going to the same place. No reason to think we aren't there to do anything but fuck too. We'll kill the engine, light some smoke, make it look like we broke down. We can basically get as close as we want. Shit we could almost walk through the front door," Mike said.

"Shit, man, I don't know," I said, taking my own turn with the documents.

"He's right," Jax said.

"What?" Mike and I said in unison.

"He's right. It'll be natural camouflage. We'll insert like Mike said, a half click out. It will make for an easy get away in case this goes sideways. If anyone fucks with us as we peel off, we can neutralize them in the relative cover of the foliage and bug out if we get bogged down without having to fight our way back to the vehicle," Jax said.

"This can work," Mike said. "We hit the fuel once we're over the wall. Cut them down as they exit their cover."

I nodded and scowled over the maps one last time, "Yeah that sounds pretty good." I had no fucking idea what I was talking about.

"Well, that leaves just one last thing then," Jax said. He found a small yellow note with a phone number. Handing it to me he said, "Make the call."

I entered the number and hit dial.

Chapter 16

"Goddamnit, Mike," I said. The map bounced in my hands as our aging Toyota Land Cruiser took the dirt highway without regard for its passengers. We had been on the road for several hours. That was after Mike had spent the better part of the morning learning how to drive on left side of the street. That was probably the most terrifying experience of my life. We careened around sharp corners, missing pedestrians, street vendors and on-coming traffic as he slowly learned the subtleties of the English mode of driving.

We had made arrangements with James' contacts to meet just before sundown in a rural and remote highway intersection just north of the city. Greatly misjudging our ability to navigate a foreign road system, the relatively poor signage and Mike's terrible sense of direction, we were laughably behind schedule and in danger of missing our drop.

"What the fuck is the problem now?" Mike asked, the truck picking up speed as we barreled down a hill.

"You just missed our turn," I said.

"For fuck's sake, I need to know before we get to the fucking turn!" he said. The vehicle dug hard into the mud as he slammed on the breaks; all four wheels sliding on gravel.

"You have to slow down, I can't keep up with the map. You're driving like a maniac," I said, turning the map to orient myself to our new direction.

Mike revved the engine as he found his gear and we swung around.

"Slow the fuck down, Mike," Jax said. He leaned forward from the back seat to consult the map with me.

"I can't slow down. We miss this and we don't get a second chance," he said.

"Can't make the deal if we are fucking dead, either," Jax said.

"One of you two fuckers want to drive?" Mike said.

"Just slow down," I said.

Mike pushed the truck's speed up higher as we neared our turn, then hammered the breaks and cranked the wheel hard. We all felt the center of gravity shift and inertia pull us up on two wheels. It was for the briefest moment, but enough to send a shockwave of anxiety radiating out from my skull. I felt like I was floating on a cloud of needles pricking my skin. Mike must have felt it too, because when the wheels finally came back down, he let the truck slowly

accelerate, but kept it at a reasonable speed.

"That was fucking stupid," Jax said.

No one responded. I think we all felt like that more or less

described this entire endeavor and there was no point in singling out

one specific act of recklessness. Our wheels floated along the dirt as

the heavy foliage on either side whipped by. Power lines intersected

in and out of large branches that overhung the highway. The sun laid

low in the sky and we all felt a heavy sense of anxiety that when we

arrived, if we did, it would be too late.

"When's the next turn?" Jax asked.

"About 15 kilometers. After that it should be a pretty straight

shot to the rendezvous. Assuming...," I trailed off as I looked over

the map.

"Assuming what?" Jax asked.

"Assuming I haven't been reading this thing wrong the entire

time. In which case, we will be completely fucked," I said.

"Well...fuck," Jax said.

"I know," I said.

I couldn't believe how the sunrise and sunset worked like

clockwork. Twelve hours of daylight every day, no matter what month or season. You could pretty much set your watch to it. I guess that's the advantage of being so close to the equator. Of course for us, it meant we had a very exact window to make.

"You guys have any idea who these people are? Any reason to think they won't just kill us?" I asked.

I am not ashamed to admit there was a part of me, tucked very deeply in the back of my mind that was praying for the sun to set a little quicker.

"They work for James," Mike said.

"Yes, I understand that," I said.

"They make a lot of money," Jax said, keeping his eyes glued to the far horizon.

"So, they would make a lot more by robbing us blind and leaving us for dead. I mean, what's to stop them from saying we never made it. We just disappeared out in the bush," I said.

"They work for James," Mike said.

"Goddamnit, stop repeating that. It doesn't mean anything to me," I said.

"You don't understand," Mike said.

"Clearly," I said.

"Working for someone like James; working for the U. S. government, it's the holy grail of arms dealing. Think about all the fucked up shit in the world perpetuated by our funneling of weapons to a specific group or cause. We fight hundreds of proxy wars a year and never lift a finger to do so other than selling guns," Mike said.

"So, where do these guys come in if our government is doing the selling?" I asked.

"Think about it. James and other CIA spooks aren't gun manufacturers. They don't hump the stuff over mountain ranges or fly gliders stocked with rifles into remote fields at night. They don't have to, not anymore, anyway. All they have to do is broker cash transactions. The almighty dollar is all it takes to supply a rebel group or militia. There are plenty of local gun runners who can arrange for the actual purchase and delivery and it's a lot easier to deny or cover-up than flying a C-130 into hostile territory. It's an endless stream of revenue for those who are willing to commit treason against their country," Mike said.

"What he is trying to say is that no one, absolutely no one, would blow their contract to profit off of one petty theft. Anything goes wrong and these guys are cut off; not only that, but they are instant targets for retaliation from anyone who has a grudge. If you've been doing this any amount of time at all, that list will be long. It doesn't take much time for word to get around that they are no longer protected. These guys will do anything to fulfill what was ordered," Jax said.

"The next time you see a clip on the news of a bunch of pallets being air-dropped to friendly rebels, just remember that shit was staged. Nothing but propaganda meant to make you feel good about being an American," Mike said.

I leaned back in my seat. I wasn't really looking for a lesson in geo-politics. A simple "you have nothing to worry about" would have sufficed.

"So, we're good then. Nothing to worry about, right?" I asked.

"Sure, unless James has been ordered to have us killed. In which case, we're screwed," Jax said.

"Oh, what the fuck, guys?" I said.

Jax and Mike laughed and I felt a pang of relief flutter through my stomach. But the sun continued its fall and the anxiety

301

buried in my stomach returned. I could feel that acidic worry eating away every time I swallowed.

The truck thudded against the road as we hummed along. It was an unbelievably hot day and there was no air conditioning. We had the windows down and the road noise, combined with the rush of air through the cabin was deafening. We had to shout to carry on our conversations.

"I need to say something; something I should have said a long time ago...," I said.

"Don't make this into a thing, alright?" Jax said, "We all know why we are here. We've said everything that needs to be said. Let's just get this over with."

"No, I need to say this," I said.

"Jesus, fine," Jax said.

"Thank you," I said.

"What is that supposed to mean?" Mike asked.

"Just, thank you," I said.

We sat in silence. I considered trying to make a joke, take back what I said, but there was no point. The longer the silence grew, the more comfortable it became. The foliage whipped by and I remember feeling hopeless; even foolish. How in the fuck did we think we could pull off something so profoundly stupid? How could we have let it gone so far? I didn't want to dwell on this, but there was no escaping it. Nothing to say, nothing to do, except be hot and miserable. The trees whipped by, over and over, and suddenly, a short opening appeared and for a split second. I registered another car parked off the road.

"Stop!" was the only thing my fatigued mind could muster. I began slapping Mike on the shoulder, waiting for more helpful words to manifest themselves.

"What the fuck...oh shit," Mike said, looking in the rear view mirror. He slammed on the breaks, which sent me hurtling into the seat in front of me.

"Goddamnit!" I shouted, "I think you just broke my fucking nose."

"Fuck, man, I'm sorry. Hold on," Mike said. He threw the gear in reverse and gunned the truck backwards.

"Let me see that," Jax said. He tilted my head back looked up my nostrils with a pen light. He leveled my head. "Follow the light."

I moved my head and eyes in unison with his flashlight.

"Your nose might be broken, but you don't have a concussion. Just keep your nose down and let the blood drain," Jax said.

Mike slowed the truck down and parked it in the dirt next to the other vehicle we had passed. It was a relatively clean SUV. The windows were tinted dark. I opened my door and instinctively threw my head back as I felt blood trickling down my face.

"Keep your fucking head down," Jax yelled, also exiting our truck.

I can only imagine the confusion from our contacts. I'm sure they were expecting professionals who acted, well, professional. Instead they got me with a gushing face wound and my companions screaming obscenities at me. Two men, dark complexion, dark sunglasses, nice clothes, exited their vehicle. They had watched us blow past like a tourist at Disney Land, then reverse at full throttle; stumble out, bleeding and swearing at each other. What a fucking great first impression.

"I don't think you are supposed to be here," the driver said.

"Sorry, I'm John," I said, taking a few steps, feeling woozy and putting my hands on my knees. "This is Jax and Mike," I was fully hunched over now, talking to the ground. Jax checked me over again while Mike took out his phone and scrolled through Facebook. I hope the fucking he got from his bill that month, using international data on cell phone to check his status on a social media platform, was so complete it could be considered a manifesto.

The driver watched us in silence. I couldn't see his eyes because of the glasses, but I will go ahead and assume they conveyed an otherworldly level of annoyance.

"You boys are definitely lost," the passenger said.

"No, it's cool, we're the guys from the thing. He doesn't understand. Tell him," I said, motioning to Jax, while I remained hunched over.

"You might actually have a concussion," Jax said sitting me down on the ground.

"No shit, asshole," I said.
Sitting helped and the spinning in my head slowed enough to be tolerable.

"Golf, foxtrot, umbrella, whiskey, tango…motherfucker," Mike trailed off at the end, apparently upset with something.

The men seemed to respond to Mike's nonsense words. They

looked at each other through their solid black glasses for a moment and then the passenger walked to the rear passenger door. He opened it and started talking to someone I couldn't see. Their conversation was either too quiet, in a foreign language or I was too fucked up to understand.

"They're FOF greetings," Jax said, kneeling back down and helping me stand.

"What does that mean?" I asked.

"Friend or foe. Easy way to identify strangers; easier to walk away if you get blank stares. James must have posted them on 4chan or Reddit; some anonymous social collecting site that Mike knew to check," Jax said.

"Do they mean anything?" I asked, regaining my legs.

"Yeah, it means James is an asshole," Jax said.

The passenger took a step back as a well-dressed white man exited the SUV.

"Gentlemen, glad you could make it," he said. His accent was hard to pinpoint, but it was vaguely European. "I don't normally wait an hour passed the scheduled delivery time, but our mutual friend is my best customer. Consider this a courtesy," he said.

His blue eyes and light hair; just something about them made me hate him. He walked toward Mike with an outstretched hand. They shook and he walked over to me and Jax. We all exchanged greetings under the watchful eyes of his two companions, who I noticed, were well armed.

"I'm sure you're just as eager to get on with whatever it is you have planned as I am to get back to my office," he said, his hand outstretched pointing to the back of his SUV. The driver had opened the tailgate and was moving items around in the rear hatch.

I started, "We're planning on...," but trailed off as Jax and Mike both threw jagged looks at me.

"Now, I have no reason, nor desire to know your business. I make it a rule. I'm merely a simple merchant. Information rarely does me any good and often causes me a lot of trouble. So, if you don't mind, we can conduct our transaction and be on our way," he said.

"Alright, I'm sorry, I didn't catch your name," Jax said.

"No names," the man replied.

I felt stupid for having already blurted out ours. Mike and Jax took the lead and I followed to the back of the SUV. I stumbled along, trying to wipe dried blood from my aching face.

"So you do this often," I said.

The man turned and looked at me, "Often enough," he said after a long pause. Then turning to Jax and Mike, "All of this is straight from the manufacturers. It's been weather tested and held in dry storage. They will shoot no matter what you do to them," the driver said.

There were multiple black rifles, all of which looked like they were straight from an action movie. There were magazines, pistols, ammo, everything a burgeoning terrorist would need.

"Holy shit," I said.

"How long has this been in storage?" Mike asked.

"Not long," the passenger said.

I picked up a medium sized rifle. A large green rectangle sitting where the sight should be. It looked electronic, with a glass circle on the end pointing away from the operator, but no corresponding opening on the front.

Mike saw me looking it over, "Infrared; has to be paired with night vision."

There was a fore grip for better stabilization during sustained firing.

It had a secondary holographic sight for easy target acquisition. Most terrifyingly, a grenade launcher slung under the barrel. It felt substantial in my hands. It was badass.

Mike picked up a smaller submachine gun and slammed a magazine into the middle of the weapon, he cleared the breach and, pointing into the bush, pulled the trigger. It "clicked" but without the anticipated bang.

"You're gun is broken," Mike said.

"That model has always been a little finicky. Let me look at it," the blond haired man said. He took the gun and played with the action several times, dropped the magazine and reloaded it. Pointing it into the nearby trees he fired. The barrel erupted with fire. Branches fell with a crash as the tattered remains of leaves floated lazily to the ground.

"There, the bolt just needed some attention," he said, handing it back to Mike.

"This thing is a piece of shit," Mike said.

"Yeah, I don't see anything here that doesn't t have rust, or heat warp. I wouldn't take these into a firefight if they came with a hand job," Jax said.

I picked up a huge gun that bristled with rails and attachments. A large box was slung underneath and a row of shiny brass rounds looped up into the gun. "Yeah and this, what is this? It's way too heavy," I said.

"Actually, that's in pretty good shape," Mike said.

Blondy looked around at his partners and we stood there for a long, long time with absolute silence. Even the breeze was scared to move. I considered what we would do if these men just opened fire; insulted by our disapproval. I pictured myself diving behind one of the vehicles and trying to crawl out of the line of fire. I imagined them just shooting me in the back as I ran away. Finally, Blondy laughed and broke the tension. I tensed, waiting for some kind of retaliation.

"I see you are experienced," he said.

He turned and chuckled to himself as he motioned to the driver. I was really starting to dislike this asshole. The driver rolled the weapons back up in the clothe they were laid on and pushed them to the back of the long rear hatch. The floor pulled up in one quick motion showing a gleaming rack of completely new firearms. I could instantly tell the difference between what we had been shown

310

and what we were being presented now. These were screaming black instruments of death. There were no wear marks, no oil splotches, no loose fittings. These were top of the line.

"This is much better," Jax said.

He retrieved a medium sized rifle, fitted with what looked like a small, rectangular brick. I later learned this was a computer controlled laser sight that automatically compensated for the weapons movement. Jax pulled the bolt back, inspecting the breach. It had a serious looking stock that made the weapon look more like a futuristic art piece than a firearm – although maybe they're not mutually exclusive. The whole thing was designed to ensure each round tore through a person with precision.

"This is some advanced warfighter shit," Mike said, "Were in the hell did you get these?"

"Our mutual friend has many top tier clients. Only the best," Blondy said.

"These platforms were rumored to be in develop while I was deployed. This is a $20,000 rifle," Mike said.

"Who are you?" Jax asked, looking back at Blondy. There was something in his voice I had never heard before; fear maybe?

"Gentlemen, like I said, information is not my business. Who I am and what I do are really not that important. None of that will help you execute, whatever it is that you are doing, and certainly won't help me. The only thing I am concerned about and, what is actually important in this moment, is that you have the money to pay for the merchandise," Blondy said.

Mike and Jax looked at each other.

"How much?" Jax asked.

"That depends entirely on what you are buying," Blondy said.

Mike looked over the cache. He picked out three rifles, all equipped with advanced looking attachments. He also selected three pistols, Kevlar helmets, magazines, boxes of ammunition, a few grenades and several other exotic looking pieces of gear and set them aside.

"How much for all of this?" Mike asked.

"200," Blondy said.

"$200?" I asked.

"$200,000," Blondy said.

"Fuck that," I said. "We don't have anywhere near enough for that."

I felt like I maybe shouldn't have said that – as soon as the words left my mouth. I know, had we not been in the middle of negotiating, the verbal assault from Mike and Jax would have been so violent and filthy, it would have been studied by maniacal dictators for generations to come. I felt their anger radiating off of them.

"Well, we have a problem then," the driver said. He placed his hand on the pistol strapped to his hip. I wasn't sure if this was an actual threat or just him posturing, either way, it sent a jolt of ice through my gut.

"Wait, wait, when we talked with James, he said our package was set for $10,000. This is horseshit," Jax said.

"He doesn't set my prices. I do," Blondy said.

"The fuck you do," Mike said.

The driver and passenger took steps towards us. Mike shouldered the rifle in his hands. Keeping the muzzle pointed at the ground, but taking an aggressive posture.

"Don't fucking move," Mike said.

"Mike, stand down," Jax said. Turning to Blondy, he said,

"Look, we all want the same thing here. You want to get paid and we want our fucking guns."

"Agreed," said Blondy. "But you're not walking away with all of this for $10,000."

"OK, what would be a reasonable amount for all of this?" Jax asked.

"I couldn't possibly part with that for less than $150,000," Blondy said.

I stood there, confused and frustrated, but silent; unsure of how we were going to leave this situation with our gear, and more importantly, alive.

"Give me a minute to discuss this over with my associates," Jax said

"Come on, you have already kept me waiting. I have better things to do than stand in the sun all day," Blondy said.

"Just one minute," Jax said.

We huddled up a few feet away from the SUV.

"How much total do we have?" Jax asked.

"$20,000 and that's if we don't eat for the next three days," Mike said.

I have an idea," Jax said. We turned around and walked back to the SUV, following Jax. Mike must have had more faith in him than me because he leaned the rifle against the side of the truck. "We agree to your price of $150,000," he said.

Stunned by this, I blurted out, "What?"

"Wonderful. Can I see the money?" Blondy said.

Mike threw our envelope of cash. Blondy caught it, his face instantly showing disappointment; not needing to count our cash to know it wasn't enough – the package being too light.

"What is this?" Blondy asked. "This isn't even half of what we agreed."

"We both know how this goes," Jax said.

"Oh yeah, and how is that?" Blondy asked.

"If we give you the full amount right now, you might be tempted to share with your buddies about how three Americans are buying high end weaponry for some clandestine mission. We don't need any extra ears listening in on what went down here," Jax said.

"That is ridiculous, I would never…" Blondy started, but Jax cut him off gruffly.

"But, if we pay you part now, and, once the job is done, the
315

remainder plus, say 10% retainer fee for keeping your mouth shut, I'd say that's enough incentive to keep our business confidential," Jax said.

"You must think me a fool. Talking about a deal; what absolute nonsense. It would absolutely ruin my business and likely be a death sentence," Blondy said; his face a startling shade of red. His hands balled into fists and trembling.

"You say information isn't your business, but a man of your position didn't get there just by running guns. We all know information is more valuable and more deadly than any weapons system. We would be the fools to rely on your sense of honor to keep your mouth shut without any type of insurance," Jax said.

I knew Jax was just bullshitting, but I have to admit, even I started to think it was a pretty good argument.

Blondy clenched his jaw, "I have no guarantee you will even survive whatever the hell you have planned. You want me to front you a small fortune when you clearly have no idea what you are doing."

"We have already made arrangements with our in country contact. He'll disburse the remaining funds only after he receives the all clear from me," Jax said.

"So, it's in my best interest if you survive," Blondy said.

"Very much so," Jax said.

"I could just walk away. Be done with this whole idiotic situation," Blondy said.

"And renege on a deal? From what I understand, that would destroy your business overnight," I blurted out.

Mike turned to me with a scowl, but Jax understood what I had insinuated and kept his eyes locked with Blondy. He had to say yes if he wanted to continue his relationship with the CIA or whoever the hell James worked for. There were way too many other men willing to make a handsome profit selling guns on behalf of a foreign government to risk backing out of a deal. Saying no would be tantamount to shooting himself in the head. No reason he would be trusted again, regardless of the reason why he had cancelled the sale. There was a long, long pause, again considering it would be much easier and economical for them to just shoot us and claim we never showed up. No reason to think James would give a shit.

"Fine. Let's get this over with," Blondy said. "And I want 20% on top."

The relief crashed over me like an avalanche. Jax put his arm around my shoulder; whispering, "You lucky motherfucker."

Mike and Jax began loading rifles and gear into our truck. Their weight putting a noticeable dip on the rear springs. I picked up a small sub machine gun and checked the magazine; fully loaded. The passenger and driver helped move heavy boxes of ammunition, clothing and survival gear.

"You know, its people like you who make me want to quit the business," Blondy said, lighting a cigarette.

"Oh yeah?" I asked.

"You Americans and your incapacity for following the rules, sticking to a deal. It's always a favor, a special exception. It's like you are all incapable of being professionals." He took a long drag.

"Yeah, we kind of fuck the rules…as a rule," I said, instantly embarrassed by my own stupidity. I blame the concussion.

He snorted out a laugh and threw a glance out of the corner of his eye that only reinforced my sense of shame. I felt awkward, letting the silence hang between us; I said the first thing that came to mind. It was like a clandestine first date.

"So, what else would you do if you weren't running guns? I

doubt you're the kind of guy to open a pizza place and settle down," I said, leaning on a large rock, testing the sights of the MP5 in my hands.

He laughed, I guess amused by my childish capacity for conversation and said, "I have other ventures."

"I'm guessing the illegal kind," I said.

"I own a small resort," he said.

"Oh, that seems nice," I said. "You right on the beach?" His companions laughed, but I couldn't tell why.

"No, nothing like that. We cater to a specific clientele," he said.

"Oh," I said.

"Things you can't get back in the States," he said.

"Must be nice," I said.

We stood like this for a few minutes. The sun was almost completely set. The car lights had been switched on to provide more light. Mike and Jax were taking one last inventory of our purchase before we left.

Bored and exhausted, and looking for any reason to distract myself from the fact I hadn't had a drink in a few days, I asked, "So, like drugs?"

"Girls," he said.

"Well, I hate to piss on your business model, but we have girls back home, too," I said.

"Very young girls," Blondy said.

It took an embarrassingly long time for his words to connect in my mind. My first instinct was to laugh, a mindless reaction when confronted with an uncomfortable moment. But then I put together what he was insinuating and the rage ignited. It was a hatred born out of everything that I had felt since Kat had died. A wave of nausea and adrenaline and pain came washing over me.

Blondy took one last puff of his cigarette and threw it on the ground. His head exploded. The body going rigid and then crumpling to the ground; shrouded in a red mist. The barrel smoked, but not as much as I had anticipated. The gun itself vibrated as my grip tightened; my attempt to stop the tremors in my muscles. The passenger and driver were frozen; their bosses body twitched slightly on the ground; blood flooding the grass around my feet. They looked at me, at him, back at me and then finally reached for their weapons.

I opened fire on the driver, struck him three times in a line across his chest. I turned, fired at the passenger, missed and dove behind their SUV. He took one step and Mike grabbed him by the forehead and ran a knife across his throat. He gulped, gasped and then crumpled to the ground. I stood up, taking stock of the situation. Three dead bodies with ragged, gushing wounds. I felt my stomach turn and I vomited into the grass.

"What the fuck, John?" Mike screamed at me.

Jax stood motionless staring into the distance.

"Did you hear?" I asked.

"Hear what? I mean for fuck's sake, do you have any idea what you have done?" Mike asked.

I ran a shaky hand through my hair and tried to breathe deeply. My heart was pounding so hard, I thought it would explode in my chest.

"He was, it. He was one of the guys," I stammered.

"What?" Mike asked. Turning to Jax he said, "Are you getting any of this?"

Jax stood motionless. He didn't respond and after a moment, I started to wonder if he was hit. I hadn't aimed particularly well. I could have easily missed. I could have just shot my friend. Holy shit, what did I do?

321

"Jax, are you OK?" I asked.

He didn't answer.

"Jax?" Mike yelled.

He walked calmly to our truck, retrieved a pistol and shot the passenger in the head. "What?" he asked, very calmly, like nothing had happened. It scared me. "He was still breathing."

"Are you OK? You're freaking us out a little," I said.

"Help me move the bodies," was his only response.

He started dragging Blondy's body into the bush. Mike and I looked at each other and joined him. We loaded the bodies into their SUV, took the remaining supplies, sorry, stole the remaining supplies we wanted and pushed the vehicle into the heavy brush. We cut the gas line and threw a road flare under the vehicle. It erupted in flames and I noticed I was completely numb to everything around me. I thought I would feel something profound; maybe a sense of accomplishment or regret. Instead, just calm.

When we were finished destroying evidence, we piled back into our truck and headed back onto the empty dirt road. Mike took the driver's seat and I was crashing hard in the back. The chemical cocktail that had overridden every circuit in my brain was leaving and it left me exhausted. I felt like I should say something, again the silence flaring my anxiety like a bellow. I also felt like I needed to justify my actions. Like Jax and Mike might judge me if I didn't offer a reasonable explanation for murder.

I said, "He was the guy, he runs one of the brothels."

"No shit?" Mike asked; seemingly uninterested. He was checking his phone again; swiping through menus. That damn phone - he was on that thing more than anyone I had ever met. It was like talking with a brick wall that also somehow used memes as a response to normal conversation. You would think he was not paying attention, until he would whip the screen around and show you some disgusting internet picture; usually some clever way of tricking you into looking at a penis.

"Yeah, he was bragging about it," I said.

Mike closed his screen, turned around and said, "Fuck 'em."

This made me feel better, but I still felt like the whole situation was spinning out of control, I was out of control and I didn't know how to stop. Mike went back to his phone and the silence returned. I was too tired at this point to care.

We hadn't gone much farther when Jax started laughing to

323

himself. He had been completely silent since ordering us to load the SUV, but was now chuckling over and over; seemingly from nothing. Mike and I shot each other glances.

"You...uh...OK, buddy?" Mike asked.

"James is going to be so pissed," Jax said.

Chapter 17

I pulled the tactical vest over my shoulders and zipped it. The weight was more than I had anticipated. Looking at myself in the mirror, I saw a person I didn't recognize. He was thin and muscular, but tired and sad.

"You get that shit locked down?" Mike asked.

"Yeah, I'm good to go," I said.

"Perfect," he said.

"Twenty mikes," Jax said.

"Holy shit," I thought. "Only twenty minutes left until we start something we can never take back; never undo."

I'd be lying if I said I was nervous. No, it was feverish, nervous dread that I was afraid would make aiming impossible. The jittery energy making my whole body tremble.

I double checked my pack, my ammo. I must have racked my rifle and pistol a hundred times, having to replace the round that ejected each time. I knew Mike and Jax were watching me, but they were silent. Just letting me go through this improvised ritual.

"Ten mikes," Jax said.

I started to feel almost out of body; like I was watching a movie, only it was myself on the screen packing all these instruments of death. I hadn't slept in almost 24 hours. The intensity of it all washing over me in perpetual wakefulness. I had eaten a lot of Oreos over the last couple of days; fulfilling my every whim in anticipation of my certain death.

"Five mikes," Jax said.

"Jesus," I said out loud. I don't know if this was a call to the deity or just my subconscious expressing its terror. I shouldered my pack, felt the weight pull me down. Gravity working no matter what I was about to do. I shouldered my rifle. Jax had given me gum, saying it would help with the adrenaline. He was right. I focused on moving my jaw up and down, felt the soft confection work between my teeth and it took the edge off of the huge chemical surge that was pounding in my brain.

"Move out," Jax said.

We threw open the door to our motel and sprinted to our truck. In a matter of seconds we were in and moving. Our weapons stationed at the ready; the butts on the floor; muzzle pointing to the ceiling. My pack rested next to me on the seat; one arm still in a sling, ready to be thrown on at any moment. I reached for my seatbelt, thought of Mike's story of being trapped, and reconsidered. The truck sped down the highway and we exited quickly onto a small rural road. The pavement gave way to dirt and we rumbled down the mud and gravel.

Mike pushed the accelerator and the needle crept up. It was a completely different feeling than our last time out in the bush. We were ready. We were set. I grabbed one of the roof handles and held on as the road bounced our truck.

"We're about twenty clicks out. Check your mags one last time. We're switching to night vision in five mikes," Jax said. He studied our map one last time.

I dropped my mag for what felt like the thousandth time and confirmed it was, in fact, loaded. I slammed it back into my rifle and pulled my pistol. I dropped the mag; fully loaded. Slammed it back into the grip and holstered it.

The truck lights shut off and our world was dark. I slid the goggles down off my helmet and powered them on. A bright green flash and then a subtle layering of different shades. My rifle gave off

327

a distinctive shimmering line from the sights. The infra-red laser zeroed in for maximum efficiency in a firefight.

"When we hit the tree line, stay in a single file," Jax said. "Watch your step, there's all kinds of creepy shit out here that would love to bite you,"

His voice was even; collected. He was use to this.

"Who is taking point?" I asked.

"I will," Mike said.

"John, you're in the middle. I'll take up the rear. Keep your muzzle pointed at the ground unless I tell you otherwise. Keep your eyes fixed on the back of Mike's gear and walk where he walks," Jax said.

I shook my head "yes" and we returned to silence. I thought about Sephie and suddenly wondered what the hell I was doing. This was the most fucked up thing imaginable and here I was actually going through with it. I felt myself about to speak, to stop the truck, call the whole thing off, runaway back home and bury myself in her.

But then Kat's voice whispered in my ear. "I love you, daddy." I didn't so much hear this as feel it in my head, and it all came back to me. Why I was here. What the point of it all was. The months of planning and training and pain. It was for this – to make someone who merits death, die. The rage re-ignited in my heart. I had lost everything. It was stolen from me and I would never get it back. No amount of pleading, or tears or hate would change it. But, I could channel it; direct it all towards those that deserved to hurt as I had hurt.

"What the hell is that?" Mike asked.

I was shaken from my thought. My eyes burned as a bright string of lights snaked its way through the pitch dark of rural Africa. I ripped off my nightvision and rubbed my eyes, trying to soothe the piercing pain of sudden exposure to bright lights. I shut my eyes tight and waited for relief; praying I hadn't been blinded. I blinked slowly, relieved that I could still see. Mike and Jax had flipped up their goggles, which were attached to mounts on their helmets.

"It's fucking rush hour," Jax said.

"Where are they all going?" I asked.

"Same as us, I think," Jax said.

It suddenly hit me how big an industry this was. We weren't hitting some hidden cocaine factory in the mountains of Columbia, completely isolated from the outside world. This was an integral part of the community. It was known. I think it was the hubris that really sent me over the edge. These men weren't cowering in fear of being discovered, but likely relished the exposure – something akin to advertising for their industry. They weren't afraid, didn't operate in secret. They existed openly. If I hadn't had the resolve before now to finish our mission, this cemented it for me. I wanted to tear these men down and piss on the rubble.

"No changes, this might actually provide good cover. We'll just be one more truck in the line," Mike said.

We followed, bumper to bumper, for what felt like hours. As the time passed, all that adrenaline, all that focus and intensity, faded and I felt myself becoming more and more tired. The body, with all its evolutionary advantages, is still a machine that gets run down from over use, like an engine that gets run too hot for too long. After a while, it has to just shutdown to save itself from breaking. This must have been what is like for them, all those years in the Army. Just hurry up, wait, sleep when you can and then bam! you're in a firefight. I'm not sure what the long term health effects of that kind of stress are, but they're probably not good.

I drifted some. My mind wandering again and I could feel

longing for what might have been, had my life gone any other direction. It wasn't so much that I felt like my present situation could change. No, it was that quiet reserve knowing that it couldn't.

I leaned my head against the glass and watched as the terrain inched by. Sleep pushed itself on my eyelids and suddenly I felt comfortable; a warm rush of dopamine as my brain coaxed me into unconsciousness.

I woke with Jax tapping my knee with his fist.

"Get switched on," he said. "We're almost there."

Sitting up, it took several seconds to remember where I was, what I was doing. That disorienting first moment of waking in which the whole world seems new.

"Alright, any place in here," Jax said.

He pulled on a thin, metal cable that had been run through the glove box. There was a quick, muffled pop and smoked oozed out of the front grill. Mike angled the truck into the dirt and killed the engine. We all exited on the driver's side, Jax having to climb over the gear shift. I knelt down, pulled my gear on and shouldered my rifle. Crouched by the rear wheel, I was pretty well concealed.

Mike set his helmet on the seat and popped the hood. A

plume of silver smoke caught the headlights as it floated into the atmosphere. He puzzled over the engine, waiting for the few cars behind us to pass our seemingly broken down transport. All we had to do was wait for a break in traffic and we would be free into the night; just had to sell this show for a few more minutes. There were longer and longer breaks between passing vehicles; traffic growing thinner. The other cars kept moving and, with them, a sense of excitement and confidence grew inside me.

"We are actually going to get away with this," I thought. "Not long now."

I caught a faint reflection of myself in the paint of the truck and felt badass. Then I heard the mechanical creak of brakes; tires crunching dirt as they rolled to a stop and the blood froze in my veins.

I heard the mechanical whir of a vehicle window and then, "Hello, friend, you need any help?" a voice called from the road. It was a thick accent, again not something I could pin down, but English seemed to be his native tongue. I tried to inconspicuously look through the rear window of our truck, but ducked down as soon as I saw movement.

"No, just a radiator leak," Mike said. "I'll get it patched."

"Well, a Yankee. Don't get many of you out this way. Just in town for a visit?" the man asked.

"Yeah just doing a little site seeing. Truck broke down; that's all," Mike didn't make eye contact with the other driver, instead focusing on the truck.

"Ah, that's terrible. Although, you are a long way from nothing as far as sightseeing. I guess you might be here for something else?" his voice gave an ironic rise. Just based on that, and mind you, I couldn't see it, but I imagined a playful look in his eye and small smile. Something you might see in teenage boy ready to commit mischief.

"Nope, just got lost I guess. How do I get back to the highway?" Mike asked.

"Come now, no reason to be ashamed. I know why you're out here," the voice said. "You sure you don't need a hand? This is no place for a break down."

I looked under our truck to the road and saw an old Jeep, with no doors and no windshield stopped just ahead of us.

"Yeah, I'm good. Shouldn't take long," Mike said, looking

over the engine compartment. He really was trying to play the detached motorist.

"I'll tell you what, I have a spotlight. I'll keep it lit for you while you work," the voice said.

I heard a click as the vehicle shifted into park. The engine stopped and the man exited his vehicle; leaving the headlights on. He came into view as he rounded the front of our truck. He was older, maybe 70. His gray hair, tanned skin and floral patterned shirt gave him a tourist appearance, but his apparent familiarity with the area meant he must be a local or, at least, a frequent visitor.

Mike took a step back; letting the old man inspect the engine. He moved slowly, like his hip cracked with each lumbering move. His light hit me; freezing in a moment of terror. I raised my rifle to fire, but before I could react, Mike pulled a nylon wire from his wrist and dragged the man down to the dirt. He thrashed, fighting for air, but was completely overmatched. After a moment, he was rigid and dead. We moved him into the bush and pushed his car after him.

Mike slid his helmet on, taking a good minute to lock the straps down. We kept low as a few vehicles came over the hill, but they quickly passed. Our truck was just another broken down vehicle on a dusty highway in the middle of nowhere.

We waited a few more minutes, made sure no one had doubled back around, or that any stragglers came rumbling down the road. We positioned our vehicle in cover; angled it for an easy getaway.

"Night vision on, radios on. Make this quiet," Jax said.

I switched my goggles on and was once again greeted by shades of green. All of our infrared sights creating streaks into the darkness. Jax had a wrist mounted GPS that he kept a close eye on. Each step was like walking on coals. The adrenaline thundering through the muscles in my body again, making it feel like I was weightless. I think I was hot. It's hard to remember. I could have been freezing, burning alive, I wouldn't have felt any of it. I was so focused on what we were doing that every other sensation disappeared.

I concentrated on my breathing, my heart threatening to beat out of my chest. I kept a steady rhythm, counting my steps in an easy pattern, 1, 2, 3, 4, 1, 2, 3, 4 trying to take control. I suddenly realized why every war movie showed soldiers running to a cadence. I remembered Jax's advice to step where Mike did. I felt for the imprints of his boots and tried to fill them exactly. I do remember

trying to listen, but there was so much noise from the wildlife, it was

deafening. A combination of bugs, birds, probably bats, and the

distant growls of predators. My radio headphones also worked as ear

protection, but it only magnified just how loud the world was. I felt

very alone.

Jax raised his arm, bent at the elbow, his fist clenched. This

was the sign to stop. We all three knelt and put our backs together;

our rifles bristling out.

"We're five clicks out; a little behind schedule," Jax said.

"That old bastard put us behind," Mike said.

"Yeah, did you really have to strangle him?" Jax asked.

"He nearly blew the op," Mike said.

"Couldn't you just hit him over the head and knock him

out?" I asked.

I could feel Mike and Jax staring at the back of my head,

something I had become accustomed to.

"Really?" Mike asked.

"What?" I asked. "It just seemed overkill."

"You weren't worried about overkill three days ago when

you blasted those other fuckers." Mike said.

"Yeah, but, that's different," I stammered.

"Shut the fuck up, both of you," Jax said. "Hydrate and let's get moving."

I gulped down a few mouthfuls of water. We moved again and I was electrified by another surge of adrenaline. It was my whole world. I tried breathing deeply, but my lungs wouldn't cooperate and I felt myself taking shallow breathes with each step. Mike was ahead of me, moving deliberately; quickly. I was amazed at how easy it was to keep up. I simply willed my body to run faster and it complied.

The bush was uncooperative, though. It was thick and dry and somehow wet at the same time. I could feel movement at my feet and prayed that it was nothing poisonous. We had read up on all the things that can kill you out here and let me say there is plenty. I imagined walking into a spider web; one that no amount of light amplification would show in the dead of night. The deadly inhabitants making a quick rush to my jugular as I screamed and twirled around, ineffectively. Mike's steady pace was unhindered, though. He had a sturdy machete he used to cut through whatever obstacle he encountered. I never turned around to check on Jax, but I assume he spent the entire hike wondering why I wouldn't hurry the fuck up.

We came on a small hill, well it looked small when we were at the bottom, even with the chemical cocktail fueling my new found superpowers, it was a bitch to climb. It just kept going up. We moved rock to rock and when we finally reached the summit, I realized where we were. Night vision tricks the eyes. What seemed like just a haze in the distance was actually light...bright light.

Jax went down to a knee and then a crawl and we all followed, finishing the last 30 yards or so tearing up our stomachs. At the edge, we could see into the camp. Groups of armed men standing around large open fires. Between them and the flames, drunken assholes were using old couches and recliners as lawn furniture. There was shouting and laughter; loud music drifted from somewhere. What looked like Christmas lights were strewn between light poles, giving the whole area a club feel. People were milling around from fire to fire. There were tables set up with long rows of bottles. Whole pigs were being roasted on spits. It was a party.

A large colonial house sat in the middle of the grounds with smaller, dorm style buildings across the yard. Several small sheds sat in the corner. The compound wall was pretty imposing. The ground slopped sharply back from our position and ended at a severe angle with the concrete and wire. In the very far corner, with all of the revelers between us, sat 50 or so steel drums.

"There," I said, "look." I pointed to the drums. Mike and Jax followed my direction. "I bet that's fuel," I said; silence for a long moment.

"Yeah, I think you're right," Mike said.

The fuel depot was our first objective. Hitting that would cause a panic. Everyone would be too drunk or too disoriented to put up much of a resistance. Plus, it would make moving around a whole hell of a lot easier.

"Those building have to be where they're keeping the girls," Jax said.

Watching closely, I could see people walking in and out, some alone, some their arm wrapped around a much smaller frame.

"Actually, that's perfect. They'll scramble to that one side, trying to put out the fire. We can infil. from here and work our way back to them," Mike said.

"I like that," Jax said. He looked at me. "When we get in there, you keep absolutely quiet."

I nodded.

"Mike, you keep overwatch," Jax said.

"Roger that," he said.

Removing his pack, Mike unzipped the main pouch. He retrieved a medium sized hard plastic case and went about unlatching the cover. Inside black gunmetal and hard composite caught the moonlight.

It's easy to forget who Mike really is. Between the general drunken fuckery and the occasional genuine expression of human empathy, you get lost. You find yourself half a bottle in, laughing and enjoying life and your mind overlooks the fact that his stories are tragic. There are moments, though, like watching him assemble that rifle, in the span of a single breath, you glimpse behind the booze and dick jokes. His mind had this determination that his hands carried out without hesitation. Within an instant, it was racked, ready to fire. His pack under his chest and a large rock bracing the bifold on the front of the stock. Mike is a killer.

Checking the scope, he gave us a thumbs up and we climbed

down the outcrop. Well, climbed is kind of generous, it was more like a controlled slide down the loose dirt and grass. I felt sharp pieces of rock grab my skin through my ballistic vest and my stomach sank as gravity accelerated my descent. I watched Jax cushion his stop on the wall with his legs and did my best to replicate it. I probably would have broken my ankle, but the ground leveled out just enough slow my fall.

We both stood and Jax gave me a hand signal to turn around and kneel. I obeyed and kept my rifle pointed into distance, watching for any sign of movement. We could hear the voices of probably a hundred men carrying over the wall. While I kept watch, Jax pulled out nylon rope and scaling hook. He carefully swung it onto the edge and gave it a sharp tug. He leaned on it with all of his weight to test its ability to hold us. Satisfied, he tapped my shoulder and I stood, putting my back to the wall and resumed my watch.

The wall had to be 20 feet high and was topped with razor wire. On reaching the top, he used a foot loop to hold himself at eye level. I couldn't quite tell everything he was doing from my angle, but I assume he was scanning the area right over the wall to make sure we had a good place to drop in. He climbed back down, flicked the rope and caught the grapple as it fell. He motioned to move farther down the wall. We took about 30 more steps and he repeated the process of climbing and surveying. Putting my back to the wall, I looked up to see Mike's barrel protruding over the edge of the hill. It was really comforting knowing he was up there. Where I couldn't see anything beyond the wall and only a few yards in either direction, he had the whole world in his view and that gun was big enough to kill an elephant.

I heard a metallic clink and looked up to see Jax snipping the wire with a folding pair of bolt cutters. After a few slices, he very carefully removed the wire from the top of the wall and let it drop behind him. I watched the whole way as it fell, my mind playing the gruesome fantasy of it landing on my head. I looked up again and Jax was gone. I took this as my cue to climb and made quick work of the rope. I pulled myself over wall, careful not to lose the rifle slung on my shoulder or get my boot caught in the remaining razors. I looked down below, holding my weight with my hands, but did not see Jax. I took the counter rope he had deployed on the other side and slid down, careful not to dislodge the first grapple.

Inching my way down took longer than I liked, being

completely exposed. I imagined just letting go, but unlike in the movies, falling two stories would have meant fractures or worse. By the time I finally reached the bottom, I was in a full blown panic. Jax had vanished and I had no idea what to do. I came in behind one of the utility sheds and I must have walked circles around it three or four times, hoping I had somehow just missed him standing nearby.

I thought radioing him. I knew that was the wrong thing to do, but not doing anything was worse. If I was heard, I would die. If Jax was heard, he would die. If I stood here and did nothing, I would die. I felt hopeless. I crouched, pressed the microphone diodes on my neck and was almost about to speak, when a hand grabbed my shoulder.

"Ahh!" I grunted. I spun around with my rifle barrel pointing at my assailant.

"It's me asshole," Jax whispered.

"Oh my god, you scared the hell out me. Where the fuck where you?" I asked, lowering the barrel.

"I scouted ahead a few yards; let's go," Jax said.

I nodded and waited for him to get about three steps ahead of me. We held our weapons at our shoulders. I walked almost sideways, keeping watch behind us. We kept a steady pace, keeping in the shadows and using random pieces of junk for cover. Jax raised his fist and we ducked behind a few crates piled up near one of the dorms. Men with AK47s and shotguns walked past us, almost close enough to touch. I could smell their sweat, hear the rustling of their clothes. The adrenaline and the fear were so intense, I could barely control my breathing. I wanted to scream, to run, to let loose all the swirling trauma in my mind. All I could think to do, was to bite my lip so hard I tasted warm copper in my mouth.

One of them stopped, the rifle hanging from his shoulder by a soft belt. He lit a cigarette and took a few draws. Jax raised his rifle and I followed, waiting, praying he wouldn't see us. I thought to myself, "Holy shit, this is it. I am actually going to die, right here in this moment. I am going to die, and this whole thing is my fault." I waited the longest minute of my life. He just stood there, stupidly. Smoking his cigarette completely ignorant of his own brush with mortality. Slowly, he took his last breathe, flicked the butt and started off towards the group that had passed us.

I released the breath I had been holding. Jax signaled to keep moving and we I followed. We were able to keep pretty close to the wall, following the perimeter of the compound to circle around to the fuel depot. When we came to the outside of the main house, we used the space between the windows and the ground to keep ourselves concealed. The windows were open and we could hear loud fits of laughter and the high pitched screams of teenage girls. Jax stopped us again and we leaned just over the bottom sash of the window. Inside, three men were hunched over a woman lying on the floor. We couldn't see her face, just her legs as she kicked and bucked in vain. Two holding down her arms while the third was on top of her. Jax and I never really practiced any complex sign language but he gestured something to the effect of "we are coming back to kill these motherfuckers." I nodded "yes" and we kept moving.

Just past the main house, more people drunkenly carousing and laughing. Two men tried to finish clear bottles of some sort of alcohol. Both vomited before the bottles were emptied, laughed and then resumed drinking. Very young girls sat on the laps of several middle aged men. Some seemed interested in what was going on. Most seemed tired. One little girl was crying, saying something in a language I couldn't understand.

I was lost in the scene; again experiencing that out of body feeling, like I watching myself from a screen. This all seemed so surreal. It couldn't actually be happening. People didn't actually do things like this. It was all just a nightmare and any minute, I would wake up, go to work, live my life; tell Mike and Jax about this bizarre dream I had. Jax tugged on my vest sharply and it got my attention. He motioned a direction and we were moving again. Out of my peripheral, I saw men dragging the crying girl, kicking and screaming off into the night.

It took us about an hour to get from where we entered over the fence to the fuel depot. Between the patrols, random revelers and the occasional unescorted girl, we had to constantly stop, hide, and wait. There was a steady stream of people, but enough noise and distraction that movement wasn't impossible.

Our last sprint to the fuel depot was completely uncovered. There was no way around it. Bright stadium lights on a telephone pole bathed the drums in light. About 30 yards of completely open and unobstructed grass between us and cover. I kept expecting to hear gun shots; rounds whizzing by my helmet, but 30 turned into 20, then 5 and then we were hidden again, tucked behind the gasoline. Of course, if anyone had actually shot at us, we would have burned to death, but you can't shoot what you can't see, so, you know.

Anyway, I can't express the excitement I had when we finally made it to the depot. We had come so far and we were finally, finally able to do something...and this was going to be big. Jax signaled for me to start and he took up a defensive position as I worked. I started by retrieving a brick of plastique. Now, in your typical action flick, the bad guys might have 40 bricks of this stuff all strapped to a busty blonde or some stupid shit. But it only took a quarter of what I had now to level those trees back home. I had more than enough to kill everyone in the compound, although hopefully not us and hopefully not the girls, but nothing was guaranteed when working with this much explosive.

I used a box cutter razor to cut off about an inch thick piece and stick it to the first drum. I repeated this until the brick had been more or less evenly cut up and stuck to about 15 barrels. I placed detonator pins in each piece and very, very carefully ran the attached electrical lines back to a radio receiver. Since the whole thing didn't vaporize us immediately, I switched the receiver on, again holding my breath; expecting to just stop existing. I waited a moment and,

347

once satisfied it was set, tapped Jax on the shoulder.

We took our time; waiting for a small patrol to pass, then sprinting back to the nearest building. We spent another solid hour working our way back around to the dorms and the crate stack where we had almost been seen a while earlier. By now, the night had grown long and some of the crowd had dwindled, but there were still many men wandering around the compound. We settled into our firing positions and Jax looked at me.

"You ready?" he asked

"Yes," I said.

I looked at the detonator in my hand and squeezed the trigger.

Chapter 18

Duma slumped in his chair and scooted it slightly closer to the fire; easier to keep the flies away. He watched as the flames danced on piles of dried brush. A log collapsed sending sparks swarming into the night. He sipped his coffee and did his best to ignore the drunken carousing that surrounded him. It was Friday night and the compound was absolutely full. White men, black men; men from every dark hole on Earth. All eagerly indulging their most carnal sins.

He watched as a girl no older than 11 was led inside her dorm. Tears running down her face. He lit a cigarette and took a long draw. The acrid smoke filled his lungs and he wished it would kill him just a little bit quicker. Taking another sip of coffee though, the nicotine/caffeine cocktail swirled in his mind and he felt better. There's a reason they're two of the most addictive and combined drugs available. They have a powerful way of just taking the edge off.

It had been almost a month since he held Aleela down and

helped her rapist finish. She hadn't spoken a word or even made a sound since then, but that hadn't stopped the endless stream of men eager to pay for her. Some even preferred the silence. His job had gotten a lot easier, too. She didn't resist anymore, just laid there, silent, staring off into nothing. He would have been concerned, but she ate and bathed, and really, that's all that anyone cared about. A young man, his rifle slung across his back with a leather sling, sat down next to Duma and said,   "Have you heard the news?"

"What's that, Alex?" Duma said.

"Josef is missing. It's been almost three days," Alex said. "He had some business in town and just hasn't come back. Emile and Samir where with him. No one has heard from them; they're not answering their phones."

"Oh," Duma said, drawing on his cigarette; staring into the fire.

"What do you think it means? Do you think he just left?" Alex asked.

"I don't know, Alex," Duma said.

"I mean, do you think he is coming back? What will happen if he is really gone?" Alex asked.

Duma turned to Alex, finished his cigarette, threw it into the fire and said, "I don't care."

He stood, throwing his coffee cup into the fire. It glowed green for a moment as the Styrofoam burned. Alex watched, silent and somewhat confused as Duma walked into the darkness. He stopped about 10 yards away and lit another cigarette. He puffed it as the end glowed to life. An odd twitch pulled at his mind and the hairs on his neck stood up. He felt like he was being watched. Turning, slowly, he scanned some palettes that were stacked a few yards away. He watched for movement, but saw none.

Puffing smoke from his cigarette, he kept walking. He stopped at the dorm where Aleela stayed and stood for a moment. He threw his spent butt to the ground and walked in. The muffled sounds of sex floated around the room. It was much hotter inside. Piles of blankets twitched and writhed as he stepped through the rows of beds. At the back of the room, he found Aleela. She was dressing as a teenage kid walked passed him; a stupid grin wrapped around his face. His fancy clothes making it obvious that dad had bought him something special for his birthday.

Duma sat down in a chair next to her bed.

351

"Jesus, they get younger every year," he said.

Aleela finished putting her dress on. The light fabric was nearly sheer in the light of the overhead bulbs.

"Are you going to be silent forever?" Duma asked. She did not respond. "That might mean entertaining a more specific clientele. That's rarely a good thing."

She sat on her bed; her back to Duma.

"They tell me you're still eating well. That's good. If they think you're sick, they likely kill you before you have a chance to die," Duma said.

Aleela remained silent.

"There's quite the party out there tonight. You're likely to be busy. You're not going to buy yourself a few minutes talking with me?" Duma asked, leaning forward in his chair.

Aleela continued to face away from him.

He leaned forward in his chair, "Girl, answer me."

Silence.

"Girl, this is only making things worse for you. We all have a job to do; none by choice. We do what we have to. You had a bad go of it in this life. Maybe the next one will be better," Duma said.

352

Silence.

"Damnit, girl, answer me." Duma slammed his fist down on the chair and Aleela flinched, but remained silent. Duma breathing his frustration out in short, punctuated puffs. He waited for her to turn, to respond. Several minutes passed and Duma loosened his clenched fist and sat back in chair.

Eventually, he stood, placing a cigarette in his mouth. "I can see you're in a talkative mood tonight. I'll leave you to your own misery, then." He took several steps towards the door and turned, "I thought you'd want to know. Josef is missing. No one knows where he is or if he is coming back." He continued toward the door.

"Is he dead?" Aleela asked.

Duma stopped and turned, "I don't know."

She had turned on the bed and was now looking at Duma, her face flush.

He almost exited, but decided to return to his chair; she followed him with her eyes, "What do you mean you don't know?"

"He's just gone. No one knows where," Duma said.

Aleela searched Duma's eyes for anything else, but found nothing. She turned away.

"I'm sure he's just out on some damn holiday. He does that, from time to time," Duma said.

"I hope he's been torn to pieces," Aleela said.

Duma didn't say anything. They sat for a while in relative silence as moans from the others kept a low ambiance of noise in the room. A man walked in from outside, his face a nervous smile.

He spoke to Duma, "How much?"

Duma just shook his head 'no' and the man left, his face downcast. Aleela turned around.

"Why did you do that?" she asked.

"We are having a conversation," Duma said.

"I don't have anything to say to you," Aleela said.

"And?" Duma asked. "Maybe I have something to say to you."

She hesitated, unsure how to make him leave, but then said, "Say it then."

Duma studied his cigarette and leaned forward in his chair. He looked like he had something heavy weighing on him. He had aged since Aleela had first seen him. Thick lines creased his skin and his eyes, they looked so tired. Like he had never slept. He was

354

smoking now too. Something she had never seen him do before.

"I know all…this, wasn't what you wanted. That your family did this to you. I just wanted to say, this is what it is. There's no point in feeling…there's no point in fighting it. You can spend your entire life feeling sorry for yourself. Make the most of it. Don't let them take everything…" he trailed off and started smoking again. "Anyway, I just wanted to say that. I'm leaving tomorrow. I won't be back. It's time for me to move on to something else."

Aleela's eyes were wide and her breathing was short and shallow. Duma stood, having said his goodbye. There wasn't anything left to say or do; just to leave and start the next part of his life. Aleela sprinted down the aisle of beds. She hit the door with the full force of her body and threw it open. Duma, stunned momentarily, ran after her and reached the door as it swung close. He pushed it open with such energy that it slammed against the exterior wall, startling a small crowd standing around the dorm. He scanned the yard, searching for Aleela. He walked to a group of men and girls standing around the fire laughing and drinking. He shoved several of them roughly aside, whipping his head around.

Duma's heart was pounding; rage boiling in his gut as he

searched. Nearby revelers watched as he flipped over couches and tables, spilling people and drinks on the ground. Guards came running, alerted to the commotion.

"Duma, what the hell are you doing?" Alex asked. His rifle at the ready.

"She's out here somewhere!" Duma shouted.

"What? What are you talking about?" Alex asked.

"Aleela, she's out here somewhere, hiding," Duma said, his eyes going back and forth frantically, pouring over the faces in the crowd.

Alex laughed, "Where does she think she's going. I'm sure she hasn't gotten far." Duma pushed him aside. "That's enough, now. Calm down."

"Don't tell me to be calm. What if she escapes?" Duma asked.

"You know that's not possible. She can't climb a sheer wall. Even if she did, where would she go? She'd die very quickly out there," Alex said.

"Of course." Duma stared into Alex's eyes, "Help me find her."

"We have better things to do than chase one girl around the comp..." before Alex could finish this sentence, Duma caught a glimpse of Aleela's dress in the distance, rounding the corner of one of the maintenance shacks. He shoved Alex and ran after her. His boots kicking up clouds behind him. Those standing near watched in stunned surprise as he ran off into the night. Silently, they sipped their drinks, each waiting for someone else to restart the party. Gradually, one voice joined another in conversation until the volume returned to its normal level of festivity and the whole scene was forgotten. Alex leaned his rifle on his shoulder, laughed and mingled with guests, reassuring them all was well.

Duma stopped when reached where he had seen Aleela turn. Footprints in the dirt led to the door on the side of the building. He realized he was alone. This part of the compound didn't have any fires or food or beds; no reason for anyone else to be over here.

"What are you doing out here?" Duma asked loudly into the night air.

He waited, but was only met by the distant sound of music. He followed the footprints. The door creaked as he opened it. Moonlight illuminated enough of the interior for him to step inside. Besides this small shaft of silver, the shack was pitch black. He blinked, trying to gain a little vision. Slowly, shadows blurred into recognizable shapes as he stepped around objects on the floor.

"Are you in here?" Duma asked.

A long silence. Then a whisper floated from the darkness, "Yes."

Duma spun around the voice echoing softly behind him.

"Why are you here, girl?" he asked. Again, he waited for a response, but when he got none, he said, "There's nowhere left to run. Come back with me. I won't let anyone else touch you." Silence filled the room. Duma stepped tentatively; going farther into the darkness.

"Answer me!" he shouted.

He realized how heavily he was breathing and tried to slow it and listen.

"Why did you care about me?" another soft whisper echoing around Duma. He spun again and crossed the moonlight into the other darkened half of the shack. Stepping around rakes and axes and hoes, he tested the ground with each step to avoid the sharp metal instruments in his path.

"I don't; this is a job. I couldn't care less about you, girl," he shouted.

"That's not true. You loved me. You protected me," The whisper said.

"Ha, don't lie to yourself, Aleela. You are just a piece of meat to me," Duma said.

Sweat oozed down his forehead and soaked his shirt.

"You're lying," The whisper said.

Duma laughed nervously, "Why would I lie?" he asked. "There have been many, many before you. I've done this a long time, girl. You're nothing to me."

"Why did you follow? Why not just let me go? Why not send someone else?" the whisper asked.

Duma strained his eyes, trying to pinpoint where the sound was emanating from.

"Because I still have a job to do," Duma said.

"That's not it," The whisper said.

Duma laughed again, "Really, and what is?"

"You know why," The whisper said.

"No more games, girl. Come out right now," he said.

"Not until you tell the truth," she said.

Duma felt around with his hands, trying to find Aleela. He caught hold of fabric and pulled with all of his strength. A heavy bag of sand tumbled off a pile and landed on Duma's foot. He cursed in pain, checking the bones for breaks.

"Enough!" he shouted. "Show yourself!"

"No," she said.

There was a long stillness. Just the darkness and the hum of a hundred people far away. Duma did not move. Then, he started shaking. His hands and arms vibrating, uncontrollably. He screamed "I hate you! You're nothing! I wish you had died your first day here. I hate you. I hate you!"

Duma's chest heaved, blood thundering by his ears. He trembled with fury. Aleela stepped out from the shadows and he could just make out her form. She walked slowly, deliberately towards him. He watched as she closed the distance to almost within arm's length. Duma burst into tears. He slid down to his knees and wept as she stood there, her arms behind her back.

"I hate you so much," he said between sobs.

"Why do you hate me?" she whispered.

"Because, for first time since my family was taken from me, I felt human. I felt something real in my heart. You…did this to me. You made me feel and then you made me hold you down and watch as some son of a whore had his way with you."

Aleela took one step forward and placed her hand on his head.

Relief crashed in waves over him as he felt her touch, "I'm sorry Aleela…I'm so, so sorry," Duma wept, leaning his head into her stomach. He sucked in huge gulps of air; expelling them in short, sharp gusts. He gripped her dress and kept her close; afraid she might run away again; leaving him alone in his humiliation.

Finally, Aleela broke the quiet with, "I have something for you." She talked in a low, quite voice.

"What?" he asked; choking back tears.

"I have something for you," she said playfully.

He looked up at her, a wrinkled smile on her face. She slowly pulled her other hand from behind her back. There was a small wooden box with a wire latch holding it closed.

"Open it," she said.

He smiled awkwardly and reached for the box, "What is it?"

"A present, something I found for you," she said.

"Is that why you ran back here? To give me this?" he asked.

She shook her head "yes," pushing the box closer to his hand. He bent the metal wire wrapped around the clasp of the box and slowly opened it. A snake lunged and sunk its fangs deep into the flesh between his thumb and finger. Pain erupted in his hand. The snake pulled back and lunged itself again, this time striking him on the bicep and again on the shoulder. It fell to the floor and slithered towards him.

Duma screamed and kicked at the snake, catching its head with his boot. It recoiled, hissed and retreated into the shadows.

"What have you done, girl?" Duma lay on his back, his right arm useless; the muscles no longer responding. Agony roared up and down his shoulder.

Aleela, still with a smile on her lips stepped forward. Duma used his good arm and his feet to push away, inching towards the door. He screamed, "Help!" but the sound just died in the darkness of the shack. She found a shovel on the wall and, raising it above her head, brought it down with all of her strength on his head. Blood erupted from his nose and mouth. Duma lay completely prone, his

362

legs moving slightly, but he made no attempt to get up or move farther. His breathing was labored, almost like the muscles in his chest were tightening.

"How dare you?" she asked. "You could have protected me. You could have saved me from all this. 'Just doing your job.' I am utterly broken and it's your fault!"

He spat blood, "Aleela, please."

The words were choked and horse.

"All those walks, all that time spent searching. I finally found what I was looking for," she said, watching the snake move along the far wall.

"Please!" he choked.

She knelt over him, "I have lost my home, my family, my brother, my life, my innocence, my future…my humanity. For what? For money? Because you wanted an easy life."

She stood, raising the shovel and brought it down on his arm, now swollen and oozing. He screamed.

"I am empty inside. I am empty of everything!" she screamed; bringing the shovel down hard on his chest. He coughed blood; wheezing through the fluid in his throat.

363

"No, it's not true," he strained out with the last bit of energy he had.

"You're right, not completely empty." She raised the shovel again, ready to bring the blade down on his face and the ground shook beneath her feet. A sound like the world ending filled her body. She dropped the shovel; steadying herself on the wall. She heard screaming and realized it was her own voice. A terrifying moment and then the quaking stopped. She leaned out of the doorway to see a huge plume of fire, almost as bright as day, rise into the air. New screams could be heard echoing in the distance and a *puck, puck, puck* sound she could not identify. She looked back. Duma' eyes were rolled into his head; his legs spasming, but no other sign of life.

She stepped into the cooler air outside and felt refreshed. Bloodied blisters were forming on her trembling hands. The friction of swinging the shovel had worn down the skin, but she hadn't felt it until now; adrenaline had hijacked her senses. She felt compelled to wash and walked to a nearby pump. She ran the water and winced as it stung her open cuts. She had nothing to use as a bandage, nothing even to dry with. So she waved her hands in the air, feeling the water evaporate off her skin.

Without any plan or sense of direction, she walked towards the now huge fire now burning in the far end of the compound. Girls were huddled together, crying behind overturned tables or behind walls. They seemed unaware of her presence, content to comfort each other. Drunk men were running while trying to button their pants, often falling over, swearing and then getting up only to fall again. Some just stayed down.

One man with a rifle came running towards her, screaming something she couldn't quite make out. He raised his rifle at her and she stopped; waiting to see what he would do. He continued shouting and it sounded like, "lay down". She had no intention of obeying. Instead she planned to pivot and dive behind a nearby couch. Before she could talk or move or think, she heard a hiss and then low crunch, like a watermelon falling off a roof. The man in front of her fell backwards.

This surprised Aleela; unsure why he had collapsed. She waited for him stand, but when it was clear he was not moving, she walked around him. His head was split open, blood gushing from the wound. She looked around, trying to identify who or what had done this, but could no one else anywhere close. She bent down and pulled out the knife strapped to his hip.

Walking a little further, she came to one of the abandoned food tables; the guards all moving towards the explosion. An obese man, his pale skin looking like it was ready to burst; his girth forced into linen pants and shirt. He stood, absolutely gorging himself on barbecued beef. He was eating it by the fist full. Everything in this man's world had just gone to shit. People were dying around him. Things were exploding and he was apparently trying to eat himself to death. Maybe he wanted to die.

Aleela stood next to him, unaware of her presence; too focused on the food to notice anything else. She drove her knife it into the man's thigh. He howled with pain, dropping his chunk of meat, and collapsed. He tried to reach it, to pull it out, but his swollen stomach prevented him from sitting up. He rolled from side to side, trying to lift himself. She stepped over him.

Her stomach growled and she suddenly became aware of just how hungry she was. She wolfed down cuts of meat. Grabbing a glass, she choked down a strong beer. The man was still screaming, begging Aleela to help, but she kept eating, ignoring his pleas.

After eating her fill, she decided to continue toward the now dying flames. After a few steps, she looked back, the man still begging her for help. He seemed to be clutching his chest and breathing in very shallow gasps.

"Please…don't…leave…me," he said in a shallow, gravelly voice.

"Have the decency to die," she said; turning her back on him.

"Please…" he pleaded, but Aleela was already too far away for her to hear.

The smoke was black and acrid. It burned her throat as she coughed. She was about 50 yards now from the flames and, even at that distance, the heat was intense. It wafted over her in waves as the wind blew. It also carried the smell of burnt human flesh. She realized that black mounds on the ground around her weren't rocks, but smoking corpses. Things flung outward from the explosion. Her stomach turned. She dropped to one knee and vomited up everything she had just eaten.

As she knelt, she thought she saw something, or, someone sprinting from shadow to shadow. She tried to focus, maybe it had been a trick of the eye with the moving flames not far away. Her concentration was broken when a group of armed guards ran out from the main house. It appeared that they had been trying to extinguish small brush fires; buckets in hand. One of them was wearing a backwards baseball cap and she recognized him as one of her pursuers that night at Uncle's.

He shouted at her "Stop where you are or I'll shoot." Apparently, they didn't want any of their livestock wandering into the night. They were more concerned about their profit than if their house burned. Or maybe he recognized her; thought this might be a good opportunity to repay her for all the pain he had suffered that first night. She took a step and he fired a few rounds into the air. "Don't move!" he screamed, walking towards her; the others following.

She twisted again to run and he dropped his rifle barrel even with her head. She took a step, expecting to hear the bark of gunfire, expecting to die right there. She wondered if heaven waited for her, or hell. Instead there was that *puck, puck, puck* sound, only louder and more intense, like the air was being punched. She turned; her pursuers all lay on the ground, bleeding from their chests and head. She was splattered with gore.

A black figure emerged from the darkness. It had an oddly shaped head, like it was too round. There were flashes, like lenses where its eyes should be. As the shape got closer, she could see it was bristling with metal and its face was covered. It carried a rifle, but seemed to have weapons hung all over its body. She knew at any moment it would raise the gun and kill her. She pictured her brains splattered on the ground like she had seen earlier. She wanted to run, to scream, she wanted disappear into the night, to just vanish, but watching him kill three men and now almost close enough to touch, she was rooted to the ground in terror.

With only a few steps left, she did the only thing she could think of, she just shut her eyes and wished to not exist. This thought comforted her; no matter what lay on the other side, nothing would compare to what she had already suffered.

She felt something heavy on her shoulder and jumped in surprise. She opened her eyes to see a swollen, punctured hand. Her heart stopped. His broken face caked with blood. His arm swollen and pussy. His eyes filled with rage. Duma stood, breathing with great effort. She realized that she had, in fact died, and it was much, much worse than she could have imagined. She had fallen into hell, and he was waiting there for her.

He raised his hand, a machete clinched in his fingers and *puck, puck, puck*. Aleela was covered in blood again. Duma slumped over, his head and chest torn ragged with bullet holes. She stared, his body gushing into the dirt.

She felt another hand on her shoulder and screamed. The ghost did something to his face and the lenses vanished. He pulled down his mask revealing pale skin, blue eyes and bearded stubble. This was a person, actual flesh and blood.

"Holy shit, are you OK?" the man asked in a thick American accent.

Chapter 19

"Was…Was that a zombie?" I asked, confused and blinded by muzzle flash. "Are you OK? Holy shit."

A small, shell shocked girl stared at me, covered in blood. I felt pretty bad about that. The disfigured, shambling thing that had just about cut her in half had misted brain and tissue all over when hit by the high velocity rifle rounds.

"Come back, did you say zombie?" Mike asked over the radio.

His voice was annoyed, to say the least.

"Yeah, uh, you wanna provide some clarification?" Jax asked, sprinting to my position from a mound of gravel he was using as cover.

The girl yelped again, unaware there were two of us.

"Well, look at him," I said pointing to the corpse.

"Shit, he does look like a zombie," Jax said, examining the body. "What happened?"

"This girl was just wandering around, just standing out in the open. I flanked this group of assholes who were shooting at anything that moved. They must have blasted half a dozen of their own guys and a few of the girls, too. I was working my way around in cover. I get into position and this one fucker starts shouting at her; fires a few rounds into the air. Well, I drop him and his buddies, and she is completely out of it, just frozen there...," I said.

The girl fainted, I'm guessing completely unable to process what was happening around her. Jax and I dropped to a knee. I kept lookout while he checked her pulse and breathing.

"Now, I try to approach as calmly as possible, I don't want to spook her. Who knows what kind of trauma she's been through, you know? So, I'm moving slowly; deliberately. Also trying to check my surroundings; trying not to get shot. Anyway, I can tell she is terrified, her eyes are as a big as dinner plates and her body is completely rigid. I was about to say something when this dick appears out of nowhere. His arm is limp. He's literally dragging himself along. He stops and I fucking kid you not, he pulls out a goddamn machete; ready to cut her fucking head off. I put him down and that pretty much takes us to where we are now," I said.

"That's the stupidest goddamn thing I have ever heard,"

Mike said over the radio.

"Fuck off," I said

"Cut the chatter," Jax barked.

"I was tracking that girl for a while. She was chased into a shed before you blew all that shit up. Some guy was following her. She was the only one to exit, though. I think she did that to him," Mike said.

"Holy shit," Jax said.

"No way, man. His skin is rotting in places. How could she do that?" I asked.

"Don't know. After she left the structure, I dropped a guard who was threatening her. She then stabbed some fucker in the leg. So, she's not afraid to fuck your shit up," Mike said.

Jax looked at me, "We need to move."

"Roger that. Take her and I'll cover you," I said.

Jax turned to me asked, "Take her? Where?"

"I don't fucking know. Out of the line of fire, for now," I said.

I could feel anxiety sour my stomach; acid crashing around in my gut.

"What would we do with her? Couldn't just take her with us, could we?" I thought. "Did it even matter?"

Shouting from a large group of men. Jax and I both heard it and snapped into cover. They were getting close.

"John, she's breathing, she'll be fine. We need to move," Jax said, putting his hand on my shoulder.

"We're not fucking leaving her in the middle of the road, asshole. Now pick her up," I growled.

"John..." Jax's words were cut off.

"He was bitten by a snake," a small voice said.

We both flinched, totally unaware she had woken.

"Jesus, you just scared the shit out of me," Jax said.

"And I hit in him in the face with a shovel," she said. "Repeatedly."

"Good job," I said. "Now get up."

I pulled her roughly to her feet and she winced in pain, like it was familiar, like she had been dragged before. I felt like a real asshole.

"Sorry," I stammered, trying to brush the dirt off of her.

She stood, her slender frame covered in a light cotton dress.

374

Her hair had been wrapped in a bun, but was now partially pulled out and caked with drying blood. She seemed coherent, but distant. Her face showing only traces of the stunned surprised it had moments ago.

"Are you, uh, OK?" I asked.

She shook her head "yes".

"My name is John, this is Jax. Our friend Mike is on the hill over there, go ahead and wave Mike," I said.

"I'm not going to do that for obvious reasons," Mike said.

"What's your name?" I asked.

"Aleela," she said.

"Guys, you are about to be fucked. There are 15 zulus about to be all over you," Mike said.

"Move!" Jax ordered.

He knelt behind a few rocks with a clear firing lane down the courtyard.

I offered Aleela my hand, "Stay with me, don't let go. You understand? Do not let go."

She looked at me hesitantly and then took my hand. We sprinted to the gravel mound. Jax's rifle erupted in hellfire. A much heavier weapon than mine, designed for suppressing crowds, the rounds hammered the air like death itself.

The assault started from the back end of the house. Men in groups of two or three, sprinting from cover to cover. Jax's weapon made a heavy *kthunk* sound each time it fired and I could see rounds impacting wood and dirt and rock. Tracers lit up the night. Each time one of the guards would try and raise his head enough to fire, molten lead slammed into whatever he was hiding behind. I couldn't really hear Mike's rifle, but I could see the damage it was doing. A few of the assholes, scared by the bark of Jax's weapon, turned and ran away from the firefight only to be cut down by heavy rifle rounds; each one tearing a fist sized chunk of flesh from their torsos.

After a few moments of sustained firing, Jax shouted, "Reloading."

"We're clear, get to cover, I'll suppress," I said. "Stay down. Cover your ears," I said. Aleela crouched at the base of the mound and put her hands on either side of her head.

"Roger that," Jax said. He shouldered his weapon and sprinted to my position.

"You have zulus trying to flank you," Mike crackled over the radio. "They just left my line of sight."

I peaked over the mound. With Jax's weapon momentarily silent, the remaining guards were getting bold. Probably tired of having their asses handed to them for the last couple of hours. Three of them were crawling behind over turned tables and couches someone had dragged outside. I used the mound to sturdy my rifle and ripped a quick burst. *Puck, puck, puck, puck.* The first guard collapsed, bleeding from his back. The others stopped, and tried to fire back. Two more bursts, a long succession of *puck, puck, puck.* The remaining two were dead.

"Zulus down. Reloading," I said.

"Roger that," Jax said.

He reached our position and finished reloading. His barrel now resting on the top of the mound, ready to fire. The last few guards were watching us from holes in their pallet stacks or from chewed corners of the house.

"Mike, where are we at? How many zulus left?" John asked.

"Uh, four, yeah looks like four left," Mike said.

"You have shots on them?" Jax asked.

"That's affirmative, but I'm going to need a little

377

encouragement," Mike said. "What are you thinking?"

"Hmm," Jax looked pensive, he stroked his chin as in deep thought. After a moment, he asked. "The Nixon?"

"What the fuck are you two talking about?" I asked.

"No, I was thinking more the Monroe," Mike said.

"At night?" Jax asked.

"Ah, good point," Mike said.

"What the fuck, guys?" I asked "We really have time for this?"

"I got it, the Clinton, Bill not Hillary," Jax said.

"Perfect," Mike said.

Jax set his rifle down and crawled to the top of the mound. "Hey, goat fuckers, how much for a blow job?"

There was muttered confusion from the other men.

"We are going to fucking kill you," one of them shouted back.

"Yeah, but how much for a blow job?" Jax asked.

"No blow jobs. You are going to die, motha fucka," the man shouted back.

"Common, isn't this a pussy shack? How much?" Jax

shouted.

"Fuck you!" the guard shouted.

"Yeah, that's the idea, but how many dollars?" Jax asked.

All four men let loose with their rifles. A hail of bullets impacting all over the mound, sending shards of rock in every direction. I flung myself on top of Aleela, while Jax slid down below the top so he was no longer exposed. Now, I didn't see what happened next, as I was cowering in mortal fear, but according to Mike, the remaining guards all left their cover and started walking towards our position, unloading round after round; magazine after magazine. Once they had committed to the open yard though, he started 'fucking them in their goddamn skulls' as he put it. The deafening roar of all four rifles being fired simultaneously sputtered and then stopped. I slowly crept back up and peaked over the top. The men lay dead about half way from us and the house; apparently the clatter of their firearms too loud for them to hear Mike's suppressed shots.

"Mike, we are headed your way. Keep us covered," Jax said.

"Reloading. I'll be online shortly," Mike said.

"Roger that," Jax said.

379

"Wait, we have to do something first," I said.

"Like hell we do," Jax said.

"No, remember," I said pointing to the main house.

Jax stared at it for a long moment; maybe deciding what to do; whether risking our lives was worth fucking over a few more bad guys.

"I'm locked in. You moving yet?" Mike asked.

"No," Jax said, looking at me. "We have one more objective."

"Roger that, I'll keep overwatch. Better fucking hurry, we are running out of night. We will be making day break in about 30 minutes and then we really will be fucked," Mike said.

"We'll make it quick," I said.

"Why aren't we leaving, please, let's just go," Aleela said, her eyes pleading.

"Trust me, we have to do this," I said.

"Please, let's just...," she tried to finish, but I took her hand and led her into the house.

"Stay behind me," I said.

She didn't fight me, but I could feel the tension in her
380

muscles. She did not want to go in. Jax took point, switching to a compact shotgun he had slung on his back. We followed the exterior wall, searching for a bedroom we knew was on the first floor. We entered a side entrance that was clearly intended for guests to wander in and out from the multiple bedrooms inside. It led to a hall that was comfortably provisioned with a small table, couch and mirror. The far end opened to a servant's staircase that was probably used to bring girls to more affluent customers, who could afford the main rooms on the top floor. The soft electric lights were almost yellow, like they weren't receiving enough power. The paint was old, but not cracked. It could have been a comfortable place to live.

The first door we came to was partially open. I motioned for Aleela to stay back and Jax peered in. He looked at me and shook his head 'no'. We kept moving. The next door we came to was completely open, the flashing colors of a TV running in the dark. A man passed out in a recliner. I considered putting my knife through his throat, but we were quickly running out of time and I didn't think it appropriate for a teenage girl to watch me murder someone with my hands.

The last door we found was completely closed. I could hear

voices from inside, two, maybe three men talking, the room muffling their voices. I again motioned for Aleela to stay back and this time put a finger to my lips. Jax and I stacked on the door, one on either side, our weapons at the ready.

He slowly turned the knob, careful to stop if even the slightest noise was produced from the rusted and worn mechanics. After an excruciating second of waiting, praying we weren't heard, the door gave and a thin streak of light crept into the hall. Jax peered into the room. Three men, all with pistols in their hands, stood looking at the window, talking with one another. Women's clothes strewn about the room along with several empty liquor bottles. Cigarettes smoldered in an ashtray on a small end table. There was a bed with a young girl on it, a look of terror on her face.

Jax froze. Realizing, much too late, she had seen him. Sweat poured down his brow, but only his eyes could be seen through his mask; the ballistic helmet taking up most of face. He slowly brought a finger to his lips and the longest moment of his life passed. All she had to do was, sigh, breathe heavily, give the men any reason at all to turn around and he would die. They would kill him before he could speak. Real life was different from movies and video games.

You don't have super human reaction time and perfect aim. Just a narrow space and a high magazine count.

The girl, very slowly, very deliberately nodded 'yes'. Jax turned to me and nodded 'yes'. He stood back from the door and raised his shotgun. I raised my rifle, took a few steps back and kicked open the door. The men stumbled in surprise. Well, surprise would be understatement; more like pure shock that melted into terror. Their bodies couldn't process what their minds perceived, there's that reaction time. I'm sure they were screaming in their heads, demanding the muscles take action, but it's a slow process. My rifle sputtered *puck, puck, puck* and two of them fell, blood and gore sprayed on the walls behind them. Jax's barrel thundered and damn near cut the last one in half. The girl screamed, tried to kick herself out of the bed. She was naked.

We marched into the room, checking the corners, moving the weapons away from the bodies. I picked up her clothes and threw them to her. She caught them and screamed again pointing behind Jax. A fourth man had been standing out of sight, along the interior wall of the room. He lunged at Jax, knife in hand, but was way off balance and collided with the floor, in a sickening thud, well before reaching his target. Jax raised his shotgun and rolled the man over.

He was dazed and bloody, the knife having caught his own arm on

the way down. I expected him to be splattered all over the floor.

Instead Jax hesitated, then lowered his weapon.

He pulled his pistol and walked over to the girl, offering it to

her. She looked at, puzzled over it and then realized what he was

asking.

She shook her head hard, "No, no," she said, recoiling from it

like poison. Jax stood there, waiting for her to accept.

"It's alright. Take it," Jax said nodding to the man on the

ground.

"No, please, no," she said.

Jax has been so focused on the girl, that he didn't notice

Aleela reach for it. She had wandered into the room, after the initial

carnage. She took the pistol and looked it over.

"It's loaded," Jax said. "Just pull the trigger."

Aleela pointed the barrel at the man and emptied the

magazine. Rounds tore through his face and chest. The last one hit

his groin. The mangled head now torn apart, oozed pink and red

slime. She gave the side arm back to Jax.

"She will, in fact, fuck your shit up," Jax said.

"Jesus," I said.

Aleela left the room silent. We followed her. The other girl crying and shaking on the floor. I caught, just as we passed through the door, a sigh of relief, like she had watched death leave.

"Where the fuck are you guys? I heard small arms fire, but can't find you anywhere," Mike said over the radio.

"We're fine, ex-filling now," Jax said.

"Hurry. The. Fuck. Up. We have maybe fifteen minutes till sunrise," Mike said.

"Roger that." To me Jax said, "We need to move." To Aleela he said, "This is as far as you go. You should be safe for now. Just stay out of the open."

"What?" she said, a panic setting in.

"We are not leaving her here," I said.

"Yes, we fucking are," Jax said.

"She will fucking die, Jax. She killed one of their people. They've seen her with us. She won't last five minutes after we leave," I said. "You know what they do here. It's not just going to be a bullet to the head. If we don't take her, you and I, not those

385

assholes, will be putting her in the ground."

"What are we going to do with her?" Jax asked. "The moment we step outside these walls, what the fuck are we going to do? It's not like she has a passport; we can't just take her out of country. We can't just hop on a plane back to the states. If we take her with us, you are going to kill us, John. Mike is going to die because of you. I'm going to die, because of you."

We stared at each other. A long moment passed. Aleela clung to my arm, tears running down her cheeks. I raised my rifle on John.

"We are not leaving her," I said, racking a round in my rifle.

There was a silence and I was scared shitless.

"Don't be a dick, Jax. Take the girl. We can figure shit out later," Mike said over the radio.

"Roger that," Jax said.

A shock of relief permeated my entire body. Aleela, wiped her tears. Jax took a step back, turned and hit me so hard I left my feet. Aleela screamed as I hit the ground, blood erupting in my mouth.

"Don't you ever fucking point a weapon at me again," Jax screamed.

"Roger that," I said, rolling over, spitting out a tooth. I was on my knees, trying to regain my composure when a hand shot into my view. I took it and Jax helped me to my feet.

"You guys have multiple contacts moving in swiftly, maybe twenty zulu all converging on your position," Mike said. "If you guys are done with the circle jerk, you might want to get the fuck out of there."

"Roger that," Jax and I said in unison.

"It's time to go," I said.

Aleela nodded and we followed Jax. I use the term heavy resistance only because it's a euphemism for shitstorm. The moment we stepped outside of the house, we were immediately hit with gunfire. The dirt and walls all around us were pocked marked with ballistic metal. Lucky for us, skinnies can't shoot for shit.

There were five or six men who had taken firing positions on the door we had entered. Jax switched back to the heavy rifle and raked the horizon. *Kthunk, kthunk, kthunk, kthunk*; the damn thing was deafening, even with ear protection. The guards collectively ducked behind cover. Even if they weren't in the direct line of fire, the gun was so goddamn intimidating. I sprinted to a nearby building, Aleela holding my hand.

Now, I tell this part as a cautionary tale. I held my rifle with one hand, and fired it off into the crowd approaching us, and hit nothing but dirt and air. It's not like the movies kids. Fire your weapon with two hands, for safety's sake.

Several guards dove behind cover as I took up a suppressing position for Jax. I leveled my rifle and emptied the magazine *puck, puck, puck.* I moved my barrel from person, to person, not hitting flesh, but keeping their heads down. Jax took this as his opportunity to move.

"Reloading," I said.

"Suppressing! Move to the next hard point," Jax ordered.

I took Aleela's hand and tried to lead her to a pile of stones being used in the construction of a latrine moat; not much in the way of stopping bullets, but enough concealment to hide behind. She stopped in the middle of the open; digging her heels into the ground.

"Fucking move," I screamed. "We have to get out of the yard!"

She pointed to a small body on the ground, a sheer dress and pigtails. She couldn't have been more than 8.

"That's...we have to help her," Aleela whispered.

"What?" I shouted, "We can't help her, now."

I squeezed off a few rounds at the nearest guard.

She looked at me, "Please, help her, she's my friend!" She just stood there staring at the body. Bullets flying past us, more guards taking up positions. The whole world was ending and she was a statue. She didn't say anything else, just stood there, in silence.

"Get to cover, what the fuck are you doing?" Jax asked over the radio.

"I'm trying!" I shouted.

"Try harder," Jax screamed.

"Fuck!" I shouted.

I pulled on Aleela's arm, but she resisted. I fired the last few rounds, hearing the distinctive click of an empty magazine. Out of patience, and afraid I would wrench her shoulder out of the socket sooner than move her, I picked Aleela up and carried her to the stones. She screamed, "Stop! Put me down! I have to help her."

We crouched down and I held her as she thrashed in arms, trying to run back out into the yard. Jax's weapon thundered, catching at least one guard between cover; his body ripped to pieces

389

by the large caliber rounds.

She stopped fighting; realizing how close to she was to her own death. I set her down and grabbed a fresh magazine.

"Was that a friend of yours?" I asked as I reloaded.

She shook her head 'yes.'

"I'm sorry," I said. "I got you, move," I yelled to Jax.

Jax's gun fell silent as he sprinted. My barrel spat fire in the night, catching two more men, tearing jagged holes in their bodies. You see, when a rifle bullet strikes your body, it doesn't go through you. No, that's the best thing that could happen. Instead, it explodes and tumbles, sending thousands of tiny, supersonic metal shards flying through your flesh. It shatters bone, tears tendon, eviscerates arteries. You don't just bleed, you liquefy. Jax was pinned down behind soft cover; rounds tearing through the thin metal of an oil drum. I kept firing, *puck, puck, puck*. My gun clicked dry and I switched to my side arm, squeezing off fifteen rounds into the distance. The other guns fell silent just long enough for Jax to move again.

My rifle suppressor had melted from heavy usage, and I screwed it off; the tip glowing in the dark. I reloaded and resumed firing, as Jax made his way to us. *Kercrack, kercrack, kercrack,* my barrel boomed with its new found freedom, breathing free for the first time all night.

"Get down!" Jax screamed. He pulled a white phosphorous grenade from his vest and tossed it into a group of men brave enough to advance on us. Willy Pete, as it's colloquially called, has to be one of the most evil things ever invented by man. It's a dry chemical that burns at 5,000 Fahrenheit when exposed to oxygen. It's often used in signal flares, but a few older munitions still exist, and they are designed for one thing.

The screams were unimaginable. It was like the devil himself had come up to drag these particular souls to hell. Aleela put her hands over her ears to try and drown out the agony of five or six men; flesh literally melting off their bones before they had a chance to die a quick death.

"Fucking move!" Jax shouted, pointing toward to the far wall we had entered from.

I squeezed of a few more rounds at the crowd now forming on us. I'm not sure they hit anything, because I was dragging Aleela behind me. We were sprinting as fast as we could, bullets whizzing by our heads, impacting everything around us. I just remember the *kthunk* of Jax's rifle behind us, the ammunition belt flinging spent brass shells off into the night.

When we finally reached the wall, I was shocked to see our rope still in place. I gave Aleela a boost.

"Climb as fast as you can!" I shouted.

She nodded and started moving up the rope. I took a defensive stance across from Jax. We were on opposite sides of two small shacks that came together almost exactly at our exit.

We poured everything we had into the twenty or thirty men pursuing us. It seemed as though the closer we got to leaving, the more determined they were to skin us alive. Maybe because we had blown up a few of their buddies and burned down their home. I don't know.

My rifle barked *kercrack, kercrack*, missing my targets, but impacting solidly on the legs of several behind them. The cries of pain did nothing to muffle the angry swears and curses that poured out of the crowd. Jax's weapon continued to piss lead into the mass of humanity hunting us, but that too seemed more of an annoyance than an actual deterrent. We had maybe a few yards before we would be overwhelmed.

I heard the crackle of gunfire and instinctively leaned back behind the wall. To my surprise though, the rounds didn't hit anywhere near me. I chuckled to myself, wondering why I had ever felt afraid, when my stomach turned to burning ice. I turned my head just in time to Aleela, just cresting the top of the wall. Small clouds of dust kicked up by bullet impacts. I heard her scream and watched as she fell behind the other side of the wall.

"Aleela!" I screamed as I sprinted toward the rope.

"Get back in position!" Jax screamed.

I ignored him. I could feel in my chest the concussion of each round he fired and it resonated in my entire body. I threw my body up the wall, totally forgetting to breathe. My muscles burned in protest as they starved of oxygen. I pushed and pushed and made the top in just a few seconds. I leaned over and saw her broken body lying on the rocks below.

That was when I felt the round tear through my back and chest. It's an odd feeling being shot. It's incredibly painful, don't get me wrong, but the sensation of being pierced from one side to the other, its indescribable. I coughed blood and threw myself over the side, clinging to rope. I don't remember exactly, maybe it was adrenaline, but I was able to let myself down without falling. I reached Aleela and called out her name.

"Aleela! Aleela, can you hear me? Say something, please, goddamnit say something!" She managed to mutter a few sounds, nothing coherent, but something.

"Jax, get the fuck out of there," I grunted into the radio. "We're outside the wall, Aleela is pretty fucked up. I'm pretty fucked up, actually. We need to get the fuck out of here."

No response. I could hear the thundering of the heavy rifle and then it fell silent. Then a bright plume of brilliant white light and more screaming. Then silence, again.

"Jax," I coughed up more blood, "come back, please." I felt tears in my eyes, somehow, in that moment, I was capable of tears. "Jax?"

I sat, bleeding, with Aleelas head in my lap. All alone, the most alone I have ever been in my entire existence. The moment I lost Kat; the moment I lost Sephie. Nothing compared to that infinite space between seconds when there was no gun fire, no orders being given, no crying girl, just my own, slowing heartbeat.

I heard a thud behind me and leveled my rifle.

"Are you fucking OK?" Jax asked.

"Holy shit, man, I thought you dead," I said.

I grabbed Jax and held his head next to mine.

"Nah, they tried but I fried a bunch of them and then hopped over the wall. I cut the ropes so between that and the threat of being burned alive should slow them down. Is she OK?" Jax asked.

"No man, I think she's hurt pretty bad," I said.

"No shit. Awe fuck, man you're bleeding," Jax said.

"Yeah, I think I've been shot," I said.

My legs suddenly went out from underneath me and fell on my ass.

"John!" Jax said. He was on me quick but before he could tend to me, some asshole was coming over the wall. Jax took my rifle and fired a few rounds, dropping him with a wet thud. He took another grenade off his vest and tossed it over the wall. I was pretty out of it at this point, but I do remember a bright white flash and more screaming.

Jax unzipped my vest and removed my helmet; pressing quick clot rags into my chest and back. He checked on Aleela, shining a pen light in her eyes.

He turned back to me, "John, listen to me, John, fucking pay attention."

Jax placed a vile under my nose which was simultaneously the worst smell ever and also the most effective jolt of energy I have ever experienced. "John, we have to get you and the girl out of here. You're bleeding a lot and I can't stop it. She has a concussion. I can't carry both of you. You need to get the fuck up."

"I can walk," I said.

I still don't know where I found the strength, but somehow, I pulled myself together enough to stand. Jax slung Aleela over his shoulder. I reached for my rifle, but Jax slapped my hand away and picked it up, instead.

"March!" he ordered. Confused, but obedient, I started walking into the night. We went about 20 yards before I collapsed again. The blood soaking my shirt and pants. I could taste copper again in my mouth and was so thirsty, it hurt my throat.

"Get the fuck up, John, you sorry sack of shit. You call yourself a fucking man? Get the fuck up," Jax screamed.

"Jesus, alright," I said, my vision swimming in the low light of pre-dawn.

We went another few yards and I heard heavy footsteps from our flank. Jax, with Aleela still over his shoulder, aimed his shotgun into the distance. Mike emerged from the bush, his rifle trained on us.

"Fuck. I thought you guys were dead for sure. I lost you after the willy pete went off; couldn't see a goddamn thing," Mike said. "This the girl?"

I slumped down again, this time, without the strength to stand again.

"What's wrong with him?" Mike asked.

"He's been shot, asshole," Jax said.

"Oh, shit," Mike said.

He knelt down, grabbed my arm and threw most of my weight over his shoulder.

"I'm not going to do all the work. You better man the fuck up," Mike said.

"Alright, no need to scream in my ear," I said.

My words were faint and drawing my next breath was difficult. I felt like focusing on anything in particular, even walking,

397

was impossible. I really don't know what happened after that. I have some hazy recollections, not so much a memory, but an impression of a moment. Like when you know you dreamed the night before, but can't quite recall what it was. There are flashes of stumbling, falling, Mike swearing, but nothing concrete. That is until we reached the truck.

Somehow, someway we made it back. I remember being folded into the rear hatch, very uncomfortably, by the way, kind of shoved in there. Aleela was there next to me, the light becoming more and more intense as the sun rose into the sky. I have vague feelings of Mike and Jax screaming at each other, demanding answers to questions I couldn't make out. There was this fading in and out of reality, like skipping time.

The last thing I remember was my chest feeling like there was solid rock on it. Taking a breath was almost impossible. Jax dug something sharp into my arm; some kind of tube running into my flesh. It looked dark, like wine and I thought a drink sounded pretty damn good, although bourbon would have been my choice.

I wasn't afraid in that moment, even though I new hell was all that waited for me. I think we all have a part to play in this world and some of us are meant for terrible, terrible things. If we choose to embrace it, we still bear the responsibility of that choice. I had made my decision, finished my part. Death and everything afterward would just be what they are. I dwelt on this as the last drips of life drained from me.

I felt a small, warm hand squeeze mine and with all my strength, opened my eyes enough to see Aleela. She was awake and crying, holding me close as I bled over everything. I pressed back with everything I had and then blacked out.

Epilogue

Central Intelligence Agency
Memorandum for Distribution
Date: August 16th, 2015
Blacksite: Nairobi
Major James Bridges
Re: Human Trafficking Incursion

...That being said, I met with the three prospective assets to evaluate their potential effectiveness in a mission oriented environment. Two of the three are known military operators, although retired. The third was a civilian with no previously known affiliation with any branch of military, paramilitary or law enforcement agency either foreign or domestic.

I was initially contacted by Asset B, which I believe is due to our perceived personal relationship. We were stationed together during certain campaigns of Operation Iraqi Freedom. He believed our shared experiences would be appropriate leverage to help secure contraband in country. I agreed on the basis of Directive 34 - Expendable Assets Program. Asset B requested materiel, specifically firearms and tactical gear, in order to assault any known human trafficking hub - none of the Assets were aware of a specific target at the time of contact. They simply had the desire and idea to carry out an armed assault on such an operation, but were completely reliant on our intel. and willingness to assist. As a personal note, this was some of the worst clandestine designing I have ever seen in my professional career.

However, quite by chance, our regional surveillance had in fact identified a local trafficking network. An increase in the severity and frequency of raids across the Somali border necessitated indigenous friendlies, which had provided an initial outline of the target. The operation traded mostly in sex work with children, although there was also moderate black market arms trade, which was the focus of our attention. Our surveillance and reconnoiter was ongoing for approximately 24 months at the time of Asset B's contact.

I would like to point out that, although no HVTs were confirmed at the site, known associates of HVTs had been identified during our frequent drone observatory flights, which made an incursion with our own personnel highly likely.

My promise of aid was readily accepted by the Assets and, in fact, was all that was needed to convince them to come in country.

We met in person one time. All three appeared to have some kind of

mental/cognitive incapacitation derived from emotional trauma.

Asset A and Asset B, have been diagnosed with Post Traumatic

Stress Disorder after their discharge evaluations. Asset C, has not

been given a formal diagnosis, but likely also suffers from PTSD,

depression and anxiety after the death of his three year old daughter.

Her death was caused by an auto accident and is unrelated to any of

the activities during their incursion.

All of the Assets had difficulty controlling their emotions,

were generally hostile, especially Asset A. They also showed signs

of alcoholism; tremors in the fingers and hands, profuse sweating,

lack of motor control. They would not qualify for standard duty

operators. However, they seemed intent and willing to go on

mission, despite the likelihood of failure and bodily harm/death, as

long as they believed the target was involved with human trafficking

and I helped secure materiel.

Surveillance of the traffickers had centered on a known

weapons dealer, Josef Maes, a Belgian national with a litany of

international charges pending in multiple European jurisdictions;

although none in the States. When the mission was approved, I decided to utilize the Assets rather than a standard tactical team - the opportunity to test Directive 34 proving more valuable than a basic raid on a small arms dealer. Maes was placed on a Kill List for weapons sales to known pirate organizations operating in Somalia and I made arrangements for the Assets to purchase weapons from him.

Because of the ease of manipulation, and their complete intel. blackout, I simply told them he was my in country contact for their needed gear. As well, I used my local persona to convince Maes that the Assets were American felons attempting to establish a criminal element in the area. Both groups were eager to engage with the other.

My analysis of the situation was - given the Assets' emotional instability, aggressive behavior, and strong desire to destroy a human trafficking network, and Maes' proprietorship of such a network, there was a strong likelihood that both groups would eliminate each other. This was partly true – the Assets did execute Maes and his entourage. Somehow, though, they survived.

After being fully armed and operational, they conducted a sloppy incursion on Maes' compound; aided by the intelligence I had supplied them during our meeting.

Despite their apparent ineptitude, lack of national and international protocol, and general inefficiency, they managed to raze most of the buildings inside the walls using HE to detonate a fuel depot. After which, they used small arms to eliminate about thirty armed personnel. They also used white phosphorous grenades to cover their escape, which resulted in about half dozen more casualties.

At some point during their operation, they kidnapped a young local. Her identity is not known at this time. They forced her to accompany them, although their reason behind this is unknown. She does not appear to provide any tactical or strategic advantage. It's possible this was intended to be interpreted as a rescue, but that is speculation, at best.

Although there is no concrete account of their whereabouts after they left the compound, as the phosphorous blinded our drones, we do know Asset C was wounded during the raid.

A small, rural clinic, about two miles from the compound reported to state police that three armed men stormed their facility the morning after the raid. They forced a doctor to treat their wounded, one of which had life threatening gunshot trauma. They were able to stabilize him, after which, the group left; stealing one of the nurse's cars. This profile seem to fit the Assets.

I have attempted contact with Asset B, but have not received a response. My intent is to lure them back to a secure facility under the guise of sympathy and continued support. After they are in custody, a decision can be made on their status.

Maes' operation, for all intents and purposes, has been destroyed. All high ranking lieutenants are either confirmed dead or MIA. Beyond a complete loss of leadership structure, the loss of reputation and sense of security for potential patrons is effectively zero based on local friendly reports. Although, demand for trafficking has not subsided and it is likely a rival network will fill the vacuum left by Maes. Threats will be evaluated as they are established, but it is unlikely such a replacement operation will hold any strategic value in our continued counter to regional insurgency.

In conclusion, Directive 34 can be deemed a tentative success. Completely deniable Assets can be acquired and directed with some efficacy – their numbers buoyed by the relative glut of exiting military personnel. I recommend further implementation.

As for the Assets in this scenario, they should be acquired if possible for further debriefing. Lethal force should be used if they resist.

54153099R00228

Made in the USA
Middletown, DE
02 December 2017